FIRST LOST

First Edition Published 2013 by: Lulu.com,
3101 Hillsborough Street, Raleigh,
NC 27607, UNITED STATES
In association with: VerdanaBee,
The Chandlery, Unit Office 501,
50 Westminster Bridge Road,
LONDON SE1 7QY,
UNITED KINGDOM

ISBN: 978-1-291-46243-2

Printed and distributed by: Lulu.com
Pictures by: VerdanaBee
Logo: by Vistaprint

ReadMeDo

VerdanaBee

Contents

Other books written by the author:

Sci/fantasy genre

Flight of Fantasy Collection - 2013

Paperback and epub editions

First Lost Risen – 2013 - paperback

DEDICATION:

To the indefatigable spirit for

righteousness and humility

Thy Will Be Done for Thy Name's Sake

Our Only Judge

In commemoration of Jamaica's 50th

Jubilee Independence Year

Introduction

This is the author's second book in the sci/fantasy genre. The author has lived in the UK since coming from Jamaica in early childhood, growing up and going to schools in London and later working in various admin positions in order to survive.

The story of "First Lost Risen" first came out of a poem called "Tears" which she wrote while on ABCtales.com in 2011. This later expanded into the story of a young girl who washed up on a Jamaican beach to be found by doctors. The mystery as to her identity and how she came to the island unfolds with time. The child is first supported and then finds her mission.

Follow Talisa as she wakes up in an ever changing world.

VerdanaBee

2/7/13

To Kevin

Thank you over and over
for your support and
encouragement
May Yah's blessings keep you
Always

Patricia

CHAPTER ONE: "TEARS"

Daniel sealed the books for The End Times

And not everything was revealed to Yochanan.

Nearing mid September 2010, one of the busiest years for hurricanes … Igor and Julia would dance by one another – it would be incredible ...

Off the coast of West Africa, Cape Verde was being lashed by waves as a wedding ceremony was ending, the bride forlorn. You would have thought someone had died but this was part of their wedding persona. The bridegroom who tied the knot for this bride accepted the solemnity of that moment.

The two storms' depressive, converging fronts brewed; air swirling though not yet detectable to the naked eye or meteorological radar even. Right now it was more of a feeling. The silky shark felt it, as did the black reef, white death …

An octopus passed over the unseemly place. Several schools of fish didn't care to loiter there either. Playful sea urchins in nearby coral, tried best to ignore it as angel fish swam by, flashing yellow and blue for sand and sea. A flat fish that had been drawn to the place, now felt uncharacteristically uncomfortable as the sand shifted beneath it, deciding to break camouflage and get the heck away from there while the going was good.

The tropical depressions forming above expanded as the sand on the sea bed moved of its own accord just around this spot. It shook and shook until a detectable skeleton was revealed; all the ribs and bones intact. The pelvic area pronounced it to be female. A forensic examination at this point would have found her to be sixteen and though of childbearing age to have not yet given birth. The storm above grew as the skeleton rose. The fish swam in avoidance. Sunlight was sparkling down on the churning Caribbean waters. The skeleton rose and as it did so, there seemed to be a noise from a breath of wind passing across the waves. Ninety feet to the surface and all manner of fleshy material was attaching to these bones. Sixty-five feet and rising, swirling gently. Organs, more flesh, forming … muscles, eyes, matted hair … Thirty-five feet, nails on toes and fingers … Seaweed wrapping around her … Twenty feet … Just ten feet left. The body slowly broke the surface tension as the tropical depression strengthened, tracking across the Atlantic, having given breath to the still unconscious body, tugging it along in its wake in a protective bubble before letting it drift loose. This lost cargo, currents finally deposit just off Negril Jamaica where the tide washed her up on the beach. The bubble finally burst.

Hopeton's eyes were transfixed on the netted heap before him. For a millisecond which seemed like hours, he was transported a decade back. He too was sixteen and in his English class. Mrs Lawrence had asked him to read it, that poem called "Tears". He had found the piece weird and challenging. This became evident as he started to sweat profusely, a couple of times having to wipe his brow, drying his hands on his well pressed trousers.

The words clanged in his ears:

'"TEARS"

Cry rain; rip tide waves, oceans,
storms, floods: tsunami of tears.

Floating, drowning, tossing;
swept up on distant shore.
Tropical dipped foresight in a pool of
unconscious insights.
Battered, bruised, exhausted, limp,
agonised: preserved in brine.
Oblivious to froth washing bare feet;
sand embedded toes.
Sirens regurgitate with screams and
spouts, what the sodden
peppered and muted form filled
garnished with seaweed
could not.

The perplexed exclaimed:

"Goodness! What have we here?"

"… Survivor … Perhaps …"

"But where is the ship?"

"That ship sailed … Some time
hence …" '

… The water lapped up on Hopeton's sandals.

Peter called to him from behind, his sun tanned skin prickling in the baking afternoon heat.

"What's that you found?"

Peter was also a doctor, English but on holiday with his young family, trying to make amends for his long hours away from home in order to stave off a threatening divorce. He had met Hopeton in New York at a neurology seminar years prior.

"It's a body," Hopeton shouted, snapping back to the present, before dipping his own 5ft 10 inch body to a squat.

"Alive?"

"I'm checking for vitals." He intoned that he had never seen such a mess.

Peter told his wife to stay back with their six year old daughter by the jeep as he ran to where Hopeton was crouched.

"Jesus! What in the world …" Agitated fingers ran through his heavy dark curly hair.

"Yeh, help me get some of this gunk off, see if there's a hint of a pulse here."

Peter took his keying out of a pocket and used the utility cutters to rip through the netting.

“How long do you think she’s been in the water?” They could clearly see the form was female.

Hopeton shook his head and laughed nervously, “Man, it looks like for ever and a day to me.” He cleared more debris from her face, and then checked the carotid artery in her neck. A sudden twitch from her now sparkling mahogany body alarmed both men. It was as if Hopeton’s sandalwood touch had ignited a spark of life.

“What?! Er, er ...” they exclaimed, as green slime and plankton oozed from her mouth.

“Clear her airway Hopeton quick!” They were both in emergency mode; CPR followed. Her slight pulse quickened as her chest inflated. The girl gasped as when a baby takes its first real breath, with eyes popping open for the briefest second as her pupils caught first light, perhaps the first for several hundred years before closing again, slipping her into a coma.

"We need to get her to a hospital fast!" They lifted her body.

"You drive up front with Brenda and Chloe as you know the way. I'll stay back with her." Peter shouted to his now distressed wife and child to get into the jeep.

Peter tried best to calm his family down. Chloe was hugging her mother tight and sobbing. Brenda rubbed her head, while keeping her turned away from the approaching men. She opened the jeep door, settling her daughter in before the men reached the vehicle.

Hopeton helped ease the damp girl into the back. Peter apologised to his wife over the roar of the engine. She sat as compassionately as she could, trying best to protect their daughter from the unfolding drama to the back. This was not what they had travelled across an ocean for.

Peter climbed into the jeep and rummaged the bags for a clean towel. Finding one, he threw it over the girl's body as Hopeton revved the engine and pressed the accelerator. They were off and rolling, kicking up sand in their rush.

Examining her body, Peter noticed dark indentations on her wrists and ankles. The incredulous thought, that perhaps she had been kept chained somewhere occurred to him. He felt a sickening surge in his stomach as if someone had walked over his grave. From somewhere in his head he heard, what was unbeknown to him, a family of talking drums, sounds that were so ghostly foreign. Hopeton heard it too, the drum beats chattering as the jeep ran over a hidden boulder which caused it to lunge into the air. Everyone except Hopeton and the comatose cargo yelled, thinking they were about to overturn.

"It's okay folks," Hopeton cried out, getting a grip of himself. "Just didn't see that coming."

CHAPTER TWO: NAMING

Hopeton drove them to a private clinic in Negril as the nearest hospital was miles away in Savvanah La Mar. They could deal with the cost details later as he worked at the clinic several times a week. The porters there knew Hopeton well. They brought a trolley and rushed the girl into a cubicle. Hopeton spotted Dr Neville who was on duty, spurting out how they found her. The doctor ordered fluids and a drip and for her to be hooked up to a heart and BP monitor. Her blood pressure was raised; she was also running a slight temperature. While Dr Neville was still examining the patient, she began haemorrhaging between her legs.

"Christ! We need to get her to theatre fast ..." He called for assistance.

Hopeton and Peter caught up in the lobby. As Hopeton brought Peter up to speed, Sister Reid made her stout matronly approach. Precious little passed unnoticed on her watch.

"Now then gentlemen, either of you two know if there are any relatives we can contact as a matter of urgency?" She was of course more addressing Hopeton, not knowing who the stranger was with him.

"Ah no Sister, we pulled her from the water. Just in time it seems like."

"Lucky for her. Any ID on her by any chance?"

Hopeton felt himself being drawn away from Sister Reid's questioning. Words flitted across his eyes, blanking out all else. They read: 'Yewe calls her Talisa'.

"Arrhmm she's plainly of African descent and her name is Talisa. Yes …Talisa, that's right," he found himself repeating.

Sister looked puzzled, raised her spectacles. "What, she tell you that her name is Talisa?"

Peter looked at Hopeton even more puzzled.

"Er, I think you'll find she'll answer to that name when she pulls through."

"Glad to know you rooting for her doctor," Sister acknowledged, writing down Talisa Africa – since it was decided by quick consensus she was no Jane Doe and evidently holding her breathing own. Her country of origin appeared to be in doubt - though she was clearly of African descent as were the majority of Jamaicans and other Caribbean nationals on the island.

"We'll have to transfer her to the hospital as soon as possible you know Hopeton. We can't afford to keep her here. There is a global economic crisis as the Administrator keeps reminding us and we are not immune."

"Sister, let me worry about the practicalities over the next few days when we know more about how she's doing if you don't mind."

"Alright, but you best speak to the Hospital Administrator yourself. I'll leave it with you."

"Fine," Hopeton assured her as she unconvincingly shuffled off. He turned to Peter who was staring at him with both hands on his hips shaking his head.

"Where'd you get that name from?" he asked as soon as the Sister was out of earshot.

“Man, it just came to me out of the blue. There’s something real strange going on here. I don’t even know where to start. Been like that since we found her,” Hopeton sighed shaking his head.

“Tell me bout it. I hope she … Talisa is going to be alright.”

“She’s in real good hands with Dr Neville believe me. I’ll square her care with him.”

“Just let me know if you need any help with this,” Peter offered. “Can’t help feeling a tug of responsibility, which I know I shouldn’t but anything I can do to assist. Hey, I need to get back to my family but call me and let me know if anything changes, good or bad.”

The two men exchanged a fraternal pat. Peter turned, following the exit signs. He rounded on the reception area, collecting his wife and child. Brenda was grateful for the decision to leave. It had been a strenuous day and for some reason she felt dirty all over, contaminated by the whole stinking episode. She needed a shower and Chloe could do with something decent to eat and a nap. More than anything, Brenda was now looking forward to the flight back to London –

eight days away. However, she wished she could leave immediately.

They had hired the jeep for the day. Hopeton could sort a ride from the clinic in his home town. The powerful sunlight and heat blasted them as they left the air-conditioned environment of the clinic. They practically ran to the jeep. It felt as if they would have to acclimatise all over again after the day's events.

Hopeton and Peter returned to the hospital the next day. Brenda and Chloe had a pre-booked water aerobics session with some mothers and youngsters around the hotel pool area for fun and fitness. It proved the antidote they needed to lift their spirits.

The Jamaican nurses came and went at Talisa's side, updating her records: temperature, pulse, checking the monitors. She was stable and in a private room.

"Any news about where she came from? Coastguard checks? Missing persons?" Peter asked.

"Bit early in the day but nothing so far. No one reported overboard as far as we know."

“Could she have come from one of the other islands?”

“Who knows …?”

It was a weekend and the area was busy. They decided to go for a quick bite and a beer for lunch at a cool little bar Hopeton occasionally dropped into on account of the owner was a family friend. He always received good service whether or not Anchorman was around. The patron had acquired the name since his running days at school. The stylish middle-aged woman behind the counter told them he had gone to pick up stock and was due back shortly. They ordered patties and two bottles of cold Red Stripe to wash it down.

Peter surveyed the pictures on the wall. Old favourites and new were on display: Don Quarrie, Merlene Ottey, the winning Jamaican Beijing squad; including Shelly-Ann, Veronica with Bolt posing his signature lightning strike. Bob Marley and the I Threes, Jimmy Cliff and Michael Manley were all representing. The West Indies cricket team of 1984 featured on another panel, joined by a signed photo of Ian Botham in a cap.

"You still playing cricket Hopeton?"

"Not half as much as I would like these days."

"Your tennis improved any?"

"Oh my game is probably a lot worse. Thinking of taking up squash instead to keep fit." Hopeton surveyed Peter's slim 6ft frame.

"Long as you don't lose any weight, if don't mind my saying doc."

"I think Brenda would agree with you." Peter acknowledged.

Anchorman returned just as Hopeton was asking Peter about how he planned to spend the rest of his holiday. The owner hailed them with a wide grin that exposed his gold tooth as he shook Peter's hand with both of his, releasing him to usher his staff to quickly wheel the stock round back.

"Glad to meet you Dr Stratford. Hold a minute." He called to someone through the beaded doorway. "Hey, Clifton, you nuh hear me seh come help nuh man. Wha? 'Ol on Hopeton. Soon come." He hooked the beads up and disappeared only to return with a bleary eyed youth reeking of ganja and who bore a striking resemblance to Anchorman.

The woman behind the counter kissed her teeth, sprawled her chest over the wood and propped up her jaw. She audibly muttered that the boy had no ambition like his mother. The doctors found a cool spot out of the way to sit.

"We need to go to a market to pick up souvenirs that sort of thing. Brenda wanted to visit Rose Hall, but perhaps she's changed her mind about that. Don't want to be spooking Chloe after everything that's happened." Peter picked up. Locals thought the place was haunted.

Hopeton nodded, understanding. "I'll get Rachel to go with you to the market. She's very good in that department. It'll be a good day out. No worries."

Hopeton had introduced Peter and his wife to his girlfriend Rachel on their third day on the island. They had been dating for almost two years and he had met her family. He confided to Peter he was thinking of popping the question sooner rather than later. Peter patted him on the shoulder, saying he was sure he would get the timing right and that Rachel seemed a good match for him.

The local couple in the corner congenially laughed out loud, as if to affectionately concur.

"So how do you juggle your General Practice, specialist duties and Rachel all in one day Hopeton? I thought I was busy!"

"Oh I enjoy the variety of patients. Why we're doctors right?" They both laughed.

"You know, the old ones know better than you because I'm just out of diapers according to them. The young ones, well most of them don't have a clue. But again they think they know it all these days because they saw it on TV so it must be good, 'til it turns out wrong and they come all embarrassed about something they've done." Hopeton stopped to consider a little. Peter regarded his clean shaven quizzical expression.

"They say the eyes are the windows to the soul Peter. Ophthalmology is what I have to keep up with so my days at the clinic cover that. Tourists come for private consultations on cataracts, but especially for glaucoma treatment with our very own Canasol from our very own cannabis sativa plants."

"Yeh, I remember reading something about that. Can't be a hit with the US FDA."

"Uh, uh. They just love playing politics with everything and everyone. But they can't keep pretending they're the only authority on this planet for ever. Anyhow, as busy as I undoubtedly am, Rachel, well, I just look forward to chilling out with her as much as I can."

Peter smiled and nodded. The two men might live miles and worlds apart but when it came right down to it, the things they valued did not seem that dissimilar.

Jamaican women saw Hopeton as a good catch, being a doctor. He was not the flash playboy type. He loved his career and was interested in finding a suitable partner who complemented and understood him. His parents had married for better or worse and he seriously hoped for the same outcome. Rachel had been introduced to him through his extracurricular community work with orphan children whose mostly single mothers had died in circumstances ranging from murder, hit and runs, illnesses. AIDS was a growing problem on the island. Like many Caribbean islands, Jamaica's young population was under twenty-four years old; there being much illiteracy with a significant amount of youngsters not finishing high school. Drugs was a big problem and a survival option particularly for those born and raised in the mushrooming garrison areas controlled by international connected drug lords. Police extra judicial killings and Police corruption was known abroad to be endemic. The Army was on constant alert to broach the rift between civilian law and armed outlaws who claimed to be offering a public service to the disenfranchised. For its size and population, Jamaica was known to be one of the murder capitals of the world and yet, the allure for tourists was unmistakable. Budding surgeons flocked there for internship outside of a war zone. The young from worldwide continents made their way there for music, frolic and drugs.

Through various crises of an internal and external international nature, since the 1960's, ruling historical minorities from European, Chinese and Indian backgrounds migrated from the island in droves. The country was further destabilised in the 1970's, its "economy screaming" death kisses with political gun running and South American drugs introduced within the breach of defunct trade agreements. This included the loss of the bauxite trade for aluminium production and the decline of the banana business. Diversity and change was needed.

Tourism was good for foreign exchange and provided jobs. However this did not make up for the loss of other local industries as globalisation transformed the fate of this once coveted island. The long-term prognosis seemed to be for the worse where self-sufficiency was concerned, with an increasing dependency on imports.

As a tourist, Peter was aware of the do's and don'ts of this paradox of an island paradise. Negril had been chosen as their holiday destination as it was known to be one of the more luxurious areas on the island and assumed safer, being further from the ever maddening town crowds as proffered. Glancing back on the pictures on the wall, some had been taken before the bad nowadays really set in Jamaica.

"Didn't you consider continuing your career in New York Hopeton?"

"Peter, tell you the truth, I did consider it. But you know what, I missed my family and country too much. Danger is everywhere these days. Been I'm a laid back type of guy you nuh, I didn't need to be swimming with all them over there in that Big Pond. I just want to be able to practise what I do in a place where I feel at home and needed. Right here."

Peter laughed, sharing the choices he had made in his own life. Ambition figured pretty high on his list of goals, but there came a time when he too had settled for options more suited to being human as well as a professional – that balancing act. That's when Brenda had walked into his life. For some reason he had been attracted to the fact she was not in medicine, that and her capacity to help him relax him with those squirrel eyes of hers, thick chestnut hair. He had been more than happy to allow her to help sort out his finances too.

CHAPTER THREE: AWAKE

Peter visited again, curious to see if Talisa was out of the coma. He could have called Hopeton for an update but for some reason he wanted to be that much closer to what was going on.

The good news was the patient had been conscious for two days, though she frequently dozed off. They had thought her delirious on account of when she attempted to speak it sounded like gibberish. This was frustrating all round, as no one could decipher what she was trying to say. For someone with remarkably bright eyes, she seemed in contrast disorientated by everything around her, responding to sounds but could not initially follow what was being communicated. Doctor Neville was trying back to basic gestures as she did not appear to recognise a single word of English. Spanish and French words also did not evoke any sense of recognition. There was the possibility of some inhibiting brain dysfunction but it was too early to tell. Given a bed pan, no bowel movement or urination had been recorded. A nurse decided to try taking her to the bathroom but the girl just stood there frozen. When the nurse flushed the chain, Talisa seemed curiously startled but not afraid. The nurse had used sounds a toddler would understand which finally worked, showing her how to wash her hands after. The patient had noticeably derived much pleasure from playing with the water, just as a toddler would in fact. Where had this teen been all her life, the nurse had noted in her report back to Dr Neville. Talisa drank water but hardly touched the food. This could not of course go on.

When Peter put his head round the door, the nurse was just about to leave. Seeing him Talisa began screaming. Fortunately Dr Neville was on his rounds and was able to calm her down by way of sedation.

"First squeak we've had out of her for a few hours. Must have taken you for the Devil," he remarked.

"Come on, I helped save her life …"

"Well she doesn't seem to know that yet."

"You have any theories as to how she got into the water?"

"I'm hoping she'll be able to tell us something when she eventually manages to say something intelligible. Seems to have lost all but basic ability to communicate. I can see that she desperately wants to. Been through some trauma, no doubt. Who knows how long this is going to take. She's beginning to respond to people a little cognitively as you yourself noticed. Not eating enough to keep a bird alive though."

"Any brain damage?" Peter asked, thinking real damage such as from a trauma or lesions resulting in some type of aphasia in the Broca area than anything psychosomatic.

"I'll have to book her in for a fMRI scan. We're a little behind at present," Dr Neville sighed.

Peter met Hopeton in the hotel beach bar later that evening just before dinner. An orange sun was setting to a warm Caribbean Sea breeze and the pounding rhythm of reggae. A chorus of creatures intonated in the wind: frogs, crickets, the odd caw of birds drifted in.

Peter ordered drinks on his tab, the strong intoxicating smell of rum and coke poured smoothly over ice and lime permeating the air, mingling with the aroma of tobacco from chilled out smokers strolling to the ebb and flow of repeating waves.

Hopeton asked him what he had enjoyed most on his trip. They had visited Greenwood Great House in Mo'Bay and Dunn's River of course – noting a lot of Japanese tourists which had surprised him: went river rafting, trekked up Blue Mountain where the famous coffee came from. Hopeton interjected.

"Now that's how come the Japanese are here. Never stopped 'til they got hold of our coffee, the best in the world," he stressed. "Now we can't even afford to buy what we grow in our own country."

Peter hadn't known. No reason why he should, as markets were not his forte. Hopeton could not help but starkly see how the world economic crisis had affected the people on the island. Runaway inflation, shortages of foodstuff, utility costs up, the increase of violence, courtesy and part and parcel of illicit drug importation and weaponry. Parts of Kingston where the garrisons were, had become no go areas ... This made life busy for doctors, who wanted to improve their surgical techniques tending multiple gunshot wounds, machete attack amputations, lacerations and deep tissue damage in an undeclared war zone in the nation's capital. The spectres meting out these deadly statistics were kept off the beaten tourist tracks. Hopeton apologised, too much talk about the dark side of life in paradise. Peter said there was no need to, they lived on one planet and it was impossible to cut oneself off completely from its circulating ills. Doctors were often caught on the frontline of life's fractures and disaster stories in one way or another after all.

"So tell me you loved the trip to the market so I can report back to Rachel. You know how women love to hear how useful they've been."

"I can actually say for real, it was another highlight of our trip," Peter nodded slowly, taking a sip of his drink. "And we have the goods as proof. Honestly, Rachel is really very sweet."

"Thank you for that."

Their conversation again turned to Talisa. Peter pressed for his theories about how she came to be in the water. Hopeton surely had an inkling of what went on in and around Jamaica's shores. Any clue was crucial to her recovery, unravelling what happened in order to trace her family as well.

The Police were also waiting for a statement but as she had lost her memory, she was unable to be of any help.

"I don't think she swam to the island," Hopeton reflected. "By the way, she miscarried you know …"

"Oh boy. That's sad. Hard to tell what all this is about. Do you think maybe she threw herself in the water? A suicide attempt perhaps? Or could be she was pushed?"

Hopeton shrugged his shoulders, he hadn't a clue.

Dr Neville had run DNA tests on the foetal remains. The patient had been in her second trimester, the foetus about fourteen weeks, male, AB genotype, mother being B. The foetus showed a HB beta-thalassaemia trait, results further established the father to be of European origin.

"Really?!" Peter pronounced, rather surprised at his own shock. "Come on, she's unlikely to have fallen off a yacht or tourist ship. Besides she's still a child."

"Ok, Sherlock, so you're that sure about what rich people get up to these days? All I know is, she screamed when she saw your ugly mug," Hopeton reminded him. "Wasn't just that you were the only white man around. You obviously triggered something. Sure she'll calm down when she realises it wasn't you!" None of this was meant to be offensive and no offence was taken.

Human trafficking was still alive in the world at large Hopeton had continued. He'd read about it in a news article that there was a thriving trade in London. Peter conceded the point. A colleague of his had dealt with an Eastern European girl who had been referred by social services for psychiatric treatment following a police raid on a house in a well to do area.

Other than agreeing the marks on Talisa's body were tell tale signs she had been restrained somehow, somewhere, it was anyone's guess what her story was. Preliminary investigations by the local police had turned up nothing. No one had been reported missing. In Jamaica, foul play aside, if a child went missing the whole neighbourhood usually knew before the Police.

The two doctors gradually chatted about developments in neurology since meeting at the seminar. This curiously led on to Hopeton asking Peter about his relationship with Brenda and how they were getting on. He knew the holiday had been an attempt to pay each other more attention. Peter responded with sardonic consideration that only time would tell. However, the thought of being separated from his daughter for longer than a night shift he was not ready to even contemplate.

“What time is your flight tomorrow?”

“Catching a 20:00 PM flight into Heathrow.”

“Sorry I can’t see you off, have a charity event in town, but I’ll keep you abreast of Talisa’s progress, promise. Love to Brenda and Chloe.”

“Thanks for everything.”

“No problem Peter. One Love.”

CHAPTER FOUR: CONNECTING

Hopeton parked in the driveway and made his way up the steps to the porch. He rang the bell. A voice called out.

"Who is it?"

"It's me Hopeton Mrs Lawrence. I called to say I was coming today."

"Ah yes. Yes Hopeton!" There was a little shuffling as the retired teacher opened the door.

"Come in man. Hopeton! Bless my days. Come in." She smiled warmly ushering him inside.

It had been a good year since he had seen his old teacher. The space he entered was teeming with memories, things collected over the course of her life. Her husband had passed away some three years prior, his pictures poised on the coffee table in front of where they sat. His widow managed to remain content with life and circumstance, was heavily involved within her Baptist community. Her love of gardening kept the flowers and fruit trees in seasonal flourish and her joints moving, all with the assistance from her trusted helper Martine.

"Lord, Hopeton so how life treating you?"

"I can't complain Mrs Lawrence, can't complain you know."

She nodded with a smile. Hopeton was one of her success stories. She had pushed him towards excellence and the result was truly beaming back at her. It had helped of course that he came from a stable family background. There was no substitute for that.

"So what breeze blow you here Hopeton? You want something to drink?"

"I'm fine Mrs Lawrence. I'm here because I have something to run by you. I don't quite know how to start." His countenance changed as he spoke, rubbing his knees as he was prone to do as a youngster. She read in his face he was deeply troubled.

"I'm listening. Go on," she encouraged.

Hopeton recounted how he had taken Peter and his family to the beauty spot where they had found Talisa and the mystery surrounding her.

“When I found her, you remember that poem you made me recite,’Tears’, it was the strangest thing Mrs Lawrence but I remembered every word of it when I saw her there on the beach.” He was perspiring and fiddled with his shirt collar.

Mrs Lawrence sat silent for a while, going over what Hopeton had imparted. She rose from her chair asking him to excuse her. She brought out a book, removing a leaflet from it which she handed to Hopeton. She intimated that if he thought the poem had been difficult, the passage might help to throw a glimmer of light on the mystery. She had thought about him when she had come across it in fact. It was an Ode of Solomon XXII. Hopeton read it softly out loud. He felt his body shiver.

“Mrs Lawrence, what do you think all this means? I want to find out who this Talisa really is and where she come from. Further, what does all this have to do with me?”

Mrs Lawrence gave out a big sigh, “Hopeton, all I know is the right person found her. Now you know them say, there are more things in heaven and earth than John reveal to us." She tapped his knee, the soothing look in her eyes calming his anxiety. "You keep the verse Hopeton and pray. By the way, how that girl of yours, Rachel? Yes Rachel."

At that precise moment Hopeton felt his cell phone buzzing. He asked Mrs Lawrence to hold on as he retrieved it from his pocket. It was Rachel, right on cue. Without rising, he told her where he was and agreed to meet her when he was done.

He turned back to Mrs Lawrence whose smile had broadened even more. "Rachel sends her regards Mrs Lawrence."

"Hmm, hmm. Hopeton, why don't you take Rachel to see Talisa. She's a school teacher isn't she?"

"Yes. She teaches juniors," he was beginning to see the sense of this.

"Then I think she'll be good for her," Mrs Lawrence forwarded.

"... It never occurred to me to do that Mrs Lawrence. But you know, Rachel is really good with people. Yeh, I'll run it by her." Something was happening but again

Hopeton did not know what. He felt in the flow of it, being carried but could not question too deeply.

"You do that Hopeton and don't take too long to come and see me again."

Rachel was closing the gate to her yard with a basket in hand as Hopeton drove up. Her hair was up in corn rows, the braids from which hung down her neck. He watched as her shapely cinnamon shaded legs strolled to meet him at the kerb.

"You didn't tell me we're going for an outing. Suppose I had other plans?" He met her gaze through the open window.

She walked round to the passenger side. "Not exactly an outing Hopeton. You're taking me to see Talisa and the three of us are going to have lunch," she announced as she climbed into the silver 2007 Toyota Mark X, throwing him one of her knowing activation looks. Hopeton could only meet her with a wide-eyed stare.

Talisa was sat up in her bed, her lunch still untouched. She smiled at Hopeton and looked searchingly at Rachel. Hopeton rubbed Talisa's hand in reassurance and removed the tray in front of her. Rachel introduced herself and started to unpack the lunch she made while Hopeton drew up some chairs. Talisa did not take her eyes off Rachel who said grace over the food while she held Hopeton's hand. Rachel dished out a plate of stewed beef, not too spicy, with a little rice and hard food. She began to eat making yummy sounds as she did. Hopeton followed suit. He encouraged Talisa to try, engaging those deep fascinating eyes of her with purpose. She looked at the plate before her and back at the couple. At length she reached for a fork, awkwardly spearing a bite sized piece of meat. She brought the fork to her mouth, her eyes trained on them as she put it a little way in, successfully removing the meat with her teeth without biting down onto the metal on first attempt. She slowly savoured the texture and began chewing. It was tender and good. She pondered the colourful plate of food, recognising yam, a green banana and okra. This time the metal met her teeth, the sensation strange but she was by now undaunted. Her stomach welcomed being nourished. She tucked in. Rachel had also made a seasonal fruit salad in case Talisa could be tempted to eat a little more. The entire meal came from local produce. By the time they reached the final course, there was little hesitation in her following suit. Rachel and Hopeton smiled at each other, holding hands at the side of Talisa's bed.

"Well it occurred to me she was eating alone and that was easily fixed."

"Thank you Dr Rachel."

"You're most welcome Dr Bennett. You think she might benefit from being out in the garden when we're done? My guess is she hasn't been outside in days and the fresh air may do some good."

"I'll arrange a wheelchair. She's still a little wobbly on her feet."

Rachel rubbed her hands in approval, smiling warmly at Talisa who appeared to sense something was about to happen. The young teacher found the robe and slippers that had been provided and placed them expectantly in position, stroking the girl's arm to reassure her. One thing at a time, she would tackle Talisa's dull and matted hair another day. It needed a good wash. For now she helped her into the robe without difficulty as Talisa had done this before. Hopeton arrived with the chair. Rachel slipped the slippers on Talisa's small feet. As soon as she was comfortable all three exited the room and turned the corner.

CHAPTER FIVE: DAY BY DAY

There were people already in the garden, including an American family of five. Their hyperactive four year old had tripped and fallen awkwardly following a sudden shower of rain, the boy ending up with a dislocated shoulder and a nasty bump on the head. He was relishing the extra attention but rearing to be that reassembled Optimus robotic Prime again.

A group of local young people were also gathered. Ambrose, Anchorman's son, who they called Brosi, was bopping towards the bench where they had congregated. Sherice whose neck was held in a collar brace, was wrapped in her peachy dressing gown, both her honey coloured legs on display on the seat. The others stood jabbering about the latest show they'd been to. This was a cross section of a more privileged set of Jamaicans, their parents owning retail shops, real estate, running franchises, in finance jobs, communications, utilities or holding government positions etc. The type of families who had enough money to buy their youngsters out of trouble, having connections and influence to ensure nothing other than scaring them to get right would in fact happen. Out of many, this particular set also dabbled with the less fortunate when it suited inclinations, including the infectious need to party and of course to smoke the best weed money could buy.

Bret and Avon were born and bred white Jamaicans, a heritage some managed to keep intact across the Caribbean by some defining design – by any means necessary. If you just heard their ghetto banter you would have been none the wiser. Ria was of mixed Asian origins, revelling in her own brand of rebellion by being a part of this crowd. April and Clayton were the youngest, hailing from more apparent African ancestry. Miss Lou's poem "Back to Africa" if you were acquainted with it, was duly represented here in colourful contrast. Cornell and Trench though physically absent, were blowing cheerful from loudspeakers having just completed a practise rally run. All this chatter was reverberating through the otherwise tranquil garden. Their youthful racket instantly drew Hopeton and Yvonne's attention, a couple of the faces being recognised, while Talisa seemed barely to register their presence.

Sherice had to turn her entire body as not to strain her neck as she looked around at the three. She hated the brace, being chronically aware of the impact it would have on her appearance and ability to get out and about over the coming weeks if not months. Thoughts of winning Miss Universe were on hold, though this stemmed more from her skin tone, which tended to reflect a caustic beauty about her that some might otherwise find repulsive.

"Kuhya! Almshouse! Den tings so bad them couldn't do someting wid dat deh head? A wonder her people can afford insurance." She was referring to Talisa's hair and the fact that she herself was recovering from a car accident days earlier but due to be discharged with whiplash injury and back pain, presenting major inconvenience to her lifestyle activities. The others once again followed Sherice's gaze, chuckling at her comment. Ria suggested Sherice should lend the girl her comb as a goodwill gesture.

"I don't know if that head ever see a comb!" she remarked, brushing her own processed hair across her forehead. Trench, her boyfriend, was now barking down her BlackBerry which had been passed to Brosi. Trench wanted to know what was going on, as he claimed to be busy and didn't have time to waste on foolishness. Sherice asked for her phone back, returning their focus to their own issues. She demanded to know what was keeping him so busy that he couldn't spare time to come and see her but once. Being sick, far from invoking his sympathy, this situation was putting her love life in imminent jeopardy as he hated hospitals. They argued.

It was a glorious day, alive with the sounds of insects, the chatter being droned out by the unnoticed drama of teeming life laced with the profusion of scented colour stimulating Talisa's senses. They found a spot in the shade next to a nutmeg tree. A humming bird made a welcome appearance, a blaze of beating colour. Talisa studied it as she absorbed the energy from the sun which seemed to set her mahogany rich skin delightfully aglow. She rose from the chair. Hopeton reached to stop her but Rachel gently stayed his hand, sensing this was part of Talisa's recovery process. Talisa ran her hands over face, her neck and rubbed her arms before dropping to the newly mowed grass, gently spreading her hands over the cut blades, then patting the ground as if searching for something and finding a spot. With her left hand to the ground and her right palm stretched out towards the sky, she murmured in her own tongue before slowly rising to her feet. She began spinning, her arms and hands spanned out as if catching shards of sun rays. The world at first revolved slowly, past and present catching up in a tangled net which she was dancing through, wading through time, wading through this concentrated historical space. A gust of wind whipped up, Hopeton was sure he could hear the whispers of Psalm 121 in it. He glanced at Rachel, but her eyes were transfixed on Talisa. The activity once again drew the set's peripheral attention. More remarks and laughter, pronunciations which failed to attract Talisa's attention.

"Maybe she belongs in the madhouse," Sherice blurted out. She squealed as her words reverberated on the front of her neck. April said it served her right, that she should stop her noise and leave people girl children alone for once. This induced Sherice to ask if they were related. April shook her head and folded her arms. Sherice was a real redibuh bitch and the crash had not dented that aspect one jot. Women hung around her because she ran a beauty salon and they would be up for anything to enhance their appearance at discounted prices if they could get it. She also knew how to throw great parties.

"If you was minding your own business, I bet you wouldn't ah crash yuh car."

"So wha? You was there? How you know what I was doing from what I wasn't eeh?"

"I know you. Bet you ena check wha some gal ena wear or a scandalise smadie pon phone." Ria blurted. Avon and Bret begged the girls to cool down before security asked them to take their noise elsewhere. They lost interest in Talisa once more.

Talisa gradually stopped spinning and finally returned to the chair. Hopeton and Rachel were then dumbstruck to hear her say quite clearly in English, "Thank you both for your help. I am most thankful. Yes. Thank you."

"You're, you're most welcome ah, Talisa, Talisa," Hopeton managed to reply, tripping over his words. "Talisa, is that your name?" He bent down to more or less her level.

"Yes. Talisa. Thank you. My father thanks you."

Hopeton gave Rachel a quick glance which she transmitted into a reassuring rub on Talisa's shoulder.

"Let's get you back inside Talisa. We seem to have come a long way in one day. Give thanks."

CHAPTER SIX: LEARNING CURVE

Dr Neville took another look at Talisa's MRI results following the dramatic breakthrough of her language skills. The results had shown remarkable activity in both hemispheres in fact which did not square with any dysfunction, quite the contrary. There were no other discernible abnormalities. He was debating whether to rerun the test. The girl had been very relaxed throughout the examination despite the then communication problems. Her English was at present functional but there was no doubt it was a huge improvement.

Rachel had spent some time introducing Talisa to drawing, which also appeared to be assisting the girl's communication achievements.

Peter Stratford's mother Bonnie had managed to secure funding for her care, courtesy of an international charity that supported children suffering from amnesia. Placing her somewhere for more long-term remedial care that would facilitate her recovery was now a priority.

The Police had also been in touch and wanted to interview Talisa as soon as possible. An intermediary was needed to assist in order to ensure this questioning would not be counterproductive to her recovery process. Having come this far, Dr Neville did not want to risk a relapse.

One male and a female officer arrived for the interview, in plain clothes so not to scare the child. Hopeton arranged for Rachel to be available as Talisa seemed to thrive in her company. The officers started off with gentle questions. She confirmed her name was Talisa, the Africa surname she did not appear to fully understand but nodded all the same. It tripped off the tongue like notes. They asked how old she was. Again she did not appear to quite understand the concept of this question. They attempted asking if she knew where her family was. She could only tell them "lost, family lost". She was informed that she had been found in the sea. Water, yes she understood this. Could she remember how she had come to be in the water? She indicated with her hands she had been on a house in the water. Rachel supplied pen and paper. At first Talisa sketched the skeleton of a ship from an aerial view, before rapidly proceeding to filling in more features. The detailed result took everyone by surprise. The amount of rigging and tiered sails on such a large wooden vessel bore no resemblance to anything remotely modern. Furthermore, the crew was entirely male and apparently European. Africans were portrayed without clothing, tied together. It looked like a scene out of a book on slavery. They simply did not get it. They were completely baffled.

"What is this?" The male officer picked up the drawing and held it up to Talisa's face, clearly frustrated, his sceptical eyes bulging, drawing breath at the end of his sentence. Rachel sensed Talisa found him intimidating. He was a big imposing figure even without the uniform.

The female officer whispered to the male in an effort to move things along. "She's drawn a ship and was found in the water. Just ask her how she got into the water to get an idea of what we're dealing with." The man agreed.

"Talisa, Talisa, do you remember whether you fell, were you pushed or did you jump into the water? Can you tell us anything about that?" This was as gentle and as simply as he could put the question. Again she seemed confused, sparking her increased agitation.

"Man push her, man push her in the water." She demonstrated with her hands, becoming so upset they had to suspend the interview. A single tear streamed down one side of her face. Dr Neville pronounced the interview over. It was all she could usefully communicate to them, which was hardly surprising under the circumstances. The officers would have to try talking to her when she was more recovered. They would keep in touch but the reality was they still had not gleaned enough to make any meaningful headway on her case other than a crime had been committed. The girl had indicated someone had tried to kill her and others were also implicated. Still, some of the details remained mystifying. At the end of it, Rachel put her arms around Talisa's shoulders and stroked the side of her face. She raised her chin up and told her she had done just fine.

As promised, Hopeton updated Peter on Talisa's progress. Peter having informed his mother of the child's condition and moved by the story, she had taken the initiative to help track down resources. He acknowledged her progress was amazing and was happy to hear how well she was doing.

Christmas was looming. With her improvement, heads were put together in earnest to find somewhere suitable for Talisa's continued rehabilitation in the New Year. Her language, motor and communication skills having made steady progress, Talisa was introduced to the novelty of radio and TV starting with children's programmes but also taking in sports events, mirroring the country's passionate pastimes. None of this appeared to overwhelm her. With this addition, her interaction and coordination improved tenfold.

Having thought it through, Hopeton approached Mrs Lawrence to be Talisa's temporary guardian, a labour she was more than pleased to accept, also having a spare room to accommodate. She was introduced to Talisa the first time Hopeton and Rachel brought her new charge to the house. Mrs Lawrence had accommodated a few youngsters this way over the years following her retirement. Looking at Talisa, her hair now in long natural braids, she immediately found her to be an unassuming little thing, for all the mystery surrounding her. However, there was something unmistakably mesmerising if you stared at her too long. It was a sense of looking beyond the beyond, that's how Mrs Lawrence experienced it. For all that, her surface assessment was that she was well behaved and curious which was just as well, as Talisa had a lot to learn and Mrs Lawrence was readily at hand for guidance.

The days passed quickly. Mrs Lawrence was a good cook and sometimes her helper Martine made meals, utilising some of the produce grown in the back yard. Sunday meals were particularly good after church. In reality, Talisa did not need to eat, the air she breathed, the water she drank and the elements she absorbed through her skin were sufficient to support her incarnation. However, everyone felt better when she ate and as her body was capable of full biological function, she indulged in eating and found it pleasurable.

There was nothing like a long sermon to work up an appetite for rice and peas and chicken. Talisa at first accompanied Mrs Lawrence on Sunday mornings. She avidly read the Bible and consumed as much information on religious beliefs as she could. One day she asked Mrs Lawrence why she attended services when it was obvious to her that her guardian did not exactly hold with everything the preacher had to say.

"Oh I don't go to church because of the Preacher," Mrs Lawrence announced. "Why

Preacher's just another lost child hoping he'll be one of the first of the risen when the time comes. In the meantime, he's just trying to do the best he can for his flock."

"So Mrs Lawrence, as knowledge has increased, even I know that, how come all these people are still calling the Creator by these false names, rather than the name he called himself? Don't you think that is truly disrespectful?"

"And what name would the Creator's real name be Talisa?"

"YHWH, the I am that I am, to be essential existence. Yah is existence itself. And Yeshua from what I've read is Maschiach, that means Messiah, so why has man changed these names? I never lost my name. Why would I answer to a name that is not my own? Abba is so merciful and people are so disrespectful."

"Girl child, it is more disrespectful than the names people like us, well perhaps not you, lost through slavery. You can't tell our Pastor though. They put him through theology programming that taught him what he should believe, but slowly and surely others are waking up. Can't blame them. A lot of confusion you see. That Devil has been tireless busy! Oh child, is just that I have a lot of friends at my church and the good Lord knows my heart. Why don't you ask Rachel to take you to one of her services? She's joined some new congregation along the lines you're speaking. Ask her bout it. I'm sure she wouldn't mind taking you along."

Talisa watched a little TV and listened to RJR radio sometimes, preferring the JBC radio debates which Mrs Lawrence listened with her occasionally. She saw the poverty in shanties across the country and in Kingston. She watched the violence, mayhem and reports of killings.

The girl troubled Mrs Lawrence with questions the old woman tried her best to answer while they waited for her to be admitted to a school. It was not Talisa's position to question The Leadership that had assigned her. Whatever her views, she would have to incorporate them in her report. It was what she was required to do.

Whenever she could, Talisa ventured out for local strolls, loving the outdoors as she did. One day, returning from one of her walks, having witnessed a crowd engaged in a heated argument, she later pressed her guardian for answers.

"Mrs Lawrence, how come some people are not like you, Rachel and Dr Bennett? They behave so aggressive. I've noticed even on TV how one person says something simple and the other person just wants to bite off the other person's head for little or no reason. Why is that?"

The old woman took a moment before responding, knowing that some situations might have a history, but there were others which were just spontaneous and opportunistic. She felt the girl had not had enough exposure yet to a large range of people and situations since leaving the clinic.

"Talisa, they say some of us have the worst of the Africans and the worst of the slave masters and pirates in us. How to mend something that started off so broken? Aye! If it wasn't for the Lord preserving us, we wouldn't even have survived thus far. All things considered child, I think we turned out none too bad for all of it. Ah girl!" she sighed. "I've been living amongst these people for far longer than you. Just you keep your wits about you when you're out and about. Ay sah!"

She hoped Talisa would be ready to take on the challenge of attending school and that the school would be able to support her tender needs. She noticed the child was very even tempered and that life seemed such a riddle to her; not too unlike the mystery she herself posed for others Mrs Lawrence pondered.

"I just wanted to sound out your thinking on the matter Mrs Lawrence. I think it admirable that you don't judge people."

CHAPTER SEVEN: INTERVIEW CONCLUDED

The child had been delivered with a suitcase of clothes. Rachel had eventually set up a computer to assist Talisa's learning while she was lodged. Steps had indeed been taken to enrol her into a local school, necessary not only for her education but also to improve her social skills. She had spent the past months primarily in the company of adults and needed to mix with peers more. Follow up appointments with Dr Neville were more than satisfactory and she was discharged into Dr Bennett's care.

The last Police interview had admittedly been a rather perplexing affair. This time they called at Mrs Lawrence's home. It was a week before Talisa was due to start school. Rachel was again drafted in to assist as was Mrs Lawrence herself. The same two officers arrived and went over the details Talisa had previously provided. This was the warm up to asking her how it was that she had become pregnant. The girl had responded by repeating the word pregnant and holding her belly. For a frightful moment Rachel thought she was going to go into convulsions as her eyes started to flicker, but on regaining her composure Talisa told them that girl had died. The female officer voiced her confusion, firmly asking what she meant by that statement. The girl appeared to be separating herself from the pregnancy. Talisa explained, in non-emotive terms, that to her knowledge, everyone in the room had been born because of similar circumstances; that they had all been born because of slavery. This surprising track took them aback, apart from Mrs Lawrence. Certainly, they were all well aware of the country's historical origins. But what did this have to do with Talisa's current predicament as she seemed to be linking them?

It was at that point that something strange happened. Seeing their obvious confusion, Talisa closed her eyes and projected visually to each in front of their own eyes, how their ancestors had come to Xamyca and events right up to their respective parents' birth. The images flashed in quick succession: men, women and children kidnapped, marched strung with others; crowded in stinking, seething dungeons in sweltering heat: the screams, whippings, blood, sores and bruises; the ships and the last glimpses of home; lying in harrowing filth spoonwise, racked with sickness. The stolen emerged from those hell holes with emaciated, shackled, dazed.

There were the marketplaces and the bartering for flesh; the irony of cutting sweet backbreaking sugar cane in day long scorching temperatures; the brandings, beatings, treading the mills, mutilations, black and tarred and left to be eaten by insects. Rape was routine, the children that died; those who survived, the sold, the powerless to prevent this triangulated tide of barbarism and depravity spanning centuries. The palpable loss of depth of feeling, the numbing to lessen the pain of plantation existence: the sanction of language to express even one's name; the obliteration of identity and the imprinting of someone else. There were the courageous who ran: those who fought back, those who took their own lives and those who endured; survivors who found hope, love and a sense of feeling, grasping for a belief in something greater than themselves, embracing this desperate hope as part of their own legacy. Mrs Lawrence's guests heard, smelt and bore witness to it all. Was it any wonder the inhumane truth of such a tortured existence was denied examination for generations, bequeathing a wealth of vile ignorance to fester, impoverish, subjugate and sugar-coat the future?

The experience left Mrs Lawrence's visitors distraught, drained weak. The male officer was in a foetal position, writhing on the floor with his companion trying to tear off her shirt, screaming and bawling as if the monstrous filth was clinging to her clothing: the rapes by the masters, the torment of the mistresses, the children bred, raised and sold; the leeching of breast-milk and the jealousies it all propagated.

It was a disturbing scene.

Rachel sat trance like, tears uncontrollably streaming from her eyes just rocking her body. Mrs Lawrence had been left out of the exercise because she was elderly and already had a grasp on what was going on. The information had been imparted at accelerated speed, being completed within a time lapse of five minutes for comfort. Mrs Lawrence tried best to calm the female officer, telling her it was Okay, it was over. She touched the man's leg which seemed chained to the spot, but he finally managed to wearily respond by raising his heavy laden off the floor, jerkily sniffing the air like a child recovering from a severe whooping. The old lady told Talisa to fetch water quick which they thirstily gulped down. Mrs Lawrence then took control of the situation.

"Well people, I would recommend that we are surely done for the day." She did not expect that anyone there needed a repeat of what they had just experienced any time soon. Her visitors simply nodded in agreement, still too dazed to speak. The two officers looked bashed in. They awkwardly gathered themselves before stumbling to the front door like two drunks. They sat in the vehicle for about twenty minutes before slowly driving away.

Mrs Lawrence told Talisa to prepare for bed. Before she went, the girl stopped to tell Rachel that she had only wanted her to understand and had not meant to hurt them. Rachel did not know what to say in response. She did not move. Mrs Lawrence hurried Talisa out of the room before helping Rachel to her feet, leading her into the kitchen and seating her on a high stool. She set about drawing some herb tea to help steady Rachel's nerves, making a cup for herself.

"Come drink this." Steam from the vervain beverage hit her nostrils before she took a sip, jolting her back to a jaded reality. She wiped her mouth.

"Hmm, hmm. That's better," Mrs Lawrence soothed. "Come again. Lean forward and close your eyes." She applied a little vervain lotion over Rachel's eye lids. "Drink up now."

"Who is she Mrs Lawrence? And how did she do that?! Make us see all that? How? I mean, I saw things my grandparents told me about. But the beginning, that terrible past, to see it unfold like that ..." she trailed off, wiping away trickles again.

The old woman shook a heavy head. "It must have been a living hell for those who lived through it. When I look at what is going on in the country now, it makes you wonder if some survived to live little better than they did then from the news." Rachel was too impacted to assimilate the contrast the old woman drew.

Hopeton had to work so could not pick Rachel up. She called a taxi, feeling too shaken to walk the mile or so home.

"But Talisa is just a child Mrs Lawrence." The taxi driver hooted his horn on arrival, Rachel gathered her belongings.

"Yes, but she's learning Rachel. Everyone comes into this world for a reason. We will know soon enough why she's here. Time girl, time." She walked Rachel out, giving her a warm hug and waved as the car drove away.

Talisa returned to her room and lay across her bed on her back, both hands behind her head, with thoughts momentarily still with Rachel. In time, she felt confident Rachel would understand there was no ill intent. She accessed the original Talisa's memories, selecting and projecting a family scene from before the abduction. Her mother was in her fifties but looked half her age. The youngest child of seven though five, was still doting around her mother's leg. On that fateful day, her father, who was a village elder, was engaged in solving a dispute between two men over the ownership of a cow. Mother had asked Talisa to fetch water from the river. It was an ordinary day, Talisa had picked up a jar, huddled it around her middle and shuffled off barefoot down the gently sloping hillside. She had greeted neighbours on their way up and called out to friends making their way back. Recent rains had swelled the current's rapid flow. It sounded louder even. Humming to herself, she crouched down and dipped her jar. She looked down, up and across the river as the jar filled. She was alone, the jar nearing full. Suddenly, she felt a hand over her mouth, almost cutting off her air. The jar slipped out of her hands as she struggled and was lifted. The jar rolled onto the rocks and was carried away with the swift current. Talisa curtailed the projection. The days were shortening, but her assignment was still on track. There was a knock on her door.

"Talisa?"

"Yes Mrs Lawrence. Come in." The door creaked as the old woman pushed it open.

"I'm just checking you alright. Rachel's gone home." There was a slight pause.

"Do you have something to ask me Mrs Lawrence, about earlier?"

Mrs Lawrence sighed, making her way into the room. She sat on the girl's bedside, her medium build resting easy on the firm mattress. She studied Talisa's face, the light of the shaded lamp shining on her dark skin and soft eyes. Talisa brushed a braid from across her face.

"Their parents missed them you know."

"I'm certain millions missed their children and loved ones."

"But children are still taken from parents in this world. In some places parents even sell their children."

"These things have continued happening over thousands of years Talisa, you know that."

"Being here is simply different from watching how life unfolds. My presence won't stop what is destined to happen. The balance is too disturbed. Too much has changed."

"What will be, will be Talisa. It is the Creator's will. We can but try." She stroked Talisa's hand and left the room.

Later that night, when Mrs Lawrence was sound asleep, Talisa decided to take a trip to west Kingston's frontline area, to Trench Town where the expectation of tragedy regularly played out to the pulse of music and indiscriminate revenge. A place where traumatised children took refuge under their beds when bullets oozed through the night air, piercing thin walls, their futures, their hopes; spawning nightmares. Under arching starlight, a rapport of Koch sprayed bodies fell; innocent souls and those of the guilty, departing in the night's gentle rain. The mental slavery Marley sang about rocked residents to a nervous sleep; water, rattling the encased in zinc warrens, burrowing into squalor and running into bleeding open sewers. Trapped, the anguished cowered in spite or silence, abandoned to fear and the love of a Don. Many gave thanks in their prayers for their enforcers and for small mercies, despite it all.

Talisa came across a gang of three giving another man a beating. It mattered not to them whether he was guilty or innocent of the alleged crime of stealing a Suzuki motorcycle he had been fingered for. One attacker, brandishing a knife, stepped forward sporting a grin. The victim was on the ground with his hands tied behind, begging for his life. Razor man yanked him up and cut his hands free. Another man caught the victim's right hand behind his back. He was dragged to a four foot wall.

"Finger stink, cuti off, You nah guh forget dis beat'n but to mek sure yeh." He shone the knife in the screaming victim's face before proceeding to deftly chop off his index finger. They threw him face down in the mud, where he writhed and whimpered in pain. They moved off slowly, laughing and cussing. As soon as they were out of sight, his friends emerged to recover him and the severed appendage.

Talisa turned away. She was by now well acquainted with the cruelties this world could exact. Her remit had strict boundaries of engagement to which she was entrusted to adhere. She could not have interfered in this instance, even if the man had been near death. She returned to Negril, where its river ran with more hope out to sea.

Passing the course of the Negril River one afternoon she happened upon some young men playing football, watched by a bunch of giggling girls, a few older encouraging adults and a rasping fit referee. An older Rasta man sat on a portable chair, stroking his beard. He her hailed her presence. She turned back and went to speak to him. She was curious about his views on hemp, having recently listened to a number of radio debates on the subject. She hoped he would indulge her encroaching on his enjoyment of the match but wanted to hear his first-hand views.

With the known historical and modern industrial uses of hemp commercially, the esteemed professors at Mona, UWI, were seeking to be able to do research without biased impediments. They were not Rastas trying to make a point about sacrament.

She introduced herself by saying she was new to the island and area.

"Hope you liking YamaiKah young sistrine." He shook his red sun bleached silver matted locks. He had meant to say Jamaica but she had allowed his tongue to slip. The sound would stay with him, resurface later.

She went straight to the point saying she'd seen people smoking cannabis on television and knew that governments across the world were against it but not against alcohol or tobacco consumption which did as much or more harm to the body as ganja. What did he think about that?

The Rasta looked at her quite soberly, introduced himself as Jah Rumble.

"Tel-e-vision, now dat is one evil someting you ah talk bout. All dem show is de wickedness of dem own pollution and de sickness of fi dem mind. De European power structure and dem wind-up toys dem have all over de world jus ah fool people. But duppy know who fi frighten, yuh hear me? Mek me ask yuh, dem teach you bout slavery ina school dese days?"

"A little" she needed to keep him on track, "but why do people smoke when your lungs were made to breathe air to sustain life? Can you explain that to me Jah Rumble?"

"Look, man drink, man smoke. Dis bring him into another state if done in a spiritual way. Nuthin' nuh wrong in dat. Now, Rasta smoke him herbs to bring him closer to the Creator. Yuh understand? Dat is part of fi we worship, seen?"

"But shouldn't His Word be enough to sustain you?"

"Dawta, you is a young girl an' I don't expect you fi understand. Sensemelia is a god given plant fi all mankind, nuh just fi de rich an' powerful. Dem devil people just want fi control everyting and everyone, yuh nuh see? But dem nah control I and I Rasta, ah ow!"

"Hmm … So do you really believe that Haile Selassie is God, when the Ethiopians say they have his body?"

"Look, dat don't mean anyting. Selassie fulfil prophecy."

"But prophecy does not say that Messiah would die twice."

“Rasta nah seh dat either.” He laughed, skinning his nicotine teeth against his otherwise soft grained features.

“He was not in line for the succession of the Ethiopian throne either.”

“No man can deny you what you are destined for.”

“So, getting back to slavery – which you did bring up - does that mean that you agree that Africans were destined to be brought to this island to be made slaves too?”

“We are and were rebellious Israelites, past, present. Yuh seh yuh watch TV suh you see de violence and killing ah tek place pon dis ya little island, like nowhere else fi we size. We too dreadful. But I an’ I know seh man must change still, cos a nuh by fi we will why tings come to pass. Jamaicans jus a wake up to de reality of dat which Rasta been telling dem for generations. Israel deh ya suh seen.” She had stirred him up. He shifted in his chair. Had she been older, he probably would have demonstrably been up on his feet at this point. She continued to press him.

"You think it possible that people of African descent can be labelled racists even on a one on one basis, taking into account what's happened across the world historically to people of colour in lands of their own heritage?"

"One on one, people will get into scraps for all kina reasons seen. Dat been going on since Cain and Abel. But when yuh check wha gwan over di past five hundred years, every picture tell a story little sistrine. Racism comes from the mighty Western power system, inflicting demselves pon indigenous populations worldwide. Dats what I an' I have fi defend against. Read up pon yuh Marcus Garvey little more yeh an' listen to some Mutabaruka seen."

She smiled at him, appreciating his even temper and candid response. One of the boys scored a goal past the makeshift goal post, causing an uproar.

"Nice one Star!" The Rasta jumped out of his chair yelling. "Him soon good enough fi go Europe yuh know," he excitedly conveyed to Talisa.

She considered this thought a moment. With a lot more training and support, Jah Rumble had hit spot on the youth's potential.

"Hmm ... Who knows ..." She remarked. He looked at her through a squint, sensing that she concurred with his assessment. She thanked Jah Rumble when he finished celebrating and turned to leave.

"Alright, respect, young sistrine. One love you hear?"

"I hear you Jah Rumble."

She had not gone far when a car pulled up suddenly to the curb. A young woman, in skimpy colourful attire with large spiral earrings emerged, slammed the door and trotted off in a huff. The burly driver tried bolting after her, passing Talisa. They stopped, blocking the way ahead, fussing.

"Hold on Cristabel. Hear me out nuh? Baby please, just hear me out one time. I'm sorry ok," the Chinese looking man, undoubtedly years her senior pleaded. Obviously what Jamaicans called a 'Boops' and a workaholic whose family had not joined the haemorrhage out of the country.

"Me nuh tell you nuh fi call me nuh baby. You ever see me ina diapa a shake rattle?"

"Alright, alright. I'll make more time for you. Promise." She breathed hard, pouted and folded her arms in an effort to calm down. Talisa passed the disjointed couple at this point, asking them to excuse her.

"Sorry. Come outa di way nuh. Mek de chile pass." The young woman pulled the man by his shirt out of the way.

"Oh sorry." He acknowledged her presence, seeming startled, as if he had been caught in some undesirable act, covering his wedding ring.

Talisa had gone about ten metres when she sensed she was being trailed. There was a distinct disturbance in tow, an intense odour of mischief. Furthermore, she could tell the presence was non-human. Glancing back, she recognised the trace of a weak signature shadow, despite no visible form. The couple were still arguing on the sidewalk.

"Archon, I command you to reveal your presence and explain why you are following me." She kept walking, while waiting for a response. "Don't let me call out your name, lest you want to battle right here right now." She spoke in the ancient angelic tongue.

The Archon obeyed, the tiniest particles of carbon falling as he revealed himself dressed casually as a fourteen year old boy of Jamaican blend.

"Why are you meddling in things that don't concern you Messenger?" He spoke with a coarse voice, way older than his apparent years.

"That disguise one of your clones?"

"I might ask you the same," he quipped.

"Not the same. Talisa died as a result of your Master's plunder and cruelty like millions like her. But she was not bred."

"Then she died because she was weak and mere flesh as these condemned mortals do."

Sonareille, her Assigned name, was swift tiring of this. "What do you want Archon?"

"For you to leave this island and this world immediately."

"Is that fear I smell or is that skunk you're wearing beginning to smoulder?"

The Archon laughed. “An Assigned with a sense of humour. That’s a first.”

Sonareille continued. “You know full well I cannot oblige your request, not now that you’ve put this whole planet in jeopardy. I will leave when I’m done. Your time is, relatively speaking, running out along with the material inducements you tempt these humans with.” The prophetic arrow of time was pulling taut.

“This dominion is ours until the full count is reached.”

“The weight of what you say is as usual only partially true. A few prophecies remain to be fulfilled. I am simply here to curtail your onslaught in relation to one soul in particular. The woman’s prayers were received and as a result you will be resisted.

“The woman did not pray to the Creator of the Universe Messenger. She prayed to my Master, the Ruler of her world.”

“As do so many others following your counterfeit observances. Must you insist on blaming them for their lack of insight, due to your meticulous rigging? A masterpiece of deception I quickly add.”

He hesitated before replying. “We may yet meet in battle Assigned but not at this hour.”

“I am but one Assigned, Archon. Be gone!”

The boy and his weak shadow vanished. Talisa continued her walk as if he had never materialised.

CHAPTER EIGHT: SCHOOLING

Before Talisa started school, Mrs Lawrence took her to see Hopeton at his surgery for one last check.

It was nearing the end of Hopeton's working day. His penultimate patient was Mr Alderton, a forty-eight year old barber, ardent rum drinking smoker who was also overweight. He was there for the results of his blood tests which confirmed he had type 2 diabetes, a growing problem for sugar loving Jamaicans. The irony of the legacy of past sugar plantations was not lost to Hopeton, in a non-medical sense.

Mr Alderton had first presented with a left eye ptosis and high blood pressure. The bad news took the patient by surprise. He sat rubbing his forehead for several minutes while Hopeton ran through the recommended treatment plan. Diet and exercise alone would probably prove problematic in Mr Alderton's case but his ptosis could possibly be helped by surgery. He wrote out a prescription and made an appointment for the patient to see the practice nurse who would take him through all the necessary details about managing his condition. He saw the man out and collected Talisa from reception.

"Talisa?"

"I'm here Dr Bennett."

"Come, come in and take a seat."

"So, how are you doing these days?"

"Much better. I think I'm recovered now."

"Sounds good to me from the report I've seen. I'll just check a few things for the all clear." He checked her blood pressure, which was fine for a young woman of her age and build.

"Like to just do a quick eye check if you don't mind. I won't put any dye in them, just that eyes happen to be my specialty and I like to have a map of my patients' visual health."

"If you like." He closed the blinds and washed his hands. He asked her to read the chart which she did without a hitch. He physically examined her eye ball and lids before using the scope to check her response to light which at first was pretty normal. As he moved closer in however, he had a bit of a shock. Instead of light, he saw himself looking back at himself.

“Something wrong Dr Bennett?”

“Ah no, no.” He stuttered, hitting the instrument in his palm. “Er, let me try that again. Sorry about that.” He tried his best to remain composed. This time he saw what appeared to be an array of stars; then further away galaxies and nebulae. He withdrew quickly, disorientated and hot.

“Ah, just hold on Talisa. Hmmm … I just need to get another one of these,” he held up the scope and feverishly searched for another. Talisa remained still.

“Let’s try again.” On the third attempt, he could clearly see the physical structures of her eyes as they should appear, moving from right to left. All was well.

“Looks fine Talisa." He stuttered. "Thank you for being so, so patient.”

“No problem Dr Bennett. Can I go now?” She looked innocently at him.

“Yes, by all means. Enjoy your time at school.”

"Thank you."

Hopeton opened the blinds again and sat at his desk. He retrieved the scope that had malfunctioned from the drawer. He shook his head, reflecting on what had just occurred; on how he had found Talisa; that poem and Mrs Lawrence giving him that tract. Rachel's account of what happened at the interview also came to mind. Two uncontrollable tears ran down his cheeks. Finally he was beginning to understand, to see how frightening and how marvellous it all was.

There was a gentle knock on his door.

"Dr Bennett? We're locking up for the night now." Iona, the receptionist put her head around the door.

"Ah yes, Iona. I'll be right out."

Talisa finally started attending school; Mrs Lawrence took her the first day. It was a mixed school. She wore a sandy coloured uniform like everyone else. The children stared at her, this strange presence in their midst. She did not make friends easily it has to be said. Mrs Lawrence felt this was probably a blessing in disguise.

Her peers also found her accent odd, though they did not tease in front of her face. She was bright and foreign, not given to the regular things that interested the average young person of her age. But for her size and build, it was sometimes hard to reconcile her age with her assessment of things when pressed in class one teacher noted. Talisa reminded him of a very old person in a young body. For example, given an assignment about tackling youth unemployment, Talisa had no compunction in saying that young people cannot be left to idleness, that society could not afford the consequences of such indolence. Some of her classmates gasped. Mr Marshall, who taught history, asked what she thought the solution should be. Talisa had no qualms in proposing a form of national service for all young people who were not in education or gainful employment, besides the fact that most of them did not know how to grow anything that passed their mouths. Mr Marshall asked her what she would do with those who had dropped out of the system prematurely. She simply said no one would be exempt under the age of twenty-one and that money should not be an obstacle in commencing such a programme. Mr

Marshall laughed, by twenty-one some of those people were already parents, the horse had already bolted and besides, Cuba had already gone that route. Talisa simply restated there should be no exemptions and that all people should know how to grow food to feed their own families at the very least. The class followed Mr Marshall's suit in branding Talisa a socialist idealist or even worse: a communist. For someone who was apparently so bright, wasn't she aware that neither China nor Russia adhered to those old models in the 21st century? Talisa's response was that socialism and communism had been designed and practised by those who already had entrenched inequalities and therefore those systems were doomed to failure from their inception. Both systems were undermined by disingenuous ideals and gross mismanagement of priorities. It was folly to even compare them to what was needed. When Mr Marshall asked how she would get people to join her programme, he was astonished to hear her say that they should be asked.

"You would just ask them?"

"Yes and show them."

"Just ask them?" The class erupted in laughter.

"Talisa, I don't know which country or planet you're from. You think you can just ask people to do something and they'll do it?"

"Yes sir."

CHAPTER NINE: UPHILL

Fortunately the school bell rang before anyone could press her further on the matter. Following that discussion however, she somehow managed to intrigue a few classmates, beyond what was formerly a touch of fear of her, they felt warmer towards her. One of these was a girl by the name of Mareka, remarkably one of the quieter ones. The history class had been their final lesson for the day. While continuing the class discussion, Mareka asked Talisa to follow her to the girls' toilet which she obliged, though not needing to go there. Mareka produced a jar of cream from which she proceeded to daub on her face while staring in the mirror.

"What are you doing?" Talisa queried.

"Oh this is just some bleaching cream I'm using to clear up some dark facial spots."

"You're using bleaching cream for that?"

"Hmm, hmm."

“Have you seen your doctor about your spots? For goodness sakes, do you really know what you’re doing?”

“I’m not going to use it for long. Besides, you don’t understand. You’ve got good even skin.”

“Mareka, some things don’t take long to do harm. I think you should see your doctor about your skin problems. At least stop using it until then. Why don’t you raise the issue of bleaching creams in science? The teacher wants us to choose a project to do. If you like, I’d do one on bleaching creams with you.”

Mareka looked at Talisa seriously. “You really think it could be harmful? Then why everybody using it?”

“Mareka, I’d stop following ignorant follow-fashion people. You want to do this project with me or what?”

She thought for a moment. “Ok, I’ll do it. I was wondering who and what to do mine about in any case.”

“Good, ‘til then, beg you please stop using that awful cream.”

"Alright."

On exiting the school gate, a car horn was blowing to riddim. Mareka recognised her cousin in the front passenger seat. She said goodbye to Talisa and made for the back seat where she slid in next to Ria. The person who looked over at Talisa was none other than Sherice, her neck still in the brace. She asked Mareka who her friend was and was simply told a classmate. Sherice had a good memory for faces but for some reason could not quite place Talisa. She asked Ria if she recognised her but she also didn't know her. Trench, who was driving her replacement car to keep her happy, turned the music up. Richie Spice was blaring out "Ghetto Girl", as they drove off with Sherice yelling at the uniformed children to move out of the road. The youngsters moved but laughed at her. She looked like a mad woman in that dark blue collar, shouting at them.

They hadn't driven too far when Trench's BB buzzed. He turned down the radio and drove the car to a kerb. The others started complaining. One glance at the display confirmed it was Backra on the line. "'Ol on, just a minute," he answered as he opened the car door and walked off to complete his call. The passengers complained even more. Sherice watched his streamlined body language keenly. He cut an alpha package; 5' 10", trim and hardy; short cut hair with the slightest side burns and even slighter moustache; what Jamaicans termed a "face man".

"Mind a nuh one a him woman friends him a talk to," Ria teased Sherice.

"Gal hush up. If you knew any ting bout man you'd read seh dat a business."

"So what kina business Trench into den Sherice?"

"None of yours that's for sure. I don't know and I don't want to know. And if trouble come, I don't know him either suh mine yuh mouth." With the last ominous comment, Ria kept quiet; nursing thoughts; at a loss as to what Trench saw in the bitch. Sherice turned the music back up.

"I have a job fi you need urgent attention. Meet me in an hour an' bring Cornell," Backra snapped.

"Be there," Trench returned. Backra's line went dead. Trench ambled back to the car.

“I’ll drop you off and pick up my wheels. Got tings to do.” The Jamerican twang of his announcement did not cushion how it was met with complete silence.

Walking home alone, Talisa noticed three children playing in the street about six or seven year olds tops with a younger one. They were barefoot with torn up clothes, but seemed happy enough for all that.

The youngest came up to her, “Beg you little someting to eat nuh Miss?” The others chuckled.

“Grandma seh you mustn’t beg! I gwan tell!”

Talisa searched her bag, retrieving a bag of peanuts in the shell and a banana she had not yet eaten. She peeled the banana, inviting them to break off a portion each.

“Thank you.”

She handed the boy who looked the eldest the bag of nuts. “You live round here?” she asked. The boy pointed up a hill.

“Over suh. Live with we grandma.”

"Your grandma know where you are?" She noted they had not said mother.

"She tell we to go play, so we come out here."

"Don't you go to school?"

"I been school couple times. Grandma seh she can't afford school fees fi all ah we."

"I think you children should be heading back home. Show me where you live. I'll walk with you." The children giggled, not quite knowing what to make of their new found friend with the funny accent but were happy about it.

The smallest girl, though shy, sported a huge grin, while hiding behind her brother's back with one finger in her mouth.

It took a good half hour to climb up the hill to where the children lived. Talisa's thoughts ran to Mrs Lawrence. A cell phone probably would not have worked up there if so had one, so she hoped Mrs Lawrence would simply sense she was fine. The children's grandmother was out in the yard gathering the last of the day's washing from the line. A couple fowls were strutting in the dirt, the woman shooed them away. Two younger children were playing hand clapping songs, twin girls around three years old. They stopped when they saw Talisa, overcome with shyness, started playing with their clothing and noses instead.

They all inhabited the dilapidated one room house that had been passed down to the latest generation. An extension would help and a lot of work was needed.

"Ah who dis unuh bring? Dena and Lena," she turned to the twins. "Stop lif up yuh skirt ah show people yuh baggy!" she chided. Talisa smiled warmly as they both lowered their little hand-me-down skirts. She had learned Jamaica had one of the highest incidents of twin births in the world. These two dimpled girls were thriving despite the obvious lack of material possessions.

"Me nuh see yuh before little Miss?" Auntie inquired once she was closer.

"I don't think so Auntie, as I'm new in the area and just thought I'd take a little look around for myself." The sound of a helicopter roar could be heard in the distance. Talisa looked up, shielding her eyes, her ears honing in on the noise some three hundred feet above the tree line over yonder.

"I like yuh uniform. Like di way yuh talk. Can tell you nuh from roun' 'ere. We nuh get much people come up yah suh, only fi boderation." The chopper was closing in on their location. "Sometime the church people come dough. Dem bring food, clothes an' shoes, books and tings fi dem pickney. Teach dem bout di Lord. Dem nuh leave we out still." She'd finished taking down the clothes, draping them over her thin sun-baked frame. She herself could not read, but it was not something she would divulge to a perfect stranger.

"Hmm hmm. Not many people visit otherwise then." It was a statement drawn from fragments of what this life beaten woman had imparted.

"Uh, uh," the woman replied. "Mostly dem man who come up 'ere a wave paper ina me face." She kissed her teeth. "Me tell dem fi tek dem paper guh wipe dem batty." She was standing akimbo, probably around sixty years old by her silver grey plaits, yet too fit to be fat from all her labours. Talisa had noticed quite a few of the children in her school were overweight and sluggish while these poor children were active and lean.

"Could I take a look at one of those papers you mentioned, that is if you kept any?" The woman studied Talisa hard for a short while. She then waved an index finger.

"It couldn't do any harm fi share what dem papers seh after all. I tink seh me did keep di fus one dem bring. 'Ol on." She disappeared into her home, emerging a short while after with a document. Talisa scanned through it. Basically it sought her agreement to give up all rights to the land and property and for her and her family to vacate on the said day of signing on receipt of monies, the final amount to be agreed, which would be payable by transfer into her delegated bank account. Talisa relayed the gist of what the paper said.

"Oh. Hmm, hmm. Well, dem can't pay me enough to move from yah. Uh,uh. Dis is home."

The chopper was closing in. Everyone looked up as it approached, now hovering just above the trees. It was near enough for Talisa to peer through the blue aluminium painted skin into the cockpit. There was the pilot and two passengers seated behind him: a German business man, Ranulf Heidrich, and Backra, an illegitimate baptised Lester Hawes, a Jamaican Real Estate Broker, come other merchandising operator. The two had earlier been at a racing event at the troubled Caymanas Park, discussing cash flow and doping issues, but now the conversation descended on the area which Ranulf, a driven bulk of a fifty-six year old, was looking to purchase to build another holiday home for his young wife to enjoy. He was depending on Backra assisting with smoothing residency issues, which he did not have time for. There remained the niggling matter of the few residents who were still living on the hill top. Heidrich did not want the wrong sort of neighbours in his vicinity, naturally. Jamaica's violent reputation did not scare him. He was used to dealing with people who knew how to start wars, ending such ventures was not so profitable. Backra was confident the neighbours would not be an issue. Heidrich smiled, counting on it.

Talisa returned the paper and her attention to the woman in front of her.

"Only few ah we lef up ya now. Dem want try throw we off we land but I nah move from ya suh. Dis land ah fi we from time. Whole ah my family bury up yah. Dem pickney mother too." The woman had continued in a raised voice, ignoring the botheration of the circling vulture high above. With the children's mother dead, their grandmother had a lot to cope with and all alone. The helicopter started veering off north of their location.

"Me nuh ave nuh help, save wah little strength di Lord gi me." She raised her head to the sky, followed the back of the chopper in the distance until it was out of sight.

Talisa surveyed the surroundings in more detail and sucked in the air. The intoxicating smell of deep roots and iron was an enchanting feast to her senses. Relative to many parts of the island, the hill top was leafy green, the soil, red and rich. It felt more natural than all the environments she had up to then experienced, more homely than the garden in the clinic or even Mrs Lawrence's back yard. This was certainly worth fighting for.

"You grow your own food Auntie?"

"Do some planting over deh" She pointed to the left of the path they had climbed. "We still mek tings fi sell to de tourists. Times hard girl, times hard." shaking a sorrowful head but still managed a toothless grin.

"Do you have any animals?"

"We have couple Hope Cow an' couple goat and dem chicken deh." She turned to the boy. "Leon, get dem chicken ina de coob nuh? People love fi buy foreign food cause it cheap, but all I can see is pure destruction fi dem an' me nuh go ah dem school. Come." She beckoned Talisa to follow her as she walked further up the path to a pasture where the goats and cows were grazing.

Auntie explained that they had breadfruit, green bananas and all kinds of fruit when in season. They grew yam, potatoes, a lot of vegetables which they shared with the few neighbours left. Up there, they pretty much lived as they did sixty years ago. They used to sell produce in town too but people didn't buy what was natural anymore and every minute running to the doctor for some ailment. They wanted everything from the supermarket because it was convenient and carried status, as if to be poor was a sin. In reality, the foreign foodstuffs were not better in quality or nutrition. Auntie didn't understand how people could be so blind. How could people not have any relationship with growing the food they ate?

Talisa watched the animals intensely. She thanked Auntie for her time, declining the offer of a drink until next time. She told the children to be good as she headed for home. Auntie called out that she was welcome any time she was ready. Talisa waved back in acknowledgement. The woman had taken to this girl's spirit in the short time they had shared.

Going back down the hill took less time of course than going up. Mrs Lawrence said she had been initially concerned that she was so late with not even a phone call to say what had happened, but for some reason she hadn't worried too tough. She sensed Talisa was safe. That feeling had been transmitted and with the assurance a phone call probably wouldn't have translated. However, Talisa still apologised, explaining about her trip up the hill.

Mrs Lawrence hummed, "Hmm, hmmm. A lot of them people moved to make way for tourist homes and the like. A wonder you found anyone left up there."

"So why do tourists need to buy homes in Jamaica in any case?" Talisa asked, "When so many people here don't even have decent homes to live in themselves and the land is good. The people should be able to make a living from it."

Mrs Lawrence looked hard at Talisa. "Oh girl child, there's so much you still have to catch up with."

The tourist industry had not been the saving grace for the island people had hoped. The negative impact on the poor in many respects had made matters worse. On the contrary, those who already had seemed to end up with a lot more, leaving many who had little to begin with even less than what their African forebears had. But the meek were indeed supposed to inherit the earth. Did the US and EU farmers represent the meek? These titanic trading blocks had dumped their cheap subsidised products on the vulnerable Jamaican market, killing off the country's own food production industry. The impact on non-service employment was devastating, giving rise to the worst poverty in generations while battles and turf wars raged in the garrison areas. Garrisons during the slave trade were places where slaves were herded, and therein dwelt a particular kind of perverse irony.

Since the 1970's, the people in these garrisons were made desperate pawns in an ever increasing toxic and impoverishing international game which maintained the global status quo and monopoly in play. A percentage of the population still lived with lack of clean running water, decent levels of sanitation, no electricity and this was also the case in the capital. Solar, non-reliant fossil fuelled green innovations and technologies were lacking or had been deliberately stifled by outsiders. The country was in desperate need of more self-sufficiency, not least in order to weather tough times ahead.

Mrs Lawrence's parents would turn in their graves if they saw what had happened to farming and fishing on the island. Talisa doubted their ancestors had lived in worse conditions prior to slavery or colonialism. This was a strange kind of progress where less quality was being peddled as more, when increasing toxicity was harmful to the environment and people. Some recognised these circumstances to be a national disgrace, perpetuated by a lack of vision, planning, greed, political sectarianism and foreign dictates for decades. Hemp was only one of the issues of course, when the professors at Mona, University of the West Indies, knew as well as anyone the historical, commercial and industrial use of the plant. Much of the control on this issue was nothing more than that; First World monopoly and this of course would not last the test of time. If your people were doomed to suffer, then surely it would be better to suffer for truth and something wholesome you could take pride and believe in, rather than something that would eventually eat you out of house and home like the leftover dregs being peddled to Jamaicans. Decent food and basic shelter were necessities for all – not mansions, swimming pools and all the craven excesses the planet and its environment could not support. Talisa knew change had to come or the people would have to face some deadly consequences either way. The planet was changing, only those who were ready to change with it would make it. Mrs Lawrence recognised Talisa knew something was happening. The old woman had read her Bible constantly. She knew the things foretold for those who would not change. She had already seen enough. If things were to worsen, she was happy for her Lord to take her than to live through sufferation.

CHAPTER TEN: ROVING

Talisa turned into her room. She didn't want to read or to listen to the radio tonight, preferring to lie still on her bed, not needing to sleep the way humans did. What the doctors identified as her brain, was constantly active. Resting was downtime, used to effortlessly remote view, selecting places deemed as restful. There was enough distress on the TV. Tonight she allowed her mind to wander to the beach near where she was found. She could hear the waves swooshing, to the sound of its fluid rhythm. She watched the crabs scurrying as if in a race. Out to sea, something caught her eye. There was a boat out there. She scanned back to see a car drive up on the beach as another a man set a canoe down on the sand.

It was around midnight, the British coastguard ship was long gone and the stretched Jamaican Marine Control was busy patrolling elsewhere and there being no other visible eyes in the sky above. The yacht signalled on cue. Trench signalled back by flashlight, instructing Kayak to collect the merchandise and hardware, handing him a TYT radio just in case there was something he needed to communicate.

The wispy dread put on his life jacket and took the canoe to the water's edge. When he had settled his weight comfortably, he gripped his paddle and steered the canoe out to sea with the next assisting wave. The trim cut a channel through the pleasant Caribbean waters, with only the stars above to spy on their nocturnal activities.

As he came alongside the yacht, Kayak was thrown a rope to help steady the canoe. He called out a brief "Thanks". The cargo was passed down to him in a basket as Spanish speakers jabbered in the background of the vessel. He evenly distributed the cargo to compensate for the extra displacement. With a simple "OK" business was concluded. He threw back the rope, turned the canoe and headed back to shore. There the merchandise was swiftly unloaded by the two men who accompanied General Trench. Trench paid Kayak who took off on foot with his canoe. The others left in the rented Land Rover.

Talisa rolled onto her stomach. Her thoughts turned to Mareka. She hoped the girl would not come to any harm, being on the peripheral edge of this pernicious matrix, with its tendency to engulf the innocent.

However, she instinctively knew something more was stirring across the world. Caribbean quakes were running more frequently as in other parts of the world. Haitians had not recovered from their mighty quake and aftermath months prior. But something huge was grating miles away in the Pacific. It was April 10th. Most Jamaicans were not even aware of a place called Fukushima, Japan. In a few days the ensuing disaster, the loss of life and the nuclear fallout would hit the world. The global impact of this would resound with economic consequences. Jamaicans would come to realise how this event would also affect their own economy and trade with their Japanese partners.

Talisa felt unsettled, deciding to venture out of town despite the rain. It was time to view Jamaica from another vantage point, to see more of the expanse of Planet Blue Water to which she had been assigned. Quietly leaving her room and out into the night air, she looked up at the vault of the sky, at the array of shifting stars. Initiating the transportal would make her invisible to the naked eye. This vehicle had no controls. Everything was initiated by thought and frequency. She invoked its transparent surround and gently rose from the ground to an initial altitude of one thousand feet, acquainting herself with the panoramic night view. She swiftly climbed higher just as the ISS swept by.

From this atmospheric vantage point, the land sprawled beneath her: streets strung with snaking beaded headlights, rolling pearls. All the romance, sadness and human dramas playing out to the night's rhythm: all the tragedies in the making under a warm blanket of darkness. A waning crescent moon shone through a cushion of grey lit weepy clouds.

She ascended higher, through the planet's thinly layered atmosphere, from where she witnessed a dance of distant thunder heads light, the ensemble spanning the curving night sky; curtains of red spikes lighting up. From a stratospheric view, geosynchronous satellites dotted in orbit; accumulating pieces of manmade debris forming a graveyard, incinerating waste on re-entry with the incalculable tons of falling grains of space dust and disintegrating meteors, sparking up the dark but posing little threat to the planet's inhabitants. Such threats were closer to the ground.

From here she could better sense the other Assignees, messengers on missions across the world. Yet higher still, she skated the gravity betwixt the planet, its tugging moon: the hidden power of the Sentinel Sun, though compromised by the Enemy, managing to maintain the system's planetary integrity, in the universal movement with other galactic bodies.

Talisa focused back on the darkened Planet Blue Water, before a rapid descent to three hundred feet, having made the gentle journey to Kingston in under three minutes. She floated, lowering above a house where a couple were arguing; heard a slap and a woman scream. A baby started crying as voices rasped shrill. To the north, a distinct rapport of gunfire and the response of sirens: reprisals, targets or indiscriminate drive-bys; the accustomed guilty blended with innocence, all dropping like flies to a high powered spray of grief and the sickening smell of blood.

She turned, moving on as cats ran here and there to get out of the rain. The dogs revelled in shaking some of their fleas; perhaps a few might even dislodge from their slippery hairs. A couple without an umbrella ran together to catch a taxi, laughing. In the hospitals, babies were being born, with mothers crying tears of joy, while others cried for the loss of a loved one. The dance of life to the sound of musical pulses permeated the air. Elsewhere wars, uprisings, turmoil and instability were engulfing the planet's inhabitants. All was far from well on this so precious world.

CHAPTER ELEVEN: ACROSS THE DIVIDE

The British were getting ready for the Royal Wedding 29th April. News of the preparations certainly had some islanders intrigued. For now the Queen was still Head of State of Jamaica, though the politics of the day was looking to sever that colonial legacy.

Talisa's studies had progressed to such an extent that both Rachel and Mrs Lawrence were convinced she would do well in programmed exams. The child just seemed to soak up knowledge as if there was no tomorrow. Within seven months she had gone from the level of a toddler to being at the top of her class.

When Hopeton had relayed this news to Peter, he could hardly believe it. Hopeton arranged for Talisa to speak to him via a video link. The child had grown accustomed to a diversity of people at the clinic and in the area at large, regularly seeing Europeans, Japanese, Chinese and others. She had picked up a lot from the internet as well. She informed Peter that she had indeed watched the Royal Wedding with Mrs Lawrence on TV and understood the relationship between Jamaica and the British historically.

"Dr Stratford," she finally said in her even, confident tone. "I'd like to thank you for helping to rescue me. I didn't mean to scare you."

"Only too glad to have been of service Talisa, and to know that you are doing so well is excellent in fact considering."

"I was how you say, disorientated I think the word is."

"Hardly surprising Talisa, hardly surprising."

She knew her mission left her little time, but she wanted to be able to see Dr Stratford again to thank him personally. It seemed incomplete to simply be talking to him through a screen. She didn't have time to travel in the conventional sense and, travelling in her own mode was not going to resolve the issue. She settled on not dwelling on the matter.

Hopeton was about ready to pop the question to Rachel. If she said yes, Peter would be sent an invitation and if he was able to attend, Talisa would be provided ample opportunity to thank Peter in person.

Peter and Brenda's relationship since returning from their holiday had had its ups and downs. Brenda worked from home as an accountant, but this night she was on the internet again having put Chloe to sleep. She had recently signed up to an online dating site just for fun. Again, she didn't seem to have enough of that lately. Her life was admittedly still as good as a gold fish bowl for three to outsiders, despite the downturn. She was toying with the idea of an affair. But why did she need this in her life? To plug the gnawing gaps opening up in hers perhaps. She was not a gold fish after all. Her life lacked excitement in reality. She had trawled for a prospective lover and had hit upon a viable candidate. As he was also married, it need not be complicated. She toyed with the pros and cons as if attempting to reconcile a balance sheet.

"How's it going?" She had been startled to find Peter standing in the doorway, hadn't heard him come in. She logged out and shutdown.

"Oh! I thought you were on lates this week."

"There's been a little shake up. They finally hired someone to fill Russell's vacancy which cuts a little slack. You didn't have to stop on my account. Didn't realise accounts was such fun." He had noticed her animated body language.

"Just a client thanking me for sorting out his paperwork. What I get paid for after all. All the excitement I get in a day round here." She rose from her chair and snuggled up to him.

"Want me to run you a bath?"

"Only if you'll be joining me. We haven't done that for the longest. Plus it would give me a chance to create a little excitement around here."

She patted his nose and pecked his lower lip teasingly. "Oh, I'm all for any excitement I can get darling. One hot bath coming up doc."

Several days later, Peter was sat at his desk in his study, reflecting on the phone call from Hopeton. He smiled and shook his head. He was about to find out what Brenda and Chloe were up to when he heard a voice.

"Dr Stratford, Dr Stratford?"

He looked around, trying to pinpoint where the voice was coming from.

"Dr Stratford." He could not be certain, but it sounded a lot like Talisa's voice. The laptop was off and the phone. He heard it again. It was coming from behind him. He turned, surprised to see what he could only describe as a holographic Talisa standing there in his study.

"Talisa? Talisa, what, how?"

The image scanned the room. "You have a nice place here Dr Stratford. A nice home, family. Dr Stratford, you need to talk to your wife more. Yes, a lovely home, a family home. But you really need to talk to your wife. Thanks again Dr Stratford."

"Talisa? Talisa? What in the world?!" The image was gone. He stood astonished. Had he just experienced a hallucination? He hadn't been drinking. He felt a little shaken up. He pointed to the computer, then to where the image had stood, he scratched his head. Nothing like that had ever happened before. He shook it off as an aberration due to the recent stress. He went to find Brenda and Chloe in the garden.

"Are we still going to your mother's for dinner?" Brenda asked.

"Ready when you two are."

They drove over to Ealing for dinner with his parents as arranged. This proved to be more of a subdued affair than usual. Brenda was a lot more reticent in conversation her mother-in-law would note with those soft engaging eyes whose lines marked years of determining when something was amiss. Peter appeared somewhat distracted too, several times not hearing what his father had said. It was usually the other way round since his dad sometimes forgot to switch on his hearing aid. She asked Peter to help her dry the dishes, something usually delegated to Chloe so they could catch up. Granddaddy Gerald was only too pleased with the opportunity to show his youngest grandchild his gardening accomplishments as a result of his retirement, while Brenda watched appreciative with arms folded and head resting on the back-door.

The kitchen was cottage-like and looked onto the garden. Peter hadn't grown up there, being a downsize option for his parents once he and his sister finally left home. Katy now lived in Canada with her international lawyer husband and children. They all wished they could see more of them but with holidays and video hook ups now allowed people to feel closer geographically than they actually were. It was less of a sever, more memorable than a phone call as it could be saved, being less time consuming than writing emails and letters; less paper in any event which was a real bonus for someone like Peter, whose life revolved around keeping up with endless streams of vital paperwork.

Peter shared his news of Talisa's progress which his mother was truly happy to hear. Then she put it to him bluntly.

"Peter, are you happy? I mean, things with you and Brenda."

"Why do ask?" He hadn't realised it was that obvious.

"Oh come on, a mother can pick up things you know that." She passed him the tea-towel.

"Well, to be honest, I really don't know. I thought the holiday to Jamaica might help bring us closer, and it did for a while but …"

“You men can get so carried away with work priorities,” his mother steered on with a knowing look which attested to what she had endured with his father before his dental surgery career finally calmed down.

“Your wife has a pulse Peter, every bit as important as those patients you tend to. You don’t have to become that Peter in that nursery rhyme.”

“Rhyme? Oh the pumpkin eater.”

“That’s that one.”

“Have you spoken to her about how she’s feeling?”

“Not lately.” Finding the right moment had not been easy what with juggling everything else.

“Well the sooner the better. Most people get one shot at happiness in a lifetime Peter, which includes you. Talk to your wife.”

Later that night, Peter had a disturbing dream. He dreamt he picked up one of the house phones to make a call and heard Brenda talking to a man about meeting him for lunch or something more which was a strange thing for someone to say to his wife. At first he thought it was a new client but by the tone of the conversation this felt way too intimate which made him feel uncomfortable. The man was telling her that he liked what she had worn the last time. Peter bolted out of his sleep. Brenda was sleeping on her stomach, her head turned away from him. He sat up, recalling the incident earlier in the day linked with Talisa's holographic-like appearance. "You need to speak to your wife".

He got out of bed and went downstairs, poured himself some apple juice. He found himself walking up the stairs to Brenda's work area. He opened the door. Her computer turned itself on just as he approached. It went through the usual loading up but on landing on the home page, immediately routed to the internet and brought up the dating site, running through images of other men before shutting down again. He stood for a while even more confused before making his way to the living-room to the couch in the dark where he sat running the cold glass over his stomach. What was going on? Was it all a product of his imagination or was something trying to tell him his marriage was in trouble, including his own mother? Was his subconscious trying to tell him his marriage was in real trouble? One thing was for sure, he now needed to talk to Brenda. He couldn't go on like this, with the constant fear of losing everything he valued in his life without knowing why exactly.

CHAPTER TWELVE: PAYING ATTENTION

Hopeton too had been busy with work and hadn't seen Rachel for a few days, though they had spoken on the phone. She mentioned she had attended the interview with Talisa and had mumbled something about what happened which wasn't too clear to him. When they at length met up, she was at first hesitant in describing what actually happened and he had had to prompt her several times to encourage her to continue. She started crying. This was not like Rachel. By the time she sobbed through the strange episode, she was appreciatively more relieved than composed. He took her in his arms and cradled her. She hadn't been in touch with Mrs Lawrence or Talisa since.

Hopeton rubbed her back and found himself wondering what effect the event had also had on the two officers, taking it for granted that they too were reasonably balanced professionals. He proffered, it might be good for Rachel to contact them, to see how they were doing.

"I know Talisa didn't mean any harm. In my heart of hearts I know that. It's just that she's so different from anyone I have ever met. You know the feeling don't you?" searching Hopeton's eyes.

"I found her remember!"

"And another thing, since the – I don't know what to call it."

"Some kind of genetic memory recall."

"That's why you're a doctor. That encapsulates the experience very well. Since the genetic memory extraction, I know there's something different about me."

"Different? Like what? I know you sounded more distant on the phone, distracted for certain. But different how?"

"I've been having more dreams that I remember. Sometimes I even know what's going to happen moments before it does."

"Oh coincidence Rachel."

"No, serious Hopeton. Like yesterday I saw this tabby run out in front of this man ahead of me, moments before it actually did. It was like déjà vu."

"Nothing unusual about such an occurrence. How did the man react to this?"

"He shouted at the puss to move out of his way. It was quite funny really."

"You see, nothing too tough to worry bout. You eating alright?"

"Nothing wrong with my appetite."

"Good. Let's go out for dinner. I want to wine and dine you tonight, if you're up to it."

After dinner, Rachel felt much more relaxed. They had delved further into the merits of contacting the officers to compare notes. Rachel converted to chancing a meeting.

The female officer was in fact glad to receive Rachel's phone call, having been on the verge of calling herself but didn't know quite what she would say for starters. The male was at first resistant to the idea but half way through their conversation, realised that actually he really did need to talk more about it. He hadn't even raised the matter with his colleague since that day. They wanted to meet somewhere discrete, not wanting nosey family members around or anywhere where members of the public might pay them attention. Rachel suggested they could drop by her school after last class, so long as they did so out of uniform. The curious would most likely assume they were parents asking about their child's progress or something of that nature, rather than Police making enquiries about someone. So it was agreed.

Rachel watched the officers approach her building from a window. Though in plain clothes, the way they both carried themselves, erect, determined, betrayed the fact that they were part of a discipline to the trained eye. They wore the mannerisms of control. Rachel wondered how controlling they were with their own children if they had any.

Constable Darlene Wade and Sergeant Earl Grant knocked on Rachel's classroom door. She called them in and drew the shutters down, leaving a slight gap for light to filter through. The room instantly cooled. The two greeted her, pulling up the two larger chairs Rachel had made available around her desk. Rachel took the initiative to smooth the way, the officers having sat down, uncharacteristically lost their former posture, perhaps wondering if this had been such a good idea after all.

"I know this is difficult but I felt we needed to talk about what happened at Mrs Lawrence's, why we're here."

It was Darlene who ventured into the breach.

"I have to say, since that day it has affected the way I do certain things. In fact, it got so bad, I even contemplated leaving the force. If it wasn't for the economic situation I would find something else to do." Her colleague looked surprised at her revelation. He hadn't realised it had hit her that hard. He put his hand to his mouth.

"To tell you the truth, it has changed me too. Made me look at the way I handled situations in the past and the way some officers behave to members of the public. Makes my position very difficult. I don't know, but unlike Darlene, I came to the conclusion that maybe I was needed more than I thought. To serve people, not just to arrest them ... kill them even. Dem seh where there is no law the people perish." Rachel nodded at both of them. She was trying to grasp the scope of the issues they faced in active service, arresting and the prospect of having to kill or being killed, feeling fortunate not to be in their profession.

Darlene pitched in again. "There is danger and there is responsibility. It is a job and someone has to do it. I had to go back in my mind and think it through all over again after what I experienced. I've made some bad decisions over my career. I know that."

The officers recounted abuses of power both had been involved in over time, without specifics. The guilt weighed heavy in the room.

"Well, only you know why you feel that way but as for myself, I don't believe that we went through that process for no reason. We all still have lives to live and a future. Change is part of being alive. How much do you remember of what you each saw?"

"Is like, I see things mostly to do with my family, though I know there was more. It is just the overall sense of it that I'm left with. My children even can see that I've changed. I'm much softer with them, whereas I was very regimented. They're asking if I'm sick or something," Darlene revealed.

"My worry is, if I can't get a grip on what I'm dealing with, I could become a liability out there, or even a target from any one of my own colleagues. You don't understand how wound up things are. Everything is interdependent."

"You'd be surprised," Rachel input. "I read newspapers you know. I know about Police corruption and closing ranks. Teachers can sometimes act that way too."

The two officers looked at each other, to the floor and back to Rachel. She was still an outsider, that's what their looks said. She smiled, understanding the distance between them despite that extraordinary shared experience.

Rachel was not finding the adjustment as hard as the other two. Her conscience was clean. As long as her students worked hard, she gave them the grades they deserved and encouraged those who needed help or those who messed around to change their ways because unless their parents had money, there was little out there if they did not make the grade.

She asked the officers if they believed in a god and whether they had prayed about the matter. They both said they attended church when they could manage. Rachel shared that she had spoken to her pastor about the whole matter surrounding Talisa for guidance. Had they raised the subject with theirs? Negative, they did not want anyone to have the impression they were going mad in their positions. She told them about the Assembly she was involved with and invited them to come along to a service. She had promised Talisa to take her to one so the pastor could meet her himself. They agreed to at least attend a service one Saturday convenient to both of them.

Rachel phoned Mrs Lawrence, telling her what she had in mind. Mrs Lawrence said she thought it a good idea as she was sure Talisa missed seeing her and would in all likelihood be keen to attend an Assembly. She called Talisa to speak to Rachel. The girl was happy to hear Rachel's voice over the phone though she would have preferred to speak to her without the technological interference face to face but gladly accepted Rachel's invite.

Mareka then called about the school project on bleaching cream. Some other students wanted to join their efforts as they couldn't come up with any viable subjects themselves. Their science teacher was most impressed with their idea, encouraging them to also include a survey. Talisa agreed to having more students on board which would mean less work for the two of them and the report they collectively had to produce.

"Have you seen your doctor yet?"

"Uh, uh. Not yet."

"What's stopping you?"

"I haven't had the time. That's all."

"But you found the time to get the cream in the first place. It has mercury in it. You should know that's poisonous."

"I haven't used it since that day! Promise."

"It's your skin."

"I know that."

CHAPTER THIRTEEN: THE SERMON

Pastor began his sermon with for her historical sins, it was generally known that Jamaica probably had more places of worship per square mile than anywhere else on the planet's surface … These mostly, Sunday's children were trying to be full of grace, while Saturday's children worked hard enough for their living, when of course they should have been resting and reflecting on their Creator. The Adventists on the island knew this and so did the new emerging Assembly communities such as their own, seeking the real truth and not that bequeathed to them by the ravaging resonance of slavery and its colonial consequences.

Such was the congregation of Pastor Josiah Young. Hopeton occasionally attended these gatherings with Rachel when time permitted. They used the term gathering, as for them the time of bringing in the harvest was nigh. The signs being visible globally for all they felt to now see, apart for the scoffers as foretold, the ones the prophets warned of and Jude revealed in his short letter so vividly.

As you would expect on YHWH's allotted day, most people were working, shopping, partying, and not giving a second thought to the deeper issues of their existence. Priority for them was indulging in everything and whatever they could lay hands on, following the stresses of the working week. Most injuries, murders and arguments erupted at weekends accordingly.

"We coming from a long way people. But we still have a way to go." The Pastor had continued.

"Yes. That's right" the members echoed as Pastor Josiah surveyed his colourful flock under the whirr of the two ceiling fans in the cool pastel blue hall. The only dress code stipulation for them was modesty. However, many chose to wear white, including some of the men. Some women tied their heads, especially the older middle-aged ones. It was still a colourful array of sheep, with a good spread from young to old, the membership a flourishing one hundred and counting, though not everyone was able to attend every week as you would expect. The Pastor was mighty pleased about the numbers of young people the Assembly was attracting.

"Jamaica was once the jewel in the crown of the British Empire, a jewel they fought the Spanish tooth and shipwreck nail for. Our ancestors were used as chattel for this enterprise on which Britain built her commercial and industrial success over centuries. But those slaves were not treated as jewels as we all know; treated worse than prized animals."

"We know how our people suffered so that we can even stand here today, to read the words of the Master, denied us at first, but left for us to decode in the End Times nonetheless."

"Yes" the congregation resounded.

"Now, though our native son, Bob Marley, never had the full understanding of what we know, he nonetheless sang about our condition Brothers and Sisters. For you will still find agents of darkness wearing all kinds of skins these days. But I am here to tell you, they have the same characteristics: murderers, liars, thieves, fornicators. Manipulators all, deceiving the whole world the Bible tells us. However, and this is where we can get caught, cause sometimes they're close, these people aren't necessarily strangers to us! So what does *The Word* tell us about this? We are told that your enemy will even be in your own household. Turn to Matthew chapter ten. You will find we are further told that Messiah came to separate out even family members. Let's read together from verse twenty-one through to thirty-six." Pages rustled as the Pastor led off with the reading.

"What a deep mystery, but history, as the powerful know all too well, is littered with the corpses of family struggles, so these things are nothing new to the world, especially where there is something to be gained of a material nature."

"Remember Joseph was sold into slavery by his own jealous brothers and though Jacob and Esau came out of the same womb, they had to separate. Esau later joins with Ishmael but that's a matter of prophecy and the times we're living in. So, we know by bitter experience that there is nothing easy in this existence people."

"No," came the response.

"My advice would be to know what is going on in your own household before you go prying in other people business, leaving trouble brewing quietly right under your nose."

"Yes. Oh yes!" There was much vigorous head nodding agreement and hands raised in the air on this point.

"And yet still we know that we must also be prepared to forgive. Yes you can turn the other cheek, seventy times seven times if need be. We do that a lot with young people especially don't we? In order for them to learn, we do that."

"Yes. Hmm, hmm."

"But we also have to remember that Jacob and Esau were brothers and they still had to separate. So these matters have to be tempered with wisdom and understanding." He wiped his forehead.

"So do you have your armour on brothers and sisters? When are you going to put it on? When the enemy is pounding at your gate? Cause if you wait until then, mind sharp him might just catch you unawares."

"Amen."

The rest of Pastor's Sabbath sermon centred on Sodom and Gomorrah, a subject he touched on many times prior. He went through what was happening in the ancient towns at the time, comparing being in the world but not participating in its beguiling sins.

"To show you how times have changed members, who here being of sound mind, would offer a virginal daughter to be raped?" There was disdainful chatter in the ranks.

"You see how times have changed? Or have they? Because these very same things are still going on around the world, probably even right here in Jamaica. And who here if besieged by wicked men, would allow the same to take your visitors to have their wicked way with them – anyone?"

"No!" came the outcry.

"Well, you note that the Creator took care of this business Himself! It was not left to Lot and Abraham. Their men were not called to give a hand. We all know how the angels themselves razed those cities to the ground because of all the wickedness and idolatry going on in them."

"Oh yes." A show of hands waved in the air.

He rounded on how one could still entertain messengers of the Creator and that he believed people unknowingly still did so in the End Times though time was indeed extremely short. He noticed Talisa sitting next to Rachel and kept looking at her. He could detect a white light emanating from her body that was so strong he kept having to adjust his spectacles. It was there whether he put them on or took them off. His attention to her did not go unnoticed. People followed his gaze. Talisa was sat on a chair at the end of a row in the seventh aisle from the front. Pastor determined to make certain to be introduced to her after service.

"So be comforted, you keep on your path Brothers and Sisters and pray, pray for guidance always. Turn to Isaiah chapter fifty and let us read again before we end with praise. HalleluYAH."

"HalleluYAH."

There was more rustling of books and shuffling in seats.

CHAPTER FOURTEEN: THE PROPOSAL

Hopeton surmised that Talisa's initial lack of responsive communication had been a temporary disablement attributable to unspecified tragic circumstances. However, she reminded him of someone very old in a young skin, though not what Jamaicans would term "force ripe". In Talisa's case the two contradictory states did not seem out of sync. He was by now convinced that somehow her fateful journey had woven itself deep into the fabric of the lives of those she came in contact with. For now though, he needed to put such thoughts aside, today would be a day for him and Rachel.

He picked Rachel up in a friend's taxi and they drove to the airport. Hopeton had been invited speak at an ophthalmology seminar in Cuba over an extended weekend. It presented an opportunity to pass on his clinical experience of retinoscopy to eager students. Having asked Rachel if she would like to attend, she had agreed most enthusiastically. They flew into Havana, capital of the indefatigable Cubans who had stood up to the Right Might Americans; because someone had to, and the Caribbean was as good a place as any,

Gitmo being the unfortunate circumstantial paradox from a revolutionary standpoint.

From the airport a coach drove them through the vibrant old colonial city, sporting 1950's American cars for a first taste, also catching a glimpse of the women in colourful attire, posing with big cigars in their mouths. They drove on to Jibacoa on the north coast.

It had been Rachel's first airplane ride ever and her first trip outside the island. Hopeton had studied in Havana after leaving Mona and had learnt Spanish. Rachel's Spanish was passable, but she was impressed by the way Hopeton effortlessly lapsed back into the lingo.

They changed for dinner and headed for the Hotel's restaurant, floating along a perfumed path, drawn to the faint tune of "My Favourite Things" as it grew gently louder. "Buenas noches," a courteous waiter greeted them at the entrance before leading them to their table after checking their reservation. The moment of truth for Hopeton had arrived before the seminar's schedule would commence the following day. They were seated at a cosy table for two, where a bottle of champagne was on ice and a beautiful neat bouquet of native flowers graced the table. A number of tourists and rising well to do locals were already soaking up the congenial relaxed atmosphere, spotted with lightly calming guava and caimito colours. He watched as her body unconsciously swayed to the waves of music.

"Having a good time?" She glanced at the jazz quartet and approvingly back to his expectant eyes.

"Hopeton, I never thought an island so near to Jamaica could be so different. But you know what, from the little I have seen so far, I believe I would love it here. How come you didn't stay man?" She didn't stop moving.

"I couldn't let the chance to go to New York pass. I would have kicked myself if I didn't take that up too. But there's no competition when it comes to Caribbean people." More specifically, he meant her.

"Well, I for one am glad you decided to come home." She reached for his hand, which slowed her motion down. The waiter brought their menus and wine list and lit their candles. Rachel hadn't noticed the champagne until the waiter popped the bottle open.

"Ooh! Hopeton do they greet all their guests like this?"

"Maybe only special ones." The waiter smiled and left, determining they were nowhere near ready to order.

"I knew coming back to Jamaica was the right decision for me where you are concerned, even though we had not even met! But Rachel, I have something to show you," Hopeton fiddled about in his pocket, made as if he'd forgotten something. He then announced that he'd found it, all the while playing around.

"Oh, what?!" She really had no inkling what it was, as she blankly stared back at him.

He offered the small box as he opened it. The alternate diamond and emerald studded engagement ring sparkled at her from its blue velvety surround. She gasped. He carefully removed its cushion and gently laid it in her palm which he caressed.

"Rachel Freeman, I'm asking, you with all my heart to be my wife." Her eyes watered with pure joy. Still clasping the ring tight, she hugged him with her free hand tight before replying through sobs as he searched for a handkerchief to dab her cheeks.

She looked him square in the eyes: “Hopeton, there is no question my answer is yes. Oh yes. There’s no one else for me but you. You know that.”

“Hmm … Pretty much,” he joked. “Just good to hear it, today of all days. Well come on my lady, let’s put it on!” He helped her slip on the ring without a hitch and kissed her lightly on the lips which she gently pressed back in acknowledgement as their hands gripped tight. This was as public a display of affection as their code would allow.

“Now that’s settled, I hope you still have an appetite for something to eat.”

Hopeton’s ten minute presentation the next day was delivered in Spanish; with a five minute Q&A session at the end. Rachel sat in the front row with the organisers who clapped their resounding approval like everyone else in attendance. She felt so proud of her fiancé, even though she had at times struggled to keep up with the technical parts of his presentation.

Weeks later in London Brenda picked up the morning post, finding a card from Jamaica addressed to her and Peter. There was also a letter from her mother which she pocketed, putting the rest on the table. She shoved Chloe through the door with her rucksack, not wanting them to be late for her daughter's tap dancing class.

Peter turned over in bed, enjoying his lie in all by himself. Thirty minutes later he roused himself to shower, and then made scrambled eggs with toast and coffee without having to rush to anyone's rescue. He shuffled off in his vest and boxer shorts to check the post, finding the usual bills and a card. He opened the card first, preferring to opt for some good news.

"Good for you Hopeton," he mouthed out loud smiling. Whether Brenda would want to travel out again would be another matter and Chloe usually spent time with her grandparents in the school holidays. He was certainly up for it if he could swing it. He had taken some needed time off work to spend with the family after his father had a heart scare. This turn of events had the effect of drawing Brenda closer.

Their heart to heart which followed proved more of a reality check than a hostage to circumstances. Taking one's partner routinely for granted probably wasn't the worst thing he could have done in their relationship.

Brenda's insecurities lay in the differences in their backgrounds, having only skirted around these in the past. He grew up in a Wesleyan household morality. Her father had worked on cruise ships which meant her mother was left alone for months at a time but in compensation always had something to look forward to with each return. Brenda had grown up missing her father when he was gone and being overwhelmingly happy when he was around bearing the gifts he brought back from exotic places and stories. Peter felt there was a correlation between this see-saw existence and her mood swings. There seemed to be something mythical about her father she shared, something intangible because he was never around long enough to grasp. Finally, when she was eight years old, he telephoned his wife to let her know he was staying in the Philippines where he had found a pint-sized love her mother would later tell her. Brenda ultimately saw far less of him over the years and his letters finally dried up too. Her mother divorced and remarried Roland, a supermarket manager and widower raising two teenage girls of his own to bring stability to all their lives. She wasn't sure if her mother appreciated her stepfather more than she loved him. Mother certainly started drinking vodka more, perhaps because it didn't smell so strong. There were a lot more arguments in their new home, probably normal family stuff but Brenda just never felt secure and accepted in the new structure. It wasn't easy going from an only child to the third in line for the bathroom because the older girls had further to travel to school.

Brenda left home as soon as she could stand on her own two feet, back then with few qualifications and before the older girls, preferring to share a flat with friends of her own choosing. Her stepfather had remarked that decision would either prove a streak of stupidity or a mark of independence that only time would tell. Brenda worked all manner of administrative jobs to prove her independence, attending night school and also acquired a lively circle of associates. Meeting Peter years later through them was as secure as she ever permitted herself to feel. She didn't blame him for the emptiness she sometimes felt; she just didn't know how to fill it. She managed not to take anti-depressants, another achievement, determined not to go down that downward spiral as a mark of having achieved her independence. How could she give that away to a pill?

Peter returned from seeing his father one afternoon after dropping Katy and his mother off at home. His sister had flown in over concerns for both her parents. Bonnie, their mother, was very good at supporting others, but slow to seek support for herself.

Chloe had insisted on waiting up for Peter to find out how granddad was doing. She also wanted to tell him about her news. Satisfied her granddad was doing well and missing her too, she showed Peter the poster the dancing school had produced for their upcoming show. 'Twinkle, Twinkle Toes'.

"What you mean like the star?" Peter tickled his daughter.

"Yes" she chuckled, rolling across his knees.

"Promise you'll come daddy and bring granddad and Nanny."

Being on-call and still working over forty-eight hours per week, Peter looked at Brenda who just shrugged with open hands.

"We'll see how well granddad is doing by the time this comes around and you know I'll do my very best to be there."

"Okay." With that, Chloe was ready for Brenda to march her up to bed.

Peter wasn't hungry but they both settled on a bottle of red wine that night. He couldn't keep it in. Uncorking the bottle seemed to help the question pop open from inside him, stopping it from festering. His eyes were suddenly surprisingly watery as if he'd been peeling onions.

"Brenda are you having an affair? I need to know."

"I promise you, no Peter, I'm not having an affair. Why ..." she began to cry, feeling guilty and foolish about having contemplated doing just that. She had betrayed his trust by not being invincible, a failure and a flaw for feeling so fractured all the time.

Her answer at first did not completely reassure. He couldn't put a realistic finger on why.

"If it is just work and the three of us, we stand a chance of working this out.

Someone else in the frame would just change everything."

"Didn't you hear me Peter? I said I'm not having an affair, believe me. You and Chloe mean everything to me. I realise how precious that is. Gerald's illness has clarified for me just how often you deal with life and death in your work and yet you don't tax us with it. I know how hard that must be, how hard you try for us. I'm sorry, sorry you married such a hard-nosed bitch Peter!" She reached for him finding his body at first rigid to her touch. She put a hand around his neck, drawing him down closer, stroking his nape, while her wet cheeks rubbed against his own. He gradually became less tense, the two of them lost for any more words to articulate it all, bodies compressing the emotions. They clung together without further utterances, gradually sinking into the carpet which received their sobs, sighs and sense of new found relief.

Afterwards, surprisingly, the first words between them related to the first letter Brenda had received from her mother.

"She sent me a letter from my Philippino teenage brother and sister. They want to meet me."

This didn't strike Peter as anything but good news. "A couple more cousins for Chloe don't you think?" He had such a capacity for seeing the positive side of any situation. Brenda simply hadn't thought through that aspect of their existence as yet.

Hopeton and Rachel had decided not to prolong their wedding plans, agreeing to a short engagement of a few months only. Though their families and friends at first found even this to be too short a notice, everyone was happy for them and coming together to chip in for the necessary planning. Hopeton's cousin, who was a Chef, was allotted the task of catering and securing the venue. Pastor Josiah agreed to perform the ceremony at the hotel.

Rachel opted for having bridesmaids and a page boy so the youngsters could feel involved on both sides of family.

Come the day, a beautiful Friday morning at the beginning of August, Hopeton held Rachel's hand lightly at the altar. Her parents were most proud to witness the marriage of their daughter, who looked elegantly stunning in her strapless fishtale wedding gown, the veil stitched with little white satin roses which fell in an arc on the left side, accessorised with a twist weave chain with matching earrings. The bridesmaids wore fleshy peach coloured dresses.

The reception also drew international relatives and friends who flew in from Cuba, the US and UK, including the Stratfords who confirmed their attendance late, but Hopeton was glad to see them. Anchorman and Brosi were also there and Bret in his capacity as a manager at the Mandrake Lodge Hotel, ensuring everything ran smoothly. They spotted April, whose mother was a family friend of Hopeton's mother. Dr Neville and other hospital staff were there; also teachers from Rachel's school. Mrs Lawrence and Talisa soaked up the atmosphere. Talisa came across Mareka who happened to be standing with April. Mareka was a distant cousin of Rachel's and was curious to know how she knew the family. Without going into too much detail, Talisa shared that she had first met Dr Bennett at the clinic in Negril. Brosi by then had joined them. No one recognised Talisa from that day at the clinic as they caught up with the recent events.

Just at that moment, someone behind called her name.

"Talisa?" The young woman who turned to regard him was a complete transformation from the person who had screamed at him from her hospital bed, but remarkably similar to the Talisa he had seen in his hallucination.

"Dr Stratford!" She was obviously genuinely thrilled to see him this time. His wife caught up with him having finished giving her congratulations to Rachel. She too had a warm smile for the girl.

"Well, look at you!" Dr Stratford continued. "You look the picture of health Talisa, I have to say."

"That really means a lot Dr Stratford. Really, it does. Thank you and congratulations." She could see Brenda was a few weeks pregnant.

"Oh for what?" Brenda asked.

"For making it out here together." The couple looked at each other quizzically but just smiled, shrugging it off as nothing significant, not knowing themselves that Brenda was pregnant.

The following afternoon, the newly weds flew to Martinique for their honeymoon.

It would only be for a week, as Hopeton's schedule could not allow him more time. It would be Rachel's second flight off the island in a year and she could not have been happier about it.

CHAPTER FIFTEEN: HILLTOP TROUBLES

Hopeton and Rachel were still on their honeymoon when Talisa had a feeling something was wrong up on the hilltop. She tuned in her senses, picking up Auntie's conversation. She was upset, arguing with some men who were being aggressive. Matters were heating up by the second. Talisa didn't have time to walk up the hill, having moments before agreed to meet up with Mareka. It was clear that more than remote viewing would be needed in this instance. A man was leading one of Auntie's Hope Cows down the hill. Talisa decided to deploy an active holographic image, how humans might describe it. However, it provided her with the ability to present in two places at once, one of her multiplex abilities. This alternate state was not without effects; even reflected light had properties that could be manipulated. Humans were just beginning to observe what they termed quantum mechanics. Their scientists had for the longest time led their species to believe in only the physical and material aspects of their surrounds. Planet Blue Water was certainly made up of a variety of matter in unusual states from microscopic single cell life forms to whales and cows. Auntie's precious cow was one for example, a creature for which humans had tasked with a variety of uses.

"Where you going with that cow? I know it doesn't belong to you. Where are you going with it?" The image mouthed.

The man was startled. He hadn't seen her coming up the hill, yet there she was, this girl blocking his way with one hand on a hip, the other just resting, legs slightly astride, flagged up in a lemon tube top, lime green shorts and a black belt. However, none of this belied the threat he felt from her casual stance.

"Ah who you?" He couldn't see her contemplative face, as her hanging braids completely covered her features until she hauled them back. A light like someone flashing a mirror in his eyes almost blinded him as he put a hand up in defence, feeling the heat.

"Uh, you mussa some duppy to ratid!" He let go of the cow and scampered down the hill without further contest. Talisa's image approached the cow. It was not phased by her presence. She ran a green light over its body.

"Hope Cow, they named you, not No Hope Cow, so you go back to your pasture and family and multiply. Go now," she instructed the animal.

When the other men saw the cow returning on its own, they were confused. The boss had told Marcel to take the cow for slaughter to teach this old woman a lesson, not to get in the way of his business. The cow made its swishing sweet-tail way back to the pasture as Auntie looked on, also surprised. The man shouted at the cow and took out his gun. The cow did not waiver from its course, busting a loud moo which he translated as meaning kiss my red hide. The boss fired a shot in the animal's direction. That is when something remarkable happened. Instead of the bullet hitting the cow, the man found himself directly in the path of the bullet, seeing it close up before it struck his right thigh, pitching him to the ground in shrieks of agony. The two other side kicks were utterly confounded. Their boss was squealing for help, eventually coming to their senses they ran to assist.

"How dat happen? You was just standing right next to us. Ah how you reach over here suh?"

"Don't worry bout dat. Yuh nuh see blood ah run? Tek me back to the car and get me outa here quick! Bloodfire!" reeling from the pain.

"Can't tek you to hospital, de Police goin' get involve. Wha we goin' to tell dem seh?"

"Just get me down de hill. Me know who fi call. Ah accident seen. Me will fill dem details later. Hurry, nuh mek me 'tan 'ere a bleed to death."

They lifted him clumsily and carried him to the parked car. None of them said another blessed word to Auntie. When they had gone, she at first thought she saw a little glimpse of that girl, Talisa. She looked again but the child had gone. She shook her head, perhaps with all the commotion her mind was playing tricks on her. Maybe she needed eye-glasses, after all, Talisa was flesh and blood and no duppy. Nonetheless she thought she heard that funny accent and calming voice telling her not to worry. She gave out an audible "whooah" shook her head and smiled.

"I'm alright little Miss. We all alright," focusing back on the day's chores.

Talisa's powers were growing daily, becoming accustomed to her body and the limitations of operating in the current dimension, density and time-frame version. She had had to quickly learn to be more like the humans, reckoning the transition to be reasonably successful being more au fait with their behaviours and processes, Jamaican stylie in any event. People's behaviours varied across the planet depending on their customs, circumstances and beliefs broadly across geographical zones, but in places these could be mixed. Humans were certainly diverse, with the capacity for great love and but also irreversible terrors and great evil for which there were long-term consequences. Unfortunately, some Jamaicans had been induced into following the wayward path to destruction. Successive politicians failed to take steps to improve areas which had succumbed to decades of deprivation and the lack of social cohesion. Living conditions personified the violent characteristics of some residents. These people appeared to be hell bent to complete on track, a path that first manifested out of poverty, becoming inflated with want and desire beyond the necessity for a healthy existence. Others who attempted to improve their habitat were thwarted time and time again by the energy sapping prevailing violence.

On a global scale, the planet had been compromised beyond anything human intervention could now achieve given the alarming loss of organisms both flora and fauna. She read in the waters how green and lush the planet once was. What was relentlessly in progress could not continue unchecked but that decision would not be hers.

Adjusting to the planet's frequencies to work with her own capabilities on such a time-limited assignment had its own peculiar drawbacks. The Watchers had breached all the rules so in terms of what she could do, the game had changed. Everything would change quickly now; the people and the planet. The fulfilment of what humans called The End Times was hurtling to its fiery consummation. The Enemy had also been subtly tinkering with the timeline, not just changing the calendar as some of the prophets attested to in prophecy. They had also been messing with the past in the current timeline which could not be allowed to continue unchallenged. Everything had consequences, the Enemy was well aware of the rules of the game.

Humans were trapped in a domino effect, following the strong, those who aligned purely to scientific realities, blind-siding other possibilities which had left them open to manipulation by the Watchers. It was time to reset the balance. Time was short. As Jamaicans said: "Who don't hear will feel". The worldwide loss of diversity and dwindling resources favoured rich nations: an absolute aberration, encroaching on the basic life-support provisions of those they saw as poor and tools to supply them with what they needed to keep them destructively competitive. This was a world where less was perversely seen as more, given where people had started from and the values they once cherished. Growth and progress had robbed and defiled a once abundant planet of extraordinary diversity. Yeshayahu's warnings Ch: 24 made plain the consequences in prophetic terms. They were warned.

Backra was recuperating back in his office, eager to resolve the interference causing him so much resultant pain. Fortunately it had only been a flesh wound, courtesy of a gaming accident he had claimed to squash awkward questions. It hurt like hell, the limp still pronounced. This anguished predicament had sparked an idea. There was an Obeah woman in the district, though he previously never entertained such dabbling, there was a first time for everything. He would try anything to rid himself of this girl, a pickney at that.

Miss Lucy they called her, a tall figure in her late seventies without any noticeable bend in her stature. She knew about Lester Hawes, Backra as he was known to associates, had clapped eyes on him when he was just a little *suck tongue bwoy*, running wild with his six toes. She could tell then that something was eating into his seedless soul. Though his women gave him *jackets*, the appearance of virility and consequent children was important to his image of manhood. Deep down he had to know the children were not his, including his wife's, who had had an affair with his first business partner. Women wanted children, a natural longing; he understood that despite the betrayal. He chose brownie women like himself so the children looked more alike. A light skin masked a multitude of sins and traits if you didn't study someone too closely. Obviously, none of the children inherited the dominant six toes which ran in his family. The men who actually spawned these children, as chance would have it, met with dubious ends; an electrocution; a fall from height. Nothing indiscriminate, strictly a matter of territorial necessity; Lester, as his wife called him, was boss in all undertakings.

Miss Lucy had read all this in his eyes, the way he stared, never satisfied, all wound up like a coil ready to spring in one once so young. She watched his approach from the doorway of her bamboo tatu hut at the back of her house, past the bushes which led to the clearing.

"So wha kina breeze blow a ram goat like you to mi yard Backra?" She grinned.

"Well, Miss Lucy, is like seh, I have dis tichi problem I'd a like fi well fix permanent."

"Ah huh. You mean she talawah."

"Yuh might seh suh. But man like me now feel seh there mus be a solution to every problem."

"Come in." She waved him inside, pointing to a wicker chair for him to sit. She reached for an earthenware jar, then told Backra to grab a fistful of stones, asking him to throw them on the floor like dice. Miss Lucy examined the result of this simple act. She looked perplexed, sighed.

"Backra, yuh mus' know disya problem well massive man," shaking her head.

"How yuh mean?" This was not music to Backra's ears.

"I don't know if I can help you wid dis. I never seen anything like it and most of it nuh even reveal to me. The girl you come here bout has protection, the likes of which I never see before. No angel's trumpet can blow pon' dis ewe lamb. You know bout them Ephramites?"

"Wha dat? I don't have time fi no riddles dis day ya Miss Lucy."

"Dis not de time to be tekking dem on yuh know Backra. Times changing fast an' nuff trouble ahead fi everybody."

"Ol' woman, wheh di backside yuh a talk seh? Anyting dat a walk an' talk can be killed ah nuh suh?"

"Yes but ..."

"No but. You jus tell me wheh fi do. I got business holding up costing millions ah US$ seen." He was cranking up like a leggo beast, heavy sweat pouring down the greedy growth of peppercorn stubble.

"Backra, how you know dis won't cost you your life man? You ready to pay dat price?"

"What don't cost life don't worth a ting! Yuh nuh know dat?" He stared beyond her. Not caring what he was letting himself in for, regardless of how far or how deep.

Miss Lucy called out for Lizzy, a light skin woman shunted into their presence, her head tied up in a scarf. She was around forty-five years old, born and bred into superstition, her eyes hazel coloured, the whites with streaks of red. She was Miss Lucy's wash-belly, the one her mother hoped would carry on the tradition.

"Lizzy bring me the red cock back deh an' quick." Lizzie glanced at Backra before replying, "Hmm hmm" and was gone for a few minutes. Backra gazed ahead into emptiness in silence, disregarding the affects that decorated. The pause was broken by a shuffling of feet and the flapping of wings in the doorway.

"Me ketch him mumm. Him well lively tonight," Lizzy proclaimed.

Miss Lucy told Backra to follow her into the yard. She took the protesting cock from

Lizzy, holding it fast by its neck and chanting some strange words while she spun slowly in a circle, her bare feet kicking up dust. The atmosphere was charging. Her face contorted as she hummed and shouted. Backra jumped backwards as he watched her face turn more animal than human. The air around swirled and he could see things emerging in the space around them, first dark spiky balls rolled out, then a succession of ram's horns and rods which grew into serpents, snaking around her, around him. The large ones opened their jaws, venomous forked tongues lashed out, threatening to strike and devour. The largest serpent wrapped itself around an enormous crown studded with gems which sparkled. Miss Lucy shouted at him to close his eyes and his mouth. He was by this time visibly quaking, so instantly obeyed her order. She took a sharp knife from her skirt pocket and deftly sliced the cock's throat. While its wings were still flapping reflexive, she splashed the warm spurting blood from the bird's body onto Backra. He wanted to curse but was too afraid an outburst might backfire on him. He kept his eyes closed tight, wishing for the ordeal to come to an abrupt end.

"You can open yuh eyes now," the old woman shouted at last. It was over.

Miss Lucy took him back to the hut where she explained the macabre details of what she felt might work for him. The girl would have to be chopped up in pieces and set alight. She concocted a liquid potion which she felt might give whoever would do the deed a chance of approaching her. Backra's countenance produced a relieved smirk. He paid Miss Lucy handsomely for her time. She stuffed the wad of notes into her bosom, instructing him not to wash off the blood for at least an hour. He left with the bottle.

Trench had just finished another rugged rally practise session. This hobby gave him a big achievement rush. He removed his helmet and gloves to speak freely with Avon, his navigator, about improvements needed to squeeze more performance out of the 4WD Focus. He had not too long turned his cell back on when Backra rang. He barked it was time Trench stopped playing the boy racer and loverman and got on with some real work. He wanted him to go to Kingston to recruit a hardcore crew for a job that needed doing back in Negril, no questions asked of course. Trench announced his early departure, leaving the racer with Avon and Clayton to sort out. He walked back to his ride.

Ria's plump biscuit body was propped up against the driver's door of the Audi convertible. She had begged him to take her with him when he'd bumped into her on his way to the course. Avon and Clayton had been taken a little aback when he arrived with her but between men, decided it was none of their business "seen as some nanny goat with run belly nuh mine when macca juk dem".

Ever the ginal, Ria signalled her intent by running her fingers up Trench's arm with her spider touch, leaving him with no doubt that she was edging for more than just a ride in the Audi. He peeled her off his door, pulling her close.

"Mind, you sure you know what you're doing?" He flashed point blank.

"There's no time like the present to find out."

Backra could wait a couple more hours and Sherice was definitely far from both their thoughts right now. He took her back to his place, driving her into the garage, away from prying eyes. She provided him with an hour's worth of tension release. He left her in bed, throwing her the TV remote.

"There's food and drink in the fridge downstairs. And I'm warning you, don't interfere with anything else. I'll be a couple hours."

"Alright."

He closed the door behind him, checking his BB as he did so.

Trench Town was where Trench had been born and baptised as Noel Defoe. His mother had taken him to the US when he was five. By the time he was twelve, he was hooking up with trouble. His mother managed to send the boy out of the country following the murder of a close friend of his when he was sixteen. She wanted him out of harm's way so sent him back to his grandmother. But the youngster was already bent on living by his wits and the quick profits and benefits that came with it. He arrived in Kingston from Canada with his favourite trench coat slung over his back, thus the name Trench stuck. After his grandmother died, his mother had refused to take him back to the States post the funeral, deciding he should stay with his father's relatives in Negril. Moving to Negril had its compensations, offering a better lifestyle and benefits for a sharp young hustler like him. It was not long before Backra reined him into service, showing him how to score some real money.

Through contacts, safe passage was arranged for Trench to enter the garrison. He was no stranger to a couple of the young men there. The eldest couldn't have been more than twenty-five tops. A strong man in this part of town was now a young man. He delivered the brief for the job in a sober tone. Said he expected their leader to send him some hardcore guys up to the job. They would be briefed with the full details when they reached Negril. Everything was on a need to know basis and was to be completed by the following weekend. The final price would be agreed once the personnel were assembled.

The six man crew arrived from Kingston in stolen vehicles with new plates all of which they planned to later dispose. They were all known by their acquired nicknames: Breezer, Bandit, Razor, Wrecker, Sparks and Dozer. To break the ice, Backra asked them how they had obtained their names. One by one each explained. Breezer was cool, laid back but deadly – not a man to cross or play with; bald Bandit loved to hold up banks and businesses; Razor, well he was a knife and carving man; Wrecka loved to “bruk-up” place; Sparks had a prominent front gold tooth and an alligator breathing fire tattoo on his right arm. He just loved to “mek tings blaze”, catch-a-fire buildings, people, animals – no matter. Dozer, the tallest at over six feet, was stacked heavy and pound for pound a brute force for any reckoning. This assault gang picked to go up against a sixteen year old girl and an old woman. It seemed to Backra these hell-hounds had the right credentials. However, of the six, Breezer opted to stay in the car to stand watch; Bandit said he would prefer to bleach the street corner as further lookout. Dozer, who was feeling betwixt and between agreed to watch the other end of the street where his speciality to block would be deployed if needed. So it was settled, Razor, Wrecka and Sparks were selected to handle the face to face business and would also be paid more for the privilege. The crew would disappear from Negril as soon as the job was completed. Locals would probably be blamed and no one would be any the wiser. Crime solving was not a given on Jamaican priorities. The Police were overstretched, ill-equipped and some could be paid off to stall things. They otherwise had enough to do, engaged in keeping domestic peace and the tourists protected for the sake of the economy. Backra could count on a mixture of all of the above, for the Police not to even bother themselves too heavy with any local wailing aftermath. He could get on with his sweet real estate business without further hindrance.

CHAPTER SIXTEEN: ATTACK

They arrived just past 03:00 AM, two cars and a jeep. The drivers remained in their vehicles as agreed. There was a full moon, the street quiet. Unbeknown to them, Talisa was outside in the front yard. She had been waiting for them and they did not disappoint, having concluded her prayer when she heard the cars arrive. She had recited an Ode of Solomon's XXVIII in Talisa's Ewe language, calling on The Creator's help, calling to Yewe for the love of the lambs still to save. Shining iridescent: in silver and gold, she drew her sword and waited for the three to enter the yard. When they reached the entrance, she erected an invisible force field around the locality which extended beyond the street corners. No one would be making any unauthorised exits or entrances. Attempts to enter would simply send those trying back where they came from. A short low frequency was enough to send other residents calmly into sleep mode without any risky situations arising, completing any actions they had been doing.

The would be assailants, being Wrecka, Razor and Sparks, were visibly stunned to find this figure stood before them: blinding, sparkling splendour from head to toe, much less holding a gleaming sword. Her gold breastplate was studded with anisotropic jewels as was the swept hilt of the sword. Her wrist amulets were gold as was the slatted green and gold short skirt and gold boots. Such was the effect that they initially had to protect their eyes and refocus from the light emanating from her body.

"What you tink? Ah she dat?" Wrecka asked off totally off balance. For an instant there was an unmistakable urge to run.

"Nuh matter. We here fi do a job an' nuting' and nobody can stand in our way," Razor finally quipped in an effort to regain a grip on the situation. He pulled a large combat knife from his commando style trouser pocket. Sweat was pouring into his bloodshot eyes.

Wrecka stamped his right fist into his leathery left palm several times to work himself up. The crew formed a predatory circle around Talisa. Wrecka decided, enough was enough, he rushed her. A discernible swish cut the air as he ended up the other side of his target, his right ear stinging. He put a hand up to it only to find his ear was missing. He groaned in shock. Talisa whispered: "Who don't hear will feel."

Razor, unaware of what exactly had happened, sprung to assail her with his knife, striking out in an attempt to slice through her encrusted stomach but missed. He too felt a sharp sting before his knife held hand left his body, the sound of metal slapping the ground resonated with his yells. Sparks remembered the bottle Backra had given him. He frantically removed it from his pocket and threw the contents at Talisa who darted well out of reach in a flash of rainbow lights. The foul smelling contents sizzled on making contact with the air before the bottle smashed. Wrecka tried rushing her again as soon as he could make her figure out but she jumped over him and he ended up stumbling out of the yard. She ran after him. The other three out in the street, turned to see what was happening. Razor, pumped with anger ran out too. Wrecka opened the trunk of the car and retrieved a semi-automatic machine gun. He started to fire at Talisa but the bullets ricocheted off her swishing sword and amulets. In his excitement, he did not see her approach but felt the sword slice his belly. His warm blood poured out as he held his gut in agony, looking into her eyes and seeing only the darkness awaiting him before his body ignited. He swiftly disintegrated into smouldering ashes.

Razor inflamed by the demise of his friend, stood with a rocket launcher aimed at Talisa. He fired, his body jerking back. With a whispered word, she reduced its mass and redirected its kinetic energy towards the vehicle which exploded, the impact noise dulled by the force field but the conflagration blast still licked orange and black; pungent, consuming tyres: acrid. Breezer, the driver, had just enough time to dive out before it struck. Razor was like a bull incensed, he tried to fire again but the mechanism jammed. He too found himself eye to eye with Talisa. Her look pierced his eyes like a lightning strike. He screamed with shock as his eyes caught fire: his body too burnt to cinders.

Seeing what happened to Wrecka and Razor, the remaining four ran to the force field's edge. Sparks and Dozer were instantly electrocuted; the air around them smoky with the smell of charred humans. Breezer and Bandit, who were by now just heaving to draw breath, had immediately drawn back from the hitting the perimeter. They turned to face Talisa who approached them calmly, the sword held to her breast, its tip pointed up in the air. Breezer, who had a goatee, felt a swift shave as the hairs were deftly pruned. Both men were then aware of a burning sting across their chests which they mistook for certain death as their vests cut away. The words carved in blood would scar their chests and minds for the rest of their natural lives. They heard her speak for the first time in that strange African accent of hers.

"It is written, 'The wages of sin is death. Choose life and live'. This be your first real Emancipation Day, but be warned; it could still be your last! Now, go tell your new boss. Get out of my sight!" She released the force field, pointing the sword directly at them. They ran, terrified, babbling like idiots.

Backra received an unexpected call from the German in the early hours of the morning.

"There's been a change in my plans my friend." He spoke nonchalantly.

"Oh? What do you mean by that?" It was 03:25 AM. Backra thought the operation was well underway. The sirens should be alarming the neighbourhood of the unfortunate house fire that had broken out unexpectedly in the middle of the night. He had been expecting another call.

There was a loud pulse from his BlackBerry and a sharp pain in his head.

Backra dropped to the floor like a heavy stone. The German hung up. Another soul harvested in their count; in the war.

Trench had tried to raise Backra when he got up, but without success. The attack had gone wrong. He was not sure what had happened. Breezer and Bandit had called him babbling something crazy that Razor, Wrecka, Dozer and Sparks were all dead. What in blazes could have gone wrong was all he could think.

Someone had later called the Police about a burnt out vehicle in the neighbourhood that needed removing. They checked the wreckage and the nearby suspicious vehicles, finding ammunition in the other car and jeep but no bodies or body parts; those remains had blown away like chaff by the early morning sea breeze.

A TV crew was on site behind which a small crowd had gathered. Mrs Lawrence explained that she did not know what had happened. She and her charge must have slept soundly through the night's alarming events. It was a miracle they had not been hurt.

Trench's phone rang. It was Cornell informing him that Backra had been found dead at his home. He had suffered an embolism that burst overnight. This news almost blew Trench away. Instead, his mind started ticking over double quick time. He nervously lit a spliff and walked to the balcony of his bedroom, failing to see the actual view in front of him. He pulled hard on the joint and rubbed his pounding open chest. Backra's death was a huge game changer. The men would be looking for the General to carry on the business, though a couple might have their own ideas of course. The rivalry could cause bloodshed even though this was not Dungle, Kingston. He knew he was smooth enough to avoid that. But why should he care about any of it? He was thinking on his feet. He went to check the Glock and the Buretta for reassurance. This would leave him with no time to be rallying around the countryside. A new reality was quickly setting in.

Sherice brought her fine lined slinky self out to join him back on the balcony, her neck now free of the brace. She hugged him around his waist and stroked his back, an opportunistic air enveloping them.

"Something bothering you Trench?" She couldn't help but notice he'd been on tenterhooks all night.

"Nothing I can't handle babe."

"Well then, how about getting round to buying a bigger place? I think you've outgrown this one." He passed her the spliff but she snuffed it out. It was a little too early in the day for her.

His door bell rang unexpectedly. He turned on the viewer, only to see Ramona of all people standing there. She was one of his three baby mothers. He told Sherice to stay put and went to meet Ramona, opening the door to also find his one and only three year old son there too behind her.

"We haven't seen you for months and Tyrell needs food and clothes," Ramona's scolding voice greeted him. The youngster smiled up at him while tugging his mum's jeans.

"Daddy! I come see you!" the child ventured coyly. Trench had named the boy after his best friend back in the States, a hero to him.

"You need to learn to be more of a father starting from today." Ramona nudged Tyrell through the doorway and whacked the child's Tom Stone doll in Trench's chest. The boy stretched out his hand to his father.

At that moment Sherice appeared, having heard a female voice, she had begun preening her hair and arms all the way to the doorway. Ramona gaped at her.

"'Scuse me for interrupting. No wonder we nuh see yuh fi months." She hadn't come to start a fight with one of his fancy women.

"You can't leave him today Ramona, serious. I got tings to take care of." Trench's mood was confused and charged.

"What kind of a mother are you? You can't just leave the child just like that?" Sherice scowled, demonstrably flashing her manicured fingernails. Ramona's response was to bend over to her son's level. She told him to put his hands over his ears before she straightened up.

"Trench, tell yuh Miss Too Stush NuhKnowWhehFiDuh to keep outa dis yeh!" She shook her index at him. "If her only work is to live to grind you, she better check yuh trailer. Oh! Like seh me nuh have tings fi tek care of tuh?" It was a clear reference to his womanising which had caused their break up.

"Look, I didn't tell you to move to Mo'Bay," Trench retaliated. Ramona just kissed her teeth, flicked her processed red dyed fringe, turned and wiggled her sassy backside, giving her halter back to them as she headed to a waiting Subaru, with the engine still running.

Though unhappy about the timing of all this, Trench picked his son up and rubbed the child's head. Somehow this had the effect of bringing him back to yet another reality for all of a few seconds. "Youth, you getting big aye boy!" Tyrell rubbed his father's cheeks as his mother drove off. He took him into the den.

"Trust Ramona to pull a stunt like this just when I need some space. Damn!" With all the American tourists in town, Trench never lost his twang. It made them feel at home, and besides, it was also good for business.

"Damn. Damn!" Tyrell repeated, making a serious face.

"Uh, uh! Don't you say that word Tyrell. See I have to be careful what I say around you little fella. I know I need to spend more time with you but today is not a good day." He turned to Sherice. "Look, I'm gonna need you and Tyrell outa here asap. Things are a little wild right now and my guys'll soon be here. Think you can do that for me?"

"No worries. We're cool. Give the baby to me." It was a wonder the child did not feel like pass the parcel. "He looks more like his bosi mother than you you know Trench."

"Now, don't start. I got no time for any foolishness right now, hear me. Gotta make some calls." He handed her a couple wads of US dollars made up of 50's. "I need you to buy Tyrell some clothes. An' get yourself a pair of shoes or something while you're at it."

She cooed. "Thanks," fanning the cash.

Sherice really didn't have time for children and had no plans to have any of her own any time soon. Besides, she had pageants to prepare for. However, being nice to Tyrell was sure to do her nothing but good in the dawn of a new chapter in Trench's charmed life. She tried to call Ria, as Ria's family had young children, then realised they hadn't linked up of late. Her call went straight to voicemail. She would have to catch up later.

"You guys ready?" Tyrell made a face like he was about to cry. He did not exactly warm to Sherice.

Trench picked him up again, kissed his cheek and told him to cheer up as he walked them to the front door. His phone rang. He handed Tyrell back to Sherice.

"Mo time." He waved them on.

"Yeh, I'm here ... Half an' hour then." He hung up.

He stood for a moment, ran his hand through his hair and rubbed the back of his neck.

"Deal with your ass later Ramona, Yeh, you'll be moving back to Negril alright. Huh! And won't be a damn thing you can do about it." He needed to get his whole mess in order. But first things first, it was time to ratchet up his game before anyone else could make a move.

His BB rang again, he answered. The voice on the line was unfamiliar, European sounding.

"Noel Defoe?"

"Who wants to know?"

"You don't know me but I certainly know of you? Through a late mutual associate."

"Ah yeh? And who would that be?"

"That'll keep."

"Okay, didn't catch your name Mr …?"

"Ranulf Heidrich."

"Yeh well, Mr Heidrich, bad timing for me currently as I'm in the middle of something." A car pulled up in the drive way.

"Yes, there's a lot going on for you."

"How'd you know about anything that's going on with me Mr Heidrich? That your name again?"

"I'll be in touch when things have calmed down Mr Defoe or should I call you Trench hmm?"

"What the …"

"Until next time." The line went dead before Trench could spit out his frustration. Car doors outside slammed shut.

CHAPTER SEVENTEEN: ROAD TO GARRISON

The original Talisa never reached the shores of Jamaica. Sonarielle was well acquainted with the details of how the life of that girl changed from that fateful morning when she was kidnapped, bundled away.

Slung, as she had been, over the shoulder of a strong running African, aware of the pounding of his companions' feet alongside him, their voices rambling in an unfamiliar tongue. Restrained by fear from the start, but yelling out; receiving hard slaps on her backside accompanied by retorts of senseless words every time she cried for help. Exhausted and hoarse, she at length settled for whimpering to herself, afraid, hoping her father, brother and betrothed would come to rescue her.

They seemed to run for some distance before she was flung from the man's shoulders, unfurling to gape on a row of tied up people, half naked, naked; men in their prime with wood blocks around their necks, chains around feet: more strangers, some with tribal markings. These strewn together: men, women and younger children than her captured self; she recognised no one. It appeared she was the only Ewe among them. These people were mainly made up of Fante and Asante, though a few looked as if they came from further north; all weary, bedraggled. The stern men guarding them carried weapons: a few guns, bows and arrows, machetes, clubs and whips with which the captured were often threatened.

Their first stop after Talisa joined them was under a canopy of merciful trees. Exhausted, here shaded from a strong midday sun, the odd ray filtering through cracks in the tree tops afforded a little respite. Thirst more than hunger gripped the captives. They sat, the women moaning. Men, particularly the fresher ones, displayed undisguised the raw anger burning in their eyes and bellies. By then, all the captives realised the stories told about people being taken, not by ghosts but by men driven by cruel purpose was true. Thoughts drifted to families, loved ones and how to escape the unfolding nightmare they had been unwillingly roped into.

She looked desperately at the faces of the people on the ground, searching for answers but their eyes were stark, or flitted away nervously. A couple of times when some chanced whispered communication in Akan dialects, the response was a quick verbal rebuke, followed by a kick, punch or slap. It was clear, there was to be no talking, no plotting to escape even in frustrated tongues. Water was provided and fruit gathered from the surrounds, hardly a belly full. They herded to squat to do their business near where they sat as eager flies buzzed. Dignity had fast begun to flow away but the air at least was still relatively fresh and earthy. They could still cover their mess with leaves and soil.

They were moved on again and had not gone far when one of the women screamed as a snake landed on her shoulder. It bit her neck as she tried frantically to shake it off but her hands were tied. The drive stopped. Others looked on helpless. Their drivers seeing what was amiss, snapped at the woman, before using a stick to remove the coiling reptile. One of these nameless men hacked the venomous viper to pieces. The woman was left gasping. She would be of no more use to them and they didn't even have to waste any time killing her. They cut her loose, leaving her to die alone without family, friends or understanding as to why any of this had happened. Talisa felt tears uncontrollably roll down her cheeks as they resumed their relentless march. Theirs had been a group of fifty-two people, now there was fifty-one. This figure would drop and rise on route to their destination.

The second night, after they had stopped to bed down, their captors started laughing. It was the first time Talisa would witness this type of camaraderie amongst them. She saw one of them grope his crotch. She felt sick, instinctively lowered her head to the ground. A couple of the women were released from the chain. They began crying, pleading in their respective languages but to no avail. They were shouted at and dragged into the bush. When the women returned, they could not look at anyone. It was understood what had happened. Words were not needed. A good price would be paid for a virgin from this bunch. Thus, all the women would not be despoiled, but none of the females were aware of this.

The march continued along tried and tested routes, places the locals feared to now broach. A wild goat was caught one day, a veritable feast for their captors, allowing more than the scraps of bush meat the captives were rarely tossed. It was hardly cause for celebration but the distraction led to one of the captive men escaping that night having slit the throat of one of the drivers. The drivers were incensed, violently lashing out at the assumed complicity of their captives. They drove them harder the next day, denying them their meagre ration of food and water as punishment.

The sun rose in the mornings and the moon shone at night. They ate and drank little and without a wash for days. Talisa's period was due, but the trauma of her ordeal affected even this. She prayed it would not come; her shame would be the more complete, afraid flies would swarm her, adding to her ever growing misery. They came to a watering place where the men were separated from the women; there they were allowed to wash themselves under close watch.

The luxury of breathing fresh air and to have running water grace one's skin; such simple pleasures she had taken for granted all of her previous precious, playful life ...

The march finally ended at the gates of the garrison their drivers referred to as Cape Coast Castle. Talisa could never have imagined the existence of such a place; this huge white building, wrapping angular with towers and red tiled roofing, perched prominent on top of a cliff, overlooking the roaring churn of the untameable ocean. An ominous greeting true, the taste of salt carried on a whipping wind. The place was a bustling hive of oxen, goats, chickens, dogs, pigs: erect black cannons and balls enough to serve and protect the foreign strutting white men in a sea of Africans.

CHAPTER EIGHTEEN: EMBRACING THE DEEP

It was the first time ever in her brief life that Talisa had spotted a white man. Some were enlisted sailors in uniform running through exercise paces; others worked for merchant trading companies. These seafaring adventurers lorded over the locals who traded wares from heavy laden pack mules, cart loads of perishable produce, timber; fishermen selling fresh and roasted fish. Buyers and sellers bartered for weapons, gold, utensils, as well as precious human lives.

Talisa had heard strange stories about these white men, stories which painted them as being mythical and dreadful. This young girl could make little sense of the confusing sights she beheld. These mythical men in strange garb also spoke an even stranger tongue. She had paradoxically entered a world in her own land where she knew no one and understood nothing. Natives were chained or tied up like those on her own forced marched. Some of these people were trussed up in neck irons with chains also shackling their feet; people of varying builds, reflecting different hues of brown from a range of tribal areas near and far: all captives in this devouring enterprise.

Grievous floggings were being meted out, some to the timed lash of subsiding howls, some to stoic resistance: sacrifices to instil fear and obedience. This was truly a bizarre and foreboding place, which nothing in her former life could have prepared her for. This nightmare, with every driven and despairing step, compounded her increasing torment and dwindling life span. They were hurried along, the men separated from the women again. Her group was pushed to the entrance of a gaping hole, a sweltering noxious stench greeting them before they were thrust deeper into its iniquitous mouth, descending from light into dank darkness.

It was Christmas Eve on the former Gold Coast now established Slave Coast 1675. The Captain's ship had been beached along the shore for more weeks than he could stand, the vessel having been damaged in heavy seas on its last triangular route back from Jamaica. The delay could cost him a month or more into the New Year. All the men, himself included, would take advantage of their stay on dry land, far from home.

His wife and three children were back in Bristol, England. He had not seen them in over a year. He paid for the provision of one of the fresh unused slave girls he'd seen arrive earlier in the day, God's gift to himself and behind the Governor's back. He simply didn't care to be alone.

An elevated Mulatto woman brought her to his room that evening. He had been working by candlelight, going over manifests and his logs, a thing he had delayed doing since arriving on the coast, also having cursory thoughts as to supplies for the next voyage. He looked up briefly, long enough to tell the older woman to go. The girl remained fixed next to the door, almost afraid to breathe the waxy air.

She had been retrieved from the hellhole, washed, scrubbed, fed and dressed; save nothing could wash the vile smell of that foul existence. It was some minutes before the Captain next acknowledged that he was indeed not alone. He called her to him but she did not budge. He beckoned to her to come forward but fear kept her transfixed, trembling inside and out.

"I'm trying to work out whether you're mute, stubborn or just don't understand." He put his quill down. "But as a new arrival I'm guessing you don't understand a single word I'm saying." There was no response to his flat rootless voice, for all the gibberish power it conveyed. Still seated, he removed his belt from his breeches and put it on the desk, unbuttoned his jacket.

He beckoned to her again, this time clearly putting a hand on his belt. Even through the dim light, highlighting his featureless white face and ghostly greying hair, Talisa understood the implied threat. She shuffled stiff legged closer to this apparition, who loomed twice as large by candlelight.

"Good, that's better. I'm not a violent man ordinarily but sometimes ..." He trailed off. "So, let me have a look at you." He walked around her. "Not seen too many like you in this place. A rare find I'd say. Lucky me." He ran a contrasting finger down her cheek, walked behind her again, grabbing her buttocks which he was delighted to find still fleshy and firm. She shuddered, could not help it, but otherwise remained fixed. He had touched her where even her betrothed had not ventured. The fear was rising in her, her heart felt as if it was wedged in her throat. The man moved back to his desk, poured himself a glass of wine. He was not yet ready for something stronger. Unsheathing a dagger from his desk, he approached her again. She flinched, shuddering, the thought that he might kill her, end her suffering or should she try to escape? Talisa closed her eyes, but he proceeded to cut down the front of the dress in one movement without drawing blood. She heard the tearing sound it made without rocking her body back, drawing a deep breath as her full breasts were revealed to him. She began to cry uncontrollably, understanding his intention. He cupped her hard young breasts in both hands, feeling his way across her belly, ripping away the rest of the frock. She stood too afraid to even breathe now. He removed his jacket and shirt, kicked off his shoes before stepping out of his breeches. He stood erect. She closed her eyes; a numbness rose from her feet. He tugged her along to his bed like a lamb to the slaughter.

"Come on, if you don't fight me, there's every chance you may enjoy this. My gift to you this Christmas," he mumbled, sitting her down, furtively mapping her young body. "Christ knows by the time you leave this god forsaken place there'll be precious little for you to look back on as good will." He laid her back on the bed and sucked her breasts like a greedy hog, the whiff of his rancid breath hitting her unwilling nostrils as he surfaced to ply his corrosive lips to her innocent mouth. He grabbed the back of her matted head and with his legs forced hers apart. She instinctively struggled with this alien assailant. “Yes, I thought you might. Not as timid as you look are you?!” He thrust his engorged member right into her vagina, rupturing her hymen like a hot poker. The shock reverberated throughout her entire being. She screamed and writhed to free herself but the pain just worsened as this hog grunted and weighted on her chest, grabbed both her legs, forcing them apart.

“Go on, fight me. That’s it!” The pain was excruciating, as if she was on fire. She gasped for breath, sore and bleeding. Where was her mother, her father? Why couldn’t anyone stop this? He pummelled away, the contorted look on his white coarse face, incomprehensive as he ejaculated his repugnant self-hatred inside her.

When he had calmed down, he wiped his blooded weapon of mass destruction on the dingy white sheet, before rising to pour himself a cup of Jamaican rum this time, swallowing a large gulp. He could hear her whimpering. He shouted at her to shut up.

“Don’t lay there sobbing, you stupid negro! Trying to make me feel guilty?! At least it was me and not some of the dogs here who have no sense of feeling whatsoever mind. You should be grateful you god forsaken heathen! Get up. Get up now!" He grabbed the dress and threw it at her. It landed on her bare feet.

"Go on, get out. Get out I say!" She understood. Glad the ordeal was over. As quickly as she could muster, she got to her feet, frantically dressed through the tears, before blindly stumbling to the door. She had barely opened it when he slammed it shut again.

"Oh no you don't you little black bitch. You'd think I was the Devil the way you're carrying on." He turned her around, with unctuous guile; he poured rum into her mouth. She spluttered as it burned her lips. "Let's get you more in the mood aye, me being the least of your woes," he snorted in utter belief. "The least. If you survive the Middle Passage, big if and plantation life in Jamaica, you could end up a right little breeder and you'd have me to thank. So you see, you will see me through this night. That you most certainly will." He dragged her back to the bloodied mess of a bed.

The Mulatto wench knocked again just before dawn, bringing with her a basin and jug of water for the Captain. Talisa could barely crawl out of the bed, covering her shame with the ripped dress, wiping the night's muck from her body, staining the dress. Captain Coster ordered the Mulatto to bring him clean sheets. Outside the door, the woman chided Talisa for staining the dress. Now it would have to be re-stitched and bleached in the sun. The filthy little new-made whore was returned the hellhole. This baptism of sheer inhumanity had barely begun.

Captain Coster stirred himself to make ready for the Christmas morning service which he would attend with a few of his own ship's company as the Governor had invited. He prided himself on being a religious man who retained much generosity under uncompromising circumstances. In church, he proudly gave thanks to his God for bringing his men and vessel safe to shore and for leading out the wretched blacks to a land where toil would hone their lazy, unrighteous backs to death if necessary under the auspices of the British realm. He did not give a single thought as to how many children he may have fathered in the pursuit of his endeavours for empire or whether any survived.

The Governor too was in good spirits. Breaking in a virgin overnight usually left him a little ill at ease, but it was Christmas Day and all sins could be wiped clean.

Over the next several days Talisa lapsed into a deranged state, despite some of the stronger women in this dejected company trying to soothe her. Every time she heard the rasp of voices, from those who came to collect for night duties, she shrunk deeper into the filthy slime in a futile attempt to hide. She was damaged goods. Her skin, her hair crawled with all things real and unimaginable. When she was able to find a wall, she dug her nails into it, scratching and scraping but nothing could ease the constant throbbing pain inside. Now and then she thought she heard recognisable words from the cacophony of wails circulating the vile hole, as women called out in abject agony. One night she was again selected, passed to several drunken dogs who treated her lower than any of the animals in her father's village, lower than the curs at the fort even. She was ready to die, to take her own useless fading life.

The Police in Negril had asked how Talisa had been impregnated; Captain Coster had had that predacious pleasure, the ignorance of his own ancestry deposited in an innocent Ewe lamb. Days later she was loaded onto one of the ships, together with five hundred other slaves. Flocks of migrating birds flew free up above them, wings catching a beguiling wind. The great expanse of what looked to her to be waves of angry water meeting the sky was fearsome to behold after passing through a gate leading further into a nightmare from whence there would be no return. The belly of this foul, rocking beast of a ship would prove far worse than the former dungeon. Shackled and immobilised in its cess pool of infectious human degradation, lacking air, lacking light or common kindness from these captors. She found herself awash in urine, faeces, vomit and vermin, barely able to keep down any of the slop given for little sustenance. Her health deteriorated faster than before, her flesh sore and raw where metal wore away her skin without pity. Unaware of the foetus she carried claiming its nourishment from her, she just simply wanted to die.

And so it was, with her body festering, wasting away, she was finally deemed unworthy for even the slop being fed, having prior tasted the whip for refusing to eat. The next fine morning when she could not manage to stand or focus in the rare light granted, she was tossed overboard with several other dead slaves and one crewman: a plunge to freedom.

Somewhere inside her semi-conscious state, she was able to welcome the embrace of the deep: her release from hell; free from fear. Captain Coster's ejaculation of death finally paid out compensation. Death, her reward for his perverse act of self-deceptive good will rape: white death.

CHAPTER NINETEEN: LAYING TO REST

Rachel, Pastor Josiah and some Assembly members had visited the old woman Talisa called Auntie, ministering to those poor souls up there on the hilltop. Offers of help with everything that needed fixing just poured her way, with Assembly members also taking the initiative to pay her to use a portion of the land as an allotment to grow more of their own provisions. Always hoping that one day "better mus' come", Auntie was nonetheless overwhelmed. The change in her fortunes also made it possible for the children to attend school regularly. Auntie had never received so much attention in her life, even getting her mouth fixed up. She gave thanks and daily sang praises for it all. There was no way she would be standing alone against any further threats to her home. For the sake of the children she was raising, life was manifestly more manageable. Auntie felt and looked ten years younger: a survivor.

Wonder of wonders, she discovered that the two Hope Cows were with calves, twins both it would later transpire. This miracle was the talk of the neighbourhood. Later, vets and scientists came from near and far to examine the animals because there were no bulls in the immediate vicinity and it was doubtful Auntie knew anything about artificial insemination. Auntie herself would frequently ask about Talisa, but was never to see her again.

Mrs Lawrence had said her heartfelt farewell at her home the night before. Talisa had been out in the backyard looking up at the starry sky.

"You thinking about leaving now?" Mrs Lawrence asked in earnest, looking at the young woman whose features now seemed to reflect the wisdom of ages.

Talisa turned to her. "My assignment here is near complete."

"Hmm. Thought so." Mrs Lawrence sighed, rubbed her bare arms and also looked to the stars. "Do you have family, I mean like people do?"

"Billions," looking upwards again, "but not, not formed like you." She turned back to Mrs Lawrence, her eyes shining. "A sick man seeks a cure, a physician for help. I was between states when I landed on this country of yours."

"I remember Hopeton telling me. Seems so long ago now … So tell me, is there anything you've learnt about Jamaica that you'll take away with you?"

Sonarielle did not have to reflect for the answer. "It is the mandated role of government to govern having outlined their strategies for their terms of office yes?"

"That's the theory, yes."

"But where there is deprivation and this breeds the breach of collective ignorance and jealous darkness of mind, it is surely the role of government to enlighten and engage residents of such localities so that there is one government and one country. Instead there are enclaves of unaffordable fiefdoms holding capital, country and residents to ransom by stagnation and the stifling of youthful aspirations."

"They would say it is easier said than done."

"Jah Rumble would say they need a livealogue"

"Who?"

"A Rasta man I met."

"Oh" the old woman nodded.

"To progress you must have a vested interest to bring change. The issues here are long overdue. I think you call it regeneration."

"It takes what government calls funding."

"What it will take is a firm resolve to tackle the issues and a direction for the future as far as allotted time will allow. How you use the time that is left is what is important. Everything is constantly in motion, the whole universe. Change is inevitable."

"Hmm, hmm. Go on ..."

"To regenerate a sense of resolve must be active, not passive. 'Yah helps those that help themselves.' Repentance is healing."

"You speaking to the converted here."

"... Things left to themselves can mushroom into disorder, spread like a virus. Paralysis is not an option in such circumstances. The spirits of your freed people did not remain trapped in their masters' cane fields for example."

"No … As we say here 'each one teach one'."

"You still can, while your eyes are still open old lady."

"From one teacher to another, thank you for opening further the eyes of an appreciative old woman."

"Thank you for giving me shelter." Sonarielle clasped the old lady's warm hand with an invigorating squeeze.

Flying the conventional way was impractical of course. Talisa had managed to say her goodbyes at the airport. Hopeton and Rachel were there to see her off. Travel documents had been sorted without too many questions being asked for the sake of formalities and to stave off awkward questions for those left behind. It was better this way.

On the morning of the Autumnal Equinox, Sonarielle's assignment was all but completed. She would have to give a full account of how the Chosen Ones were faring. Others would also give their recent mission accounts, the details of which were always enlightening. Her recommendation would be that there were enough Yamaicans seeking *The Path* to stay the hand of a major calamity on the scale of Port Royal, though more intervention was needed to give the people particularly in the garrison areas respite. Jamaicans needed to reclaim their streets and communities, reconnect them with the rest of the land. Theirs was not the history of the Wild West or the Romanesque Mafia which these areas were hell-bent on aping: 'Where there is no law, the people perish'. Community workers alone could not hope to stem the mental anguish of children forced to sleep under their beds for fear of stray bullets with some even being suicidal. This was not what was meant by: "suffer the little children to come unto thee". It would be up to The Creator to decide how the people in the locality of Jamaica fitted in with the wider unfolding events across the planet. Sonarielle's role was simply to present her report, having been tasked with engaging the Enemy to protect the innocent.

There was no allowance for scaling the Himalayas, surfing dunes in the Sahara, weaving across the Rockies or cruising the Amazon. Other Assignees had been despatched on missions, given the critical imbalances on the planet and considering they had yet to feel the full force of the furnace of affliction man courted, some to their eternal damnation as foretold: an inert state.

Ghana was in range, she adjusted her scope for the Volta Region, scanning the area and pinpointing Talisa's family graveyard in the midst of a cared for grove; the place still treated with reverence by the locals. Stories about Talisa's family were often recounted.

She stepped out of the transportal. Dawn was about to break. Apart from the vibrant calls of birds in anticipation of the rising sun, the scurrying of small mammals and the relentless movements of insects, tirelessly rustling routes in the undergrowth, not a single soul was close by. Her electromagnetic being lithely slipped from the physical Talisa casing, which remained upright like a mannequin. Sonarielle allowed it to slowly incline to the ground until level. The flesh melted away leaving the dry skeleton which sunk into the mineral rich soil. It had not been necessary to do all this but it seemed a fitting end for now. Come the end of the week, the locals would see a new growth of unusual plants, something for them to marvel at: a gift.

She re-entered her transportal, transforming it into a walnut like shape and to that approximate size before making contact with Planet Blue Water's consciousness and linking that with the Sun's. Both responded by opening a portal to assist her swift exit from the solar system. She was gone in the blink of a spatial dimensional eye.

Sonarielle's next galactic assignment was already scheduled. The life forms concerned needing guidance. She was to be born as the second son to a priest, and was assigned to help bring the population to an age when a new king would rule. She would be his trusted friend from childhood. Sonarielle was fully focussed on the assignment ahead; the life forms involved were not as biologically complex as humans which would make accessing functional orientation much easier.

There was always something new on the immortal horizon.

BONUS POETRY

Harking back to events in the past …

A Ship's Brief Mascot

The dim streets, smoky, filled with burning
brawl and cursing;
Drunken sailors staggered doused with
rum'n rolling song
To a background of laughter, tears and
quarrelsome death;
Where rude offence dragged dark women to
taste their tackle,
The night before the 7th of June 1692 …

Her cargo loaded by colourful waning crew,
The Provident's anchor raised and ship set
sail,
Cresting out southwester track from Port
Royal,
Tracing a motion way above the equatorial
line.
'Twas 8:00 past sunrise
As Jamaica receded and patience slipped
and broke and bit the morning air.

It was not a seagull that followed her wake
sir.

The cabin boy spied those dainty wings
Above the mast, where no bird had breached the morning sky.
Youth shielded eyes from the sun's stern gaze.
Rice paper wings, calligrapher's markings reflected, sparkling
As she rose and fell,
The wind lifting warm and wet,
Tossing and dipping Providence bowed to an angry sea
While sailors barked and snapped through the roar of waves.
A superstitious lot aye, but cargo full of rum, spice, sugar, cloth:
Not a belly full of slaves was she, for goodness sake providently.

"What's that?" the Captain cried out,
As the circling insect fell on washed and salted deck.
"Just a butterfly" the boy shouted in return,
The wind picking up, stirring up, flinging colourful crew aside.

A surge hit Providence near midday,
The Caribbean plate grated, frustrated,
Ordering swift tsunami out from great depths
As the ship ploughed on to safer course …

The butterfly finally was swept away,
A mascot for any other day …

The Banquet

She awoke to music, singing and laughter
Her eyes skating dancers in frolicking display
She lay on the table, head crowned with gold trimmings
Naked, cooked crisp as a stuffed roasted sow

Such dainties and pastries, the rarest of delicacies
Graced this fine gathering of merrymaking folk
Hung from the rafters, fruits from world's forests
Feathers and skins from animal kind

Dhey drunk *wid* blood mulled wine, *dem* elixir for life
With spirited cheers for more bounteous times
While far flung from feasting, gaiety and romping
The half-starved and dying who paid with their lives

"TEARS"

Cry rain; rip tide waves, oceans, storms,
floods: tsunami of tears.
Floating, drowning, tossing, swept up
on distant shore.
Tropical dipped foresight in a pool of
unconscious insights.
Battered, bruised, exhausted, limp, agonised;
preserved in brine.
Oblivious to froth washing bare feet;
Sand embedded toes.
Sirens regurgitate with screams and spouts
What the sodden peppered and muted
form filled garnished with seaweed
could not.

The perplexed exclaimed:

"Goodness! What have we here?"

"... Survivor ... Perhaps ..."

"But where is the ship?"

"That ship sailed ... Some time hence ..."

ABOI

The author, a former cereal killer, ' ːd Wheat and Special K, has ove a non-public school and Oxbridge l, well hysterical work. Arthur TS J ı-ated from the University of Bradford with a BSc.21 in Social Sciences and an M.A. in European Studies, under the expert guidance of such luminaries as Danny Kennally, Mich Le Lohe, Jack Morrell, and Dr Price. Mr Jackson boasts a record collection that includes every one of the number one singles of the 1960s. If the projected royalties of this magnum opus fail to materialise, he is threatening to one day write another publication on the relative merits or otherwise of these hits. The author lives somewhere in Northern Ireland. The precise whereabouts have not been disclosed in the absurd belief that his home will be besieged by a multitude of admirers. Currently studying Latin in an effort to become a High Court judge, Jackson devotes his spare time to constructing underwater lighthouses for submarines.

ABOUT THE PUBLISHERS

Parkbench Publications welcomes manuscripts from all aspiring authors and new writers who find their literary ambitions thwarted by other publishing companies that simply take the easy option and sponsor the 'works' of celebrity non-writers. If you have a project that is no more than 200 pages in length, submitted preferably by disc in PDF format, then Parkbench Publications will afford your proposed book the attention and respect that it deserves.

THAT WAS THE DECADE THAT WAS

Arthur TS Jackson

PARKBENCH PUBLICATIONS

Published in Great Britain by Parkbench Publications,
PO Box 1081, Belfast BT1 9EP

A CIP catalogue record for this title is available from the British Library

ISBN 978-0-9555756-1-7

Designed and typeset by Bookcraft Ltd,
Stroud, Gloucestershire
Printed and bound in Great Britain by
CPI Antony Rowe, Eastbourne

CONTENTS

For Hazel W, who can barely remember the 1960s,
and for Charlotte, Hannah, and Sophia,
who definitely don't.

INTRODUCTION

For better or for worse, the 1960s was a decade of tremendous upheaval, both culturally and economically, as well as politically and socially. This book is not intended as a pseudo-revisionist work, aiming to support the conservative reaction to the emergence of the 'permissive society' nor the liberal romanticism of the decade of love. Instead, it is merely a factual guide to the major events that shaped the development or otherwise of Britain and Ireland in the sixties. I regard this publication as a supplement to such worthy attempts to analyse the era in much greater depth as exercised by the likes of Dominic Sandbrook, among others.

Britain in the 1960s was suffering from an identity crisis. On the one hand, Britain was an exclusive member of the nuclear club, whilst on the other, she was slowly coming round to the painful realisation that she was no longer equipped to maintain an empire. Furthermore, Britain was trying to both cement her special relationship with the United States of America and at the same time cultivate a closer friendship with the countries of western Europe, only to be rebuffed by the perpetual 'non' of Monsieur de Gaulle. On top of all this, the world's leading constitutional monarchy was busy driving its own vehicle, the Commonwealth, along new paths.

Against this confusing background, Britain's economy endured the fluctuating fortunes of boom and bust, while on a social level, the once-homogeneous English nation was slowly adjusting to the pace of change, accentuated by such phenomena as immigration and the 'permissive society'. Remarkably, in spite of the economic, political, and social turmoil, Britain was 'swinging' in the sixties to new sounds and new fashions, whilst British sporting stars did their very best to preserve British bragging rights, wherever possible.

Across the Irish Sea, the irony was that just as relations between north and south were beginning to normalise, and while tensions between the Republic of Ireland and Britain started to de-frost, the dormant volcano of Northern Ireland violently erupted in the summer of 1969.

If I may be permitted to digress. I was impressed by Martin Gilbert's harrowing history of 'The Holocaust'. Aside from being a grim read of page after page of atrocities, many of which had been perpetrated long before a 'Final Solution' was arrived at in the Wannsee Conference, the book was admirable because the author merely re-told the facts without moralising, leaving the reader to draw his or her own conclusion. My project, I like to think, is constructed along similar lines. It is not my mission to sermonise about the merits or lack of them of the sixties revolution in Britain and Ireland, but simply to record the facts in chronological order, whilst resisting the large temptation to pour scorn or lavish praise on the personalities and organisations that made the news. I will allow the reader to take this liberty. Changes (good or bad) in fashion, popular music, radio, sport, television, and transport are also featured. The book is mercifully not an exposition of the minutiae of government decisions and actions. Incidentally, one illustration of the apparent upheaval in sixties Britain is that while the country 'enjoyed' only three Prime Ministers between May 1979 and May 2007, spanning a remarkable 28 years between them, such was the rollercoaster ride of British politics in the 1960s that three different individuals occupied Number Ten, Downing Street in 1963 and 1964.

Noting Oscar Wilde's observation that 'talent borrows, but genius steals', this talented genius has both borrowed and stolen from 'The Chronicle of Britain'. Mind you, I would argue that as all events form part of the public record and are thus in the public domain, any perceived infringement of anyone else's copyright on account of my literary burglary is rather untenable. After all, if a newspaper publishes the score of a football match, and I do so likewise at a later date, my 'plagiarism' hardly constitutes a breach of copyright.

If I may be permitted to finish with a naked and thoroughly shameless piece of commercialism. Please spread the benefits of this gospel far and wide to friend and foe. Otherwise I will be forced into writing a sequel, covering a subsequent decade, in order to pay my bills and debt to society. It also goes without saying, although I will say it anyway, that my gratitude goes to my publishers, Parkbench Publications, as well as to the typesetters and printers. It has been stated elsewhere that 'if you remember the sixties; you weren't there.' Draw from that what you will. This factual tour de force, if I may say so, is dedicated both to those who were there and to those who weren't.

Arthur TS Jackson, May 2007

1960

JANUARY

4th – A survey by the British Broadcasting Corporation reveals that approximately half the population of Britain watch their television sets during peak times.

12th – Nevil Shute dies at the age of sixty. Born under the name of Nevil Shute Norway, Shute wrote more than twenty novels, including 'Ordeal'(1939), 'No Highway'(1948), 'A Town Like Alice'(1950), and 'On The Beach'(1957).

13th – Nine-year-old Princess Anne performs the function of bridesmaid during the marriage ceremony of her cousin Lady Pamela Mountbatten and David Hicks at Romsey abbey.

18th – Africans boycott the Kenyan constitutional conference that takes place in London.

20th – The Macmillan government announces restrictions on the sale of so-called 'pep pills'.

26th – Street disturbances greet the visit of Harold Macmillan to Salisbury, the capital of Southern Rhodesia.

27th – The British Broadcasting Corporation declares its desire to create a new television channel to complement its current channel.

FEBRUARY

3rd – Harold Macmillan addresses the South African parliament in Cape Town where eyebrows are raised by his speech. Macmillan states that "the wind of change is blowing through this continent and, whether we like it or not, this growth of national consciousness is a political fact."

5th – Sean Lemass, the Taoiseach of the Republic of Ireland, and President Eamon de Valera attend the premiere of Mise Eire (I am Ireland), which is the first full-length feature film to be made in the Irish language.

8th – Queen Elizabeth announces that the name of Mountbatten-Windsor will be used for all of her descendants who are not called Royal Highness.

15th – The Kenyan constitutional conference approves the constitutional blueprint of Iain MacLeod, the Colonial Secretary.

19th – The Queen gives birth to her second son, who becomes known as Prince Andrew Albert Christian Edward.

21st – The Kenyan constitutional conference, held in London, draws to a close.

22nd – Aviation Minister, Duncan Sandys, announces a new project in which Britain will collaborate with either France or the United States in the development of a supersonic airliner, capable of travelling at 2,000 miles per hour.

26th – 29-year-old Princess Margaret has agreed to marry a photographer called Antony Armstrong-Jones, the son of the Countess Rose and Ronald Armstrong-Jones, QC. A wedding is planned for early May.

28th – An anti-apartheid rally addressed by the Labour Party leader Hugh Gaitskell is disrupted by fascist Mosleyites.

MARCH

14th – A government report announces plans to construct a barrier across the River Thames at a reported cost of at least £17 million as a means of preventing high tides from the North Sea flooding London.

On the same day, the radio telescope at Jodrell Bank in Cheshire sets a space-tracking record by making contact with the United States' Pioneer 5 – a mere 407,000 miles away.

17th – The new one pound note goes into circulation. On the same day, the opposition Labour Party fails to win either of the first two by-elections of the new parliament.

26th – Merryman II, owned by Miss W.H.S Wallace, wins the Aintree Grand National.

29th – Harold Macmillan reaches agreement with President Eisenhower at Camp David about nuclear test ban proposals which they will make to Soviet Russia.

APRIL

4th – Viscount Amory, the Conservative Chancellor of the Exchequer, announces in his budget that an extra twopence will be placed on a cigarette packet.

5th – President Charles de Gaulle is greeted by a reported crowd of 100,000 well-wishers on the first day of his state visit to Britain.

6th – Dr Richard Beeching is appointed to supervise a four-man team that will investigate the effectiveness or otherwise of Britain's railways.

7th – The Reverend David Sheppard, an England test cricket opening batsman, states that he will not participate on a cricket tour of South Africa.

13th – The Conservative government announces that it will abort Britain's £65 million Blue Streak missile programme. On the same day, grand prix driver Stirling Moss is banned from driving for a year as a result of dangerous driving. He is still eligible however to drive dangerously fast in grand prix races.

30th – The Blue Streak missile programme is scrapped.

MAY

3rd – The British Commonwealth conference begins, in London.

6th – Princess Margaret marries the 'commoner' Antony Armstrong-Jones in Westminster Abbey. More than two thousand guests attend the wedding ceremony.

7th – Wolverhampton Wanderers defeat Blackburn Rovers 3-0 in the English FA Cup Final.

9th – Major differences of opinion are expressed at the Commonwealth Conference as Commonwealth leaders confront the South African representatives over apartheid.

14th – Harold Macmillan joins de Gaulle, Eisenhower, and Khrushchev in Paris for a 'big four' summit, aimed at restoring harmonious relations between east and west.

16th – A bill to curb the anarchic activities of Teddy Boys receives an unopposed second reading in the House of Commons.

17th – The four power talks at Paris end without any hint of agreement or progress. On the same day, Queen Elizabeth the Queen Mother officiates at the opening ceremony of the new hydro-electric turbines of the Kariba dam, located in the Central African Federation of Rhodesia and Nyasaland.

18th – A crowd of approximately 135,000 spectators flock to Hampden Park, Glasgow to witness the first European Cup Final to be staged on British soil, during which Spanish giants Real Madrid overwhelm West Germany's Eintracht Frankfurt by the remarkable scoreline of seven goals to three.

29th – Stirling Moss records a win at the Monaco Grand Prix.

JUNE

1st – Proposals for the introduction of colour on television are "shelved indefinitely".

2nd – Planners from London County Council declare their intention to curb the recent trend of constructing high-rise buildings in the capital city.

7th – The first-ever National Health Service hearing aids are made available.

9th – An announcement is made that the Armstrong Siddeley, one of Britain's oldest quality motor vehicles, is to end production.

19th – Two British competitors, Bristow and Stacey, are killed in the Belgian Grand Prix while Stirling Moss is injured too. On the same day, the Jaguar car firm pay in the region of £3.5 million to acquire Daimler cars.

22nd – The House of Lords calls for the impending 'Press Council' to have real clout or be "given some teeth" in its operations. Meanwhile, one of Liverpool city centre's largest department stores catches fire, resulting in the deaths of eleven people.

24th – Jacob Epstein's last major work of sculpture 'St. Michael and the Devil' is unveiled at Coventry Cathedral.

26th – British Somaliland becomes independent.

28th – A pit accident in the village of Six Bells, Monmouthshire in Wales leads to the death of 28 coal-miners.

JULY

2nd – Australian Neale Fraser defeats his fellow-countryman Rod Laver in the men's singles final at Wimbledon. The women's event is won by Maria Bueno after she overcomes Sue Reynolds in the final.

6th – Former Labour Minister of Health, Aneurin 'Nye' Bevan, dies at the age of sixty-two. A formidable orator, this Welshman was a passionate, uncompromising socialist.

18th – Donald Campbell's new £1 million vehicle, 'Bluebird', receives its first test drive.

21st – 58-year-old Francis Chichester steers his yacht, Gypsy Moth II, into New York harbour, thereby sailing into the record books, having crossed the Atlantic Ocean in a mere forty days. The remarkable Chichester not only had to defy hurricane-like weather during his journey, but he has been battling lung cancer for two years.

27th – The Earl of Home is appointed as the new Foreign Secretary, while Edward Heath becomes his deputy at the Foreign Office.

AUGUST

4th – An agreement is found in London on the subject of a new constitution for Nyasaland.

13th – The price of beer increases by one penny per each pint to a new cost of 1/7d.

16th – A 21-gun salute at midnight marks the end of British rule in Cyprus, which steps out into the brave new world of independence, with Archbishop Makarios as President, and Dr.Kutchuk, a Turkish-Cypriot, as his Vice-President.

17th – Book publishers, Penguin, postpone the proposed publication of D.H. Lawrence's 'Lady Chatterley's Lover', anticipating the prospect of legal action.

19th – As predicted, Penguin Books are on the receiving end of a legal move to prosecute the publishers for obscenity in 'Lady Chatterley's Lover'.

22nd – The Edinburgh arts festival includes a new satirical review, entitled Beyond The Fringe.

SEPTEMBER

6th – Ten skeletons are found at Stonehenge in graves that date back 3,800 years.

8th – Although Penguin Books defends itself by claiming that 'Lady Chatterley's Lover' is art, the company faces trial over its proposed publication.

16th – Donald Campbell wrecks his new 'toy', Bluebird, in a 350 miles per hour crash. The record-breaking speedster at least emerges relatively unscathed.

19th – Traffic wardens and parking tickets operate for the first time in central London, with 344 tickets being brandished on day one of this new 'reign of terror' in the metropolis.

20th – Flat racing jockey, Lester Piggott, achieves the dual milestone of his 150th winner in this season and also reaches the landmark of one thousand career winners.

27th – The Bank London Underground railway station, on the Central and Northern lines, is the site of Europe's first 'Travelator', or moving pavement. Also on this day, pioneering suffragette campaigner, Estelle

Sylvia Pankhurst, dies at the age of 78. Her elder sister, Dame Christabel Pankhurst, had died two years previously.

28th – Harold Macmillan meets Britain's 'public enemy number one', Colonel Nasser of Egypt, at the United Nations assembly in New York, four years after the Suez debacle.

29th – The British Prime Minister's speech to the United Nations assembly meets with the disapproval of Russia's Nikita Khrushchev, who proceeds to thump his desk and heckle in response.

30th – Independence becomes effective in the former British colony of Nigeria at midnight.

OCTOBER

2nd – Britain and Iceland engage in discussions in Reykjavik to overcome their fishing disagreement. Meanwhile, Anthony Wedgwood Benn resigns from his position on the Labour Party's National Executive Committee.

3rd – Labour Party leader, Hugh Gaitskell, makes an impassioned speech at the party conference in Scarborough on the divisive issue of nuclear disarmament. Gaitskell labels the 'ban the bomb' enthusiasts as "pacifists, unilateralists, and fellow travellers." Making a personal plea to the party faithful, he also states that "there are some of us who will fight, fight and fight again to bring back sanity and honesty to the party we love." Gaitskell's words however are in vain as the assembled delegates vote in favour of unilateral nuclear disarmament.

9th – The south of England is on the receiving end of the worst torrential downpours for seven years.

17th – An announcement is made that the News Chronicle will cease to function, merging instead with the Daily Mail.

19th – A new 'Greater London Council' is required to operate in place of the London County Council, according to the recommendation of a royal commission.

20th – Harold Wilson declares his intention to compete against Hugh Gaitskell in a contest for the leadership of the Labour Party. On the same day, the trial of the morality or lack of it in 'Lady Chatterley's Lover' begins at the Old Bailey, London, where the assembled jury are instructed to read the controversial novel by the presiding judge.

21st – H.M.S. *Dreadnought*, Britain's first nuclear submarine, is launched by the Queen. Meanwhile, on dry land, the vertical take-off jet, the Hawker P.1127 attempts her first test flight.

24th – The philosopher, Bertrand Russell, steps down from his position as the leader of Campaign for Nuclear Disarmament.

26th – Bolton Wanderers' Bill McAdams records the first hat-trick by a Northern Ireland footballer for thirty years, but the mighty West Germany still emerge triumphant from Belfast's Windsor Park, courtesy of a 4-3 victory in a World Cup qualifying match.

NOVEMBER

1st – To the consternation of the 'ban the bomb' lobby, the Prime Minister announces a defence bill which will enable American nuclear submarines to make use of Holy Loch in Scotland.

2nd – 'Lady Chatterley's Lover' is proclaimed fit for publication by the Old Bailey jury, with the defendants, Penguin Books, preparing to issue 200,000 copies at a cost of 3s 6d to a curious public.

3rd – Harold Wilson's bid to de-throne Hugh Gaitskell as Labour leader ends in failure.

4th – Severe floods pay a further unwelcome visit to south-east England, bringing more disruption to the region.

8th – Ten Irish soldiers lose their lives in an ambush at Niemba in the Congo, where they were fulfilling their duties in a United Nations peace-keeping force.

9th – The first-ever 'hover-scooter' is given a trial demonstration in Surrey.

10th – D.H. Lawrence's 'Lady Chatterley's Lover' sells out on its first day. 200,000 copies had been shifted after the end of the novel's thirty-year ban.

16th – Broadcasting personality, Gilbert Charles Harding, collapses outside Broadcasting House in London, and dies at the age of fifty-three.

17th – William Wedgwood Benn, first Viscount Stansgate, dies at the age of eighty-three. His son, Anthony Wedgwood Benn MP, will succeed the title of Viscount Stansgate.

18th – A by-election at Ebbw Vale in south Wales, arising out of the death of Aneurin Bevan, results in the Labour Party candidate, Michael Foot, winning the vacant seat.

23rd – Anthony Wedgwood Benn returns his Letter Patent to the Queen, in an effort to renounce his new, inherited title of Viscount Stansgate.

DECEMBER

2nd – The Archbishop of Canterbury, Dr Geoffrey Fisher, has an historic meeting at the Vatican with the Pope. On the same day, Vivien Leigh is granted a divorce from Sir Laurence Olivier.

5th – An announcement is made that Leyland Motors will take over the business of the firm Standard-Triumph International.

10th – Britain's Peter Medawar is nominated for a nobel prize in medicine.

31st – The last-ever call-up cards are issued for national service. Just over two thousand civilians are enlisted today to a scheme that has recruited almost five and a half million individuals since its inception in 1939.

THE NUMBER-ONE HIT SINGLES OF 1960

Starry Eyed by *Michael Halliday*
Why? by *Anthony Newley*
Poor Me by *Adam Faith*
Running Bear by *Johnny Preston*
My Old Man's A Dustman by *Lonnie Donegan*
Do You Mind? by *Anthony Newley*
Cathy's Clown by *The Everly Brothers*
Three Steps To Heaven by *Eddie Cochran*
Good Timin' by *Jimmy Jones*
Please Don't Tease by *Cliff Richard and The Shadows*
Shakin' All Over by *Johnny Kidd and The Pirates*
Apache by *The Shadows*
Tell Laura I Love Her by *Ricky Valance*
Only The Lonely by *Roy Orbison*
It's Now Or Never by *Elvis Presley*
I Love You by *Cliff Richard and The Shadows*

1961

JANUARY

3rd – It is announced that the one millionth Morris Minor has rolled off the assembly line.

8th – Special Branch officers from Scotland Yard arrest five people on suspicion of espionage. The spy suspects, three Canadians and two civil servants, are accused of passing on confidential information from the Royal Navy's Underwater Warfare Establishment at Portland in Dorset.

9th – Relations between Britain and the Soviet Union de-frost slightly as both countries sign a culture, education and technology agreement.

11th – British Rail intends to hold an enquiry to ascertain why the Queen's train came to a halt, inconveniencing the monarch for almost an hour.

14th – Prison riots at Maidstone and Shrewsbury come soon after disturbances at Wandsworth in south London.

19th – Following the retirement of Geoffrey Fisher, Dr Michael Ramsey is appointed as the new Archbishop of Canterbury.

25th – The Daily Herald newspaper is bought by Thomson's.

30th – The oral contraceptive tablet, Conovid, is now available for purchase in Britain. The pill may soon be available on prescription via the National Health Service.

31st – The West Clare railway line in Ireland closes down.

FEBRUARY

1st – The Postmaster General announces a proposal to construct a post office tower in the centre of London.

6th – Tottenham Hotspur's captain, and Northern Ireland international, Danny Blanchflower, becomes the first celebrity to decline an invitation to have his story commemorated on the ITV show, 'This Is Your Life'.

8th – An acrimonious debate in the House of Commons on planned increases to National Health Service charges draws to a halt, but not before hostile responses from the Labour opposition members of parliament. Also on this day, the British Broadcasting Corporation declares its intention to drop the Children's Hour from the radio in April, after a run of almost forty years. The advent of television is regarded as responsible for the decline in the radio show's audiences.

16th – Robert Ranke Graves, author of 'I, Claudius', becomes Oxford University's new Professor of Poetry. Meanwhile, Cyprus applies to join the British Commonwealth.

17th – Constitutional discussions on the future of Northern Rhodesia at London's Lancaster House fail to reach a settlement.

19th – The violent death of Congo's Patrice Lumumba has prompted demonstrators to protest outside the Belgian embassy in London, a month after Lumuba's murder.

24th – Scientists at Jodrell Bank claim that they have managed to transmit telegraph signals 'down under' to Australia by bouncing them off the moon.

MARCH

3rd – Edwin Bush is the first criminal suspect in Britain to be apprehended on the basis of an 'Identi-Kit' picture.

6th – Lancashire's music-hall comedian, George Formby, dies at the age of fifty-six. Born George Hoy Booth, Formby appeared in twenty-two films, usually with his ukulele.

8th – Iain Macleod, the Colonial Secretary, announces that Malta will be granted self-government. Also on this day, Sir Thomas Beecham dies, aged eighty-one. Beecham founded the New Symphony Orchestra in 1906, and later became artistic director of Covent Garden Opera in 1933.

13th – Canadian businessman, Gordon Lonsdale, and four associates appear at the Old Bailey on charges of espionage.

15th – Dr Hendrick Verwoerd states that South Africa will be leaving the Commonwealth once she becomes a republic on May 31st. Meanwhile, Dr Richard Beeching is entrusted with the task of supervising British Railways.

16th – Michael Foot and four other rebel Labour MPs have the whip withdrawn by Labour's parliamentary party.

17th – A by-election in Cambridgeshire results in a triumph for the Conservative, Francis Pym.

20th – The Shakespeare Memorial Theatre at Stratford-upon-Avon is renamed the Royal Shakespeare Theatre.

21st – The House of Commons Committee of Privileges declares that the new Viscount Stansgate, Anthony Wedgwood Benn, is ineligible for the House of Commons.

23rd – Denis Howell of the Labour Party claims the parliamentary seat of Small Heath in Birmingham, after victory in a by-election.

25th – Nicolaus Silver, owned by Mr C. Vaughan, wins the Aintree Grand National.

APRIL

3rd – More than thirty people are arrested, following skirmishes at an anti-nuclear rally outside the United States Embassy in London.

4th – Harold Macmillan arrives in Washington for discussions with the new President of the United States, John F. Kennedy.

9th – An estimated 150 fatalities are expected after the British liner, Dara, is overwhelmed by fire, whilst in the Persian Gulf.

17th – Bill Nicholson's Tottenham Hotspur secure the first half of a potential double, by clinching the Division One championship title.

18th – 38-year-old George Blake is charged with offences under the Official Secrets Act, although details of his 'misbehaviour' have not been disclosed.

28th – It is revealed in Paris that the British government has made an application to join the European Common Market.

MAY

4th – Anthony Wedgwood Benn, otherwise known as Viscount Stansgate, doubles his majority in the Bristol South-East by-election, but as a peer it is unlikely that he will be permitted to take his seat in the House of Commons.

6th – A 2-0 triumph against Burnley in the FA Cup final renders Tottenham Hotspur the first club this century to achieve the English league and cup double.

8th – Proposals are announced by the government that would oblige pedestrians to use traffic lights as a means of crossing the road. Meanwhile, at Westminster, Viscount Stansgate is prevented from admission to the House of Commons by the principal doorkeeper. The

Labour peer will not, it seems, be accepted as an elected Member of Parliament until new legislation is enacted, which will provide him with the opportunity to renounce his peerage. Also, on this day, a former diplomat, George Blake, is handed an unprecedented sentence of forty-two years' imprisonment, on account of passing numerous sensitive documents to the Soviet Union.

11th – Following the conviction of George Blake, the Prime Minister orders an independent review of the functions of the security services.

14th – Stirling Moss secures victory on the streets of Monte Carlo, thereby winning the Monaco Grand Prix for the second successive year.

17th – Glasgow Rangers appear in the first final of the European Cup-Winners' Cup, but proceed to lose 2-0 in front of 80,000 supporters at Ibrox, in the first leg against Fiorentina of Italy.

18th – Canterbury, Colchester, and Coventry are to provide the campuses for three new universities.

22nd – The first 'pay-on-answer' telephone boxes are installed by the Post Office. The telephones provide 'pips' whenever coins are needed to prolong a conversation.

28th – The CEGB claims that human error is responsible for a major power cut that left south-east England without electricity a fortnight ago.

31st – The Epsom Derby is won by Psidium, owned by Mrs A Plesch. On the same day, South Africa formally severs links with the Commonwealth, on becoming a republic.

JUNE

4th – President Kennedy pays a flying visit to Harold Macmillan in London, en route to Washington, following his discussions in Vienna with Russia's Nikita Khrushchev. Meanwhile, on the same day, the cost of cigarettes increases by a half-penny. As a consequence, most ten packets will be sold for approximately 1/9d.

5th – Dr. Arthur Michael Ramsey begins his tenure as the new Archbishop of Canterbury.

7th – Initial figures for the 1961 population census reveal that the population of Britain has increased by almost two and a half million. Increased immigration is regarded as a contributing factor.

8th – The Duke of Kent, a cousin of the Queen, weds Katherine Worsley in the York Minster. The Queen and her mother are amongst two thousand guests at York's first royal wedding for over six hundred years.

13th – Inadequate security at the Admiralty is held responsible for allowing Gordon Lonsdale and his fellow spies to operate unhindered.

14th – Push-button controlled pedestrian crossings are to be introduced, according to a government statement.

19th – Britain's protectorate of the oil rich sheikdom of Kuwait comes to an end, but military assistance will continue to be provided.

26th – The government states that more Northern Rhodesian Africans will be granted the right to vote.

27th – Dr. Ramsey, former Archbishop of York, is enthroned as the one hundredth Archbishop of Canterbury, at the age of fifty-six.

28th – A ballot by the Electrical Trades Union is ruled as invalid by a judge, because it was apparently rigged by Marxist extremists.

30th – Queen Elizabeth pays a visit to the deprived Gorbals area of inner-city Glasgow.

JULY

1st – British soldiers arrive in Kuwait, where an attack is expected.

5th – The United Arab Republic demands the withdrawal of British troops from Kuwait.

8th – Australian Rod Laver defeats Charles McKinley in the men's singles final at Wimbledon, but his achievement was overshadowed by the staging of the first all-British final in the women's singles since 1914. Against most expectations, Angela Mortimer, a beaten finalist three years ago, overcomes the twenty-year-old Christine Truman in three sets, 4–6, 6–4, 7–5.

11th – Terry Downes from Paddington, London, seizes the world middleweight boxing crown at Wembley, after his 31-year-old opponent, Paul Pender, quits at the end of the ninth round.

12th – One million pounds is allocated by the government to help with the creation of the new National Theatre.

13th – Harold Macmillan meets new Russian space hero, Yuri Gagarin, and states that he is "a delightful fellow".

14th – The world's first spaceman, Yuri Gagarin, receives a very warm welcome from the British people, whilst on a brief visit. Included in Gagarin's itinerary is lunch with the Queen and Prince Philip at Buckingham Palace, and a press conference at Earl's Court.

16th – A train containing many holiday-makers crashes near Blackpool, resulting in the deaths of six people, while more than one hundred others are injured.

17th – The government announces that children will be learning a forty-three letter phonetic alphabet as an experiment.

25th – Cigarette prices will increase by four-pence, according to the mini-budget, which also decrees a rise of three-pence on a gallon of petrol.

28th – The High Court in London over-rules Viscount Stansgate's recent by-election triumph, declaring that his defeated opponent is the lawful Member of Parliament.

31st – Reactions on both sides of the floor of the House of Commons is mixed after the Prime Minister confirms Britain's application for membership of the European Common Market. Whether Britain's application is accepted remains to be seen.

AUGUST

4th – The government's intention to join ranks with the Common Market is backed by a majority in the House of Commons.

10th – Following the granting of Commons' approval, Britain makes a formal application to join the European Economic Community.

16th – The new post office tower in London is expected to exceed six hundred feet, an increase of one hundred on earlier estimations.

24th – A man and his girlfriend are savagely murdered on the A6.

28th – The earliest-known Roman mosaics in Britain are revealed at Fishbourne, near Chichester, in southern England.

SEPTEMBER

1st – Hampshire celebrate their first-ever victory in English cricket's county championship.

3rd – Britain and the United States demand an end to nuclear tests in the atmosphere.

4th – The Electrical Trades Union is expelled from the Trades Union Congress for ballot-rigging.

7th – The Trades Union Congress, assembled in Portsmouth, votes against a proposal for unilateral nuclear disarmament.

10th – Over eighty people are dead, after a chartered DC6 of President Air Lines plunges into the Shannon estuary shortly after take-off, in Ireland's worst air crash ever.

12th – Bertrand Russell and playwright Arnold Wesker are imprisoned for inciting a breach of the peace, arising out of their pursuit of nuclear disarmament.

13th – Moise Tshombe, leader of the breakaway Katanga state in the Congo, fails to honour a lunch appointment with Dr. Conor Cruise O'Brien, the Irish United Nations representative. Tshombe has allegedly gone into hiding.

14th – Mothercare's first shop opens in Kingston-Upon-Thames, in south-west London.

17th – Trafalgar Square, in central London, is the scene for an extraordinary 'sit-down' protest, as fifteen thousand people lend their weight to a 'ban-the-bomb' demonstration. Three thousand police react to this act of civil disobedience by arresting more than eight hundred protesters, including such celebrities as jazz singer George Melly, playwright John Osbourne, and actress Vanessa Redgrave.

22nd – The British head of the Ghanaian army is dismissed by Kwame Nkrumah, who assumes the role of Commander-in-Chief instead.

29th – The vote-rigging Electrical Trades Union is expelled from Labour's National Executive Committee.

OCTOBER

1st – The last-ever steam train runs on London's underground rail network.

3rd – Princess Margaret's husband, Antony Armstrong-Jones, is created Earl of Snowdon by his sister-in-law, the Queen.

6th – Sean Lemass's first election as Prime Minister enjoys mixed fortunes as his Fianna Fail party are returned to power, but only as a minority government. Fine Gael collect seven extra seats, but are still 23 seats short of Fianna Fail.

9th – The Conservative Party's youngest female member of parliament, Margaret Thatcher, lands her first government role, as a parliamentary secretary.

12th – Smaller ten shilling notes are now in circulation in the United Kingdom.

24th – The Mediterranean island of Malta becomes independent of Britain.

25th – British and American tanks confront Russian tanks in Berlin, in a stand-off concerning Allied entry rights.

31st – Augustus Edwin John, portrait and landscape painter, dies at the age of eighty-three. His works included Galway, as well as portraits of his wife, Dorelia, Madame Suggia, George Bernard Shaw, Thomas Hardy, and Dylan Thomas.

NOVEMBER

1st – The government announces its intention to introduce a Commonwealth Immigration Bill, aimed at creating criteria for entry into Britain. The legislation comes against a background of increasing inter-racial tension.

2nd – Extreme right-wing 'Mosleyites' attack members of parliament who have voiced their opposition to proposed immigration controls.

3rd – Princess Margaret gives birth to a boy, subsequently entitled David Albert Charles, alternatively know as Viscount Linley.

9th – A wave of bombs in Accra has not deterred the Queen from arriving in Ghana for a state visit. An ecstatic welcome vindicates her decision.

10th – President Kwame Nkrumah of Ghana, the first of Britain's former black African colonies to become independent, entertains the Queen and Prince Philip at a banquet, where warm tributes are exchanged between the heads of state.

23rd – The leader of the opposition, Hugh Gaitskell, pours scorn on Harold Macmillan for his party's sponsorship of the new Immigration Bill.

24th – President Charles de Gaulle arrives in London for discussions with the Prime Minister, amidst tight security.

29th – A white paper is issued by the government, which provides details for a proposed abolition of the London County Council.

DECEMBER

1st – Dr. Conor Cruise O'Brien is 'relieved' of his responsibility as the United Nations' representative in the Congo. The Irish diplomat had courted controversy, not least when he expressed support for the suppression of the Katanga region's breakaway from the Congo.

3rd – The south-east corner of England endures a two-hour blackout, courtesy of an electrician's error.

4th – The government announces the availability of the birth control pill on the national health service.

7th – Approval is granted by the London County Council for the building of three-hundred foot blocks of flats at Hammersmith, in west London.

8th – A cross-channel underwater cable that connects the electricity systems of France and England is officially inaugurated.

15th – Harold Macmillan meets President Kennedy for talks in Bermuda, before the American President sets off on a tour of Latin America.

19th – Decimal coinage is accepted in principle by the Conservative government.

31st – The Republic of Ireland's Radio Eireann launches a television station.

THE NUMBER-ONE HIT SINGLES OF 1961

Poetry In Motion by *Johnny Tillotson*
Are You Lonesome Tonight? by *Elvis Presley*
Sailor by *Petula Clark*
Walk Right Back by *The Everly Brothers*
Wooden Heart by *Elvis Presley*
Blue Moon by *The Marcels*
On The Rebound by *Floyd Cramer*
You're Driving Me Crazy by *The Temperance Seven*
Surrender by *Elvis Presley*
Runaway by *Del Shannon*
Temptation by *The Everly Brothers*
Well, I Ask You by *Eden Kane*
You Don't Know by *Helen Shapiro*
Johnny Remember Me by *John Leyton*
Reach For The Stars/Climb Ev'ry Mountain by *Shirley Bassey*
Kon-Tiki by *The Shadows*
Michael by *The Highwaymen*
Walkin' Back To Happiness by *Helen Shapiro*
His Latest Flame/Little Sister by *Elvis Presley*
Tower Of Strength by *Frankie Vaughan*
Moon River by *Danny Williams*

1962

JANUARY

9th – The de Havilland Trident jet aeroplane completes its debut flight.

11th – A smallpox outbreak is reported in Britain.

14th – Passengers on a BEA flight from Amsterdam are detained at London Airport as a precaution, after eight immigrants from Pakistan feel unwell. With smallpox afflicting Pakistan, there were grounds for fearing the worst, but in the end, it was merely a case of travel sickness. Nevertheless, six people have already died from the current outbreak.

15th – England cricket team are dismissed for 209 in the fifth and final test against India, thereby losing by 128 runs. Consequently, the home nation clinch a 2-0 series victory.

16th – Socialist historian, Richard Henry Tawney, dies at the age of eighty-one. Born in Calcutta, Tawney was a pioneer of adult learning, and his works included 'The Acquisitive Society', 'Equality', 'Religion, and the Rise of Capitalism'.

21st – Britain and Nigeria call a halt to their defence agreement.

22nd – The accused, James Hanratty, pleads not guilty at the outset of his trial for the 'A6 murder'.

29th – Britain and her ally, the United States, both walk out of the nuclear test ban discussions in Geneva with Soviet Russia.

FEBRUARY

4th – The Sunday Times issues its first colour supplement, featuring articles on Mary Quant and Pop Art. Despite the reservations of many critics, the newspaper owner, Lord Thomson, is confident of the new supplement's success.

7th – England cricket team's first-ever match at Karachi's National Stadium results in a draw, after Pakistan bat their way to safety in the second innings.

11th – A schoolboy from Essex has reportedly created a new world record by dancing to 'The Twist' for an unbroken thirty-three hours' stint.

16th – Ferocious gale force winds are held responsible for the deaths of eleven people in the United Kingdom.

17th – Britain's longest-running murder trial concludes after 21 days, with a guilty verdict being pronounced on the accused, James Hanratty. As a consequence of his murder of 36-year-old Michael Gregsten, Hanratty is sentenced to death.

20th – Six ban-the-bomb demonstrators are imprisoned for violating the Official Secrets Act.

25th – Renowned philosopher, Bertrand Russell, condemns the jailing of the six protesters, and describes the practice of atomic tests as "butchery".

26th – The Irish Republican Army announces a halt to its recent five-year terror campaign.

27th – The House of Commons agrees to restrict immigration from the British Commonwealth.

MARCH

3rd – The British Antarctic Territory is established in the south Atlantic.

4th – A British DC-7 aeroplane crashes in the Cameroons, with more than one hundred people feared dead. On the same day, Malta becomes completely independent.

7th – The health risks posed by cigarette smoking are flagged up by the publication of a report by the Royal College of Physicians.

8th – Dick Taverne, the Labour Party candidate, tastes victory in a parliamentary by-election at Lincoln. Meanwhile, the Bank of England lending rate falls to 5.5 per cent.

15th – Eric Lubbock, representing the Liberal Party, pulls off a remarkable by-election success, where he overturns a Tory majority of more than fourteen and a half thousand into a comfortable victory margin of almost eight thousand votes. Whether this surprise triumph leads to a Liberal resurgence remains to be revealed, but it is unquestionably a wake-up call for the government.

19th – An unexpected visitor appears at 10 Downing Street, when a three-hundred-year-old skull is discovered beneath the building.

23rd – Clement Davies, who was leader of the Liberal Party for a decade following the end of the Second World War, dies, aged 78.

28th – Marlborough House, constructed by Christopher Wren, is re-invented as the Commonwealth Centre.

31st – Twelve-year-old Kilmore secures victory in the Aintree Grand National. Fred Winter's second success as a jockey helps Mr. N Cohen's horse to triumph.

APRIL

2nd – The first push-button operated Panda crossings start to function.

4th – The A6 murderer, James Hanratty, is hanged, still protesting his innocence.

5th – William Rodgers of the Labour Party is elected to parliament, following victory in a by-election at Stockton. Meanwhile, the Radcliffe report on national security advises against the appointment of communists to the civil service. Also on this day, British spy chief, Sir Percy Sillitoe, dies, aged seventy-three.

9th – Economic experts predict a consumer boom as Selwyn Lloyd, the Chancellor of the Exchequer, produces a budget which includes decreases in purchase tax on domestic appliances and motor vehicles. Sales of 'white goods' are expected to increase.

11th – Cardiff City's Mal Charles scores all four goals in front of his own home crowd, as Wales demolish Northern Ireland in a home international match.

20th – Jailed members of the Irish Republican Army are to be released from prison as a consequence of the organisation's recent announcement of a ceasefire.

23rd – Stirling Moss suffers a broken leg, broken ribs, and serious head injuries, arising out of a 110 miles per hour crash in his Lotus Climax in a race at Goodwood racing circuit.

26th – Britain's first satellite, entitled Ariel, is launched successfully from Cape Canaveral, whilst in Britain, the lending rate is reduced to 4.5 per cent. Also on this day, Rochdale from the Fourth Division play host to Norwich City in the first leg of the League Cup final, with the visitors recording a comfortable 3–0, en route to a final tally of 4–0 on aggregate.

27th – Harold Macmillan arrives in Washington for more talks with President Kennedy.

30th – A police frogman unit is established by London's Metropolitan Police Force.

MAY

2nd – Pedestrians who do not make use of the new Panda crossings are threatened with fines for any future non-compliance.

8th – London's last trolley buses are removed from the streets.

10th – The Conservative government is presented with further cause for concern, after the party suffers more electoral setbacks, when it loses control of thirty councils.

11th – The heir to the throne, thirteen-year-old Prince Charles, arrives at the physically demanding private school of Gordonstoun, in north Scotland, to continue his secondary education.

17th – The British colony of Hong Kong establishes a barbed wire surround to prevent illegal entry by Chinese immigrants.

20th – England football team's last warm-up fixture prior to the World Cup tournament in Chile results in a 4-0 drubbing of Peru, as Jimmy Greaves plunders his third hat-trick in three consecutive years. His team-mate, fellow Londoner, Bobby Moore makes his debut appearance.

25th – The new Coventry Cathedral is consecrated, having taken six years to complete at a cost of almost one and a half million pounds.

29th – London's Stock Exchange endures its worst 'crash' since the 1929 slump, with share prices being reduced by £1,000 million.

30th – Benjamin Britten's *War Requiem* is performed in Coventry Cathedral as part of the cathedral's inauguration ceremony.

31st – Ron Flowers's third successful penalty kick from England's last five internationals cannot prevent Walter Winterbottom's men incurring a 2–1 defeat at the hands of Hungary in England's opening World Cup match.

JUNE

2nd – Britain's first legal casino, the Metropole, opens its doors in Brighton for business. Also on this day, novelist and poet Victoria Mary Sackville-West dies at her home at Sissinghurst Castle, at the age of seventy. A friend of Virginia Woolf and wife to Sir Harold Nicolson, her best-known works include 'The Edwardians' and 'All Passion Spent'.

6th – Larkspur emerges victorious in the Epsom Derby, but not before four jockeys are treated in hospital, following the collision of seven horses.

10th – Having scraped unconvincingly through the group phase, England football team meet their match in the shape of world champions-elect Brazil, who duly despatch them 3–1 at Vina del Mar in what proves to be Fulham stalwart Johnny Haynes's last cap for England.

13th – Composer and conductor Eugene Goossens dies, aged 69. Goossens shared the same name and profession as his father and grandfather. He was a conductor of the Rochester Philharmonic and the Sydney Symphony, and composed two operas.

15th – Tam Dalyell, representing the Labour Party, is elected to the House of Commons, following triumph in the West Lothian by-election.

18th – The Flying Scotsman embarks on its centenary train journey.

26th – Eighteen-year-old American tennis prodigy, Billie Jean Moffit, humbles the ladies' top seed Margaret Smith at Wimbledon.

27th – A government committee recommends a second television channel for the British Broadcasting Corporation. Meanwhile, a star of the screen, Charlie Chaplin, has an honorary Doctorate of letters bestowed on him by Oxford University.

30th – The first broadcast of 'Police Five' appears on British television. Also, it is announced that the forthcoming cricket engagement between the Gentlemen and the Players at Lord's, London will be the last such contest.

JULY

1st – The Commonwealth Immigrants Act comes into force (at midnight). The advent of new restrictions has prompted increased immigration in recent days.

4th – John Christie, founder of the Glyndebourne Opera, dies, at the age of 79. A member of a family of organ-makers, he was married to the soprano, Audrey Mildmay.

6th – Australian Rod Laver overwhelms his fellow-countryman Marty Mulligan to secure the men's singles title at Wimbledon.

7th – The ladies' singles final at Wimbledon results in victory for American Karen Susman against Vera Sukova.

10th – Ireland's first motorway opens, connecting Belfast with the dormitory town of Lisburn.

11th – American frogman, Fred Baldasare, becomes the first person to swim the English Channel underwater. Also on this day, it is reported that the first live television pictures are broadcast across the Atlantic Ocean via the Telstar satellite and a terminal at Goonhilly Downs.

13th – A series of recent electoral setbacks suggested that the Conservative Party was in danger of being evicted from government. In a drastic effort to revive his party's fortunes, Harold Macmillan dismisses seven cabinet colleagues – including Selwyn Lloyd, the Chancellor of the Exchequer. This 'night of the long knives' finds 'Supermac' re-named as 'Mac the Knife'. Liberal Party MP Jeremy Thorpe claims that "greater love hath no man than this, that he lay down his friends for his life."

20th – The estuary of the River Dee is the unlikely setting for a piece of history. Here, a hovercraft transported 24 passengers and two mailbags, containing eight thousand letters from Rhyl to Wallasey, thus becoming hovercraft's service.

21st – Historian George Macaulay Trevelyan dies, aged eighty-six. His historical works include 'British History in the Nineteenth Century' (1922) and 'English Social History' (1944).

25th – The gates of Buckingham Palace are thrown open to the general public for the first time, as large queues form to view the Queen's Gallery at a cost of two shillings and sixpence (12.5p).

26th – The Macmillan government proposes the establishment of a National Incomes Commission, nicknamed 'Nicky'. 'Nicky' is expected to make recommendations on pay disputes, but has no authority in terms of imposing its findings. Not everyone is impressed with the birth of 'Nicky', with Hugh Gaitskell, the leader of the opposition, describing it as an act of desperation.

30th – The Archbishop of Canterbury, Dr. Ramsey, pays a visit to Moscow.

31st – Britain approves the formation of a Federation of Malaysia. Also on this day, Oswald Mosley attempts to address a Union Movement rally in the east end of London, only to have his speech disrupted by violence. Meanwhile, in Dudley in the west midlands, four hundred supporters of the far right march on the local immigrant population.

AUGUST

6th – The Caribbean island of Jamaica becomes independent, having been a British colony for more than three hundred years.

8th – Police arrest American fascist spokesman, George Rockwell, and order him to leave Britain.

9th – It is announced that Sir Lawrence Olivier is to become the director of the National Theatre Company.

11th – British mountaineers reach the peak of Mount Communism – Russia's highest mountain.

20th – The government grants approval for the construction of a new London underground line, extending from Victoria in central London to Walthamstow, in the east end.

31st – The islands of Trinidad and Tobago become an independent state within the Commonwealth. Also on this day, 27-year-old Chris Bonnington and 25-year-old Ian Clough conquer the notorious north face of the Eiger mountain, not before this formidable obstacle claimed victims number 24 and then 25.

SEPTEMBER

2nd – Further street clashes take place in London between Mosleyites and east end residents.

6th – Dr. Robert Soblen, a Russian spy, attempts to kill himself, while being deported from London.

11th – Commonwealth leaders express their opposition to Britain's proposed membership of the European Common Market.

13th – William Vassall, a civil servant, is charged with breaching the Official Secrets Act.

14th – Various British distillers offer a quarter of a million pounds to assist with research into the effects of the thalidomide drug.

19th – The formation of a 'press council' is advised by a royal commission.

24th – British soldiers deploy tear gas to quell street disturbances in Aden.

OCTOBER

5th – A 'war of the cones' is anticipated, after Lyons Maid amalgamates with two other companies. A contest against Walls is expected to materialise.

8th – Judge Elizabeth Lane makes history as the first female judge to sit in the High Court.

9th – Sixty-two years of British rule in Uganda are halted by the start of independence.

15th – Amnesty International is formed as a means of campaigning against human rights abuses around the globe.

17th – Large traffic jams result from the opening of London's Hyde Park underpass.

22nd – William Vassall, a 38-year-old clerk at the Admiralty, is sentenced to prison for eighteen years, on account of his six-year campaign of passing highly important documents to the Soviet Union.

30th – The first James Bond movie, Dr. No, makes its screen debut, starring Sean Connery.

NOVEMBER

2nd – British businessman, forty-two-year-old Greville Wynne, is seized in Budapest, and flown to Moscow by the KGB, on suspicion of espionage activities.

5th – Purchase tax on motor vehicles is cut by fifty per cent by the government, in a bid to increase consumer spending.

6th – The Commonwealth Institute opens in south Kensington, thereby replacing the Imperial Institute. Also on this day, the Admiralty states that Her Majesty's Ship Cook has discovered the record ocean depth in the Mindanao trench – a mere 37,782 feet.

7th – Recent Manchester United recruit, Denis Law, records his first hat-trick in a Scotland jersey, as the home team annihilate Northern Ireland 5–1 at Hampden Park, as the Tartan Army march towards an eventual clean sweep in the British Championship.

8th – Thomas Galbraith, a junior minister, resigns from office, after his letters to the disgraced spy, William Vassall, are published.

12th – The Prime Minister claims he is now prepared to sign a partial nuclear test ban treaty with Soviet Russia and the United States of America.

22nd – The government suffers another electoral setback, when the Labour Party gain the seat of South Dorset in a by-election, overturning a Conservative majority of eight thousand.

24th – The British Broadcasting Corporation transmits the first episode of 'That Was The Week That Was' – a programme likely to irritate one or two figures in 'the establishment'.

29th – Britain and France sign an agreement to initiate a joint project to build a supersonic aeroplane, appropriately entitled 'Concorde' (or agreement).

DECEMBER

4th – Two British deep sea divers reach a new record depth of one thousand feet underwater in American waters.

6th – It is reported that the recent smog phenomenon in London has caused the deaths of approximately sixty people.

7th – The Nevada desert in the United States is the venue for Britain's second underground nuclear test.

8th – An uprising in Brunei leads to British soldiers clashing with rebels who are hostile to the Malaysian Federation.

10th – Nobel prizes for chemistry are awarded to British scientists John Kendrew and Max Perutz, while Francis Crick and Maurice Wilkins are two other British recipients of a coveted nobel prize.

11th – Oleg Penkovsky, a forty-year-old associate of Greville Wynne, is arrested in Russia, where he is suspected of spying for Britain over a period of almost a year and a half.

15th – British stage and film actor, Charles Laughton, dies at the age of sixty-three. His films include 'Mutiny on the Bounty' (1935) and 'The Hunchback of Notre Dame' (1939).

16th – Discussions between Harold Macmillan and President de Gaulle concerning Britain's proposed membership of the Common Market, end with little progress having been achieved.

17th – The Prime Minister leaves for talks with President Kennedy at Nassau in the Bahamas. Meanwhile, a parliamentary committee suggests that peers ought to be able to renounce their titles – if they so desire.

19th – Britain agrees to permit the breakaway of Nyasaland from the nine-year-old Central African Federation.

21st – Britain has been offered the use of American Polaris missiles in her submarines as part of a multilateral N.A.T.O nuclear force, suggested by President Kennedy at his Nassau conference with Harold Macmillan.

THE NUMBER-ONE HIT SINGLES OF 1962

The Young Ones by *Cliff Richard and The Shadows*
Can't Help Falling In Love/Rock-A-Hula Baby by *Elvis Presley*
Wonderful Land by *The Shadows*
Nut Rocker by *B Bumble and The Stingers*
Good Luck Charm by *Elvis Presley*
Come Outside by *Mike Sarne, with Wendy Richards*
I Can't Stop Loving You by *Ray Charles*
I Remember You by *Frank Ifield*
She's Not You by *Elvis Presley*
Telstar by *The Tornados*
Lovesick Blues by *Frank Ifield*
Return To Sender by *Elvis Presley*

1963

JANUARY

3rd – The Bank of England lending rate is reduced to four per cent.

14th – Britain's hopes of admission to the European Economic Community have been dealt a major blow, after President de Gaulle rejects the proposed move in a press conference. France's concerns about the extent of Anglo-American relations, coupled with Britain's involvement in the Commonwealth are influencing de Gaulle's 'non'.

15th – The British Broadcasting Corporation ends its censorship of politics, religion, royalty, and sex in its comedy programmes.

17th – Power blackouts result from strike action by electricity workers in London.

18th – The leader of the opposition, fifty-six-year-old Hugh Gaitskell, dies in hospital, after a brief illness. Gaitskell had been leader of the Labour Party since 1955.

25th – One of the Daily Sketch's journalists is imprisoned, after he declined to reveal his sources to the Vassall tribunal.

30th – In the wake of French opposition to British entry to the Common Market, Harold Macmillan claims that President de Gaulle wants to dominate Europe.

FEBRUARY

4th – Margaret Hunter, acclaimed to be Britain's worst learner driver, is handed a fine for failing to stop, after her instructor jumped out of the car, yelling "this is suicide". Also on this day, two more journalists are convicted of withholding information from the Vassall tribunal. There appears to be conflict between the concept of confidentiality and the duty to uphold justice.

11th – The cancellation of Princess Margaret's state visit to France is a snub for Charles de Gaulle, claims Harold Macmillan.

14th – Surgeons at Leeds General Infirmary admit that a couple of months ago, they were able to transplant a kidney from a dead person to a living one. Meanwhile, Harold Wilson defeats the mercurial George Brown in a ballot of the Labour parliamentary party by 144 votes to 103, thereby succeeding the late Hugh Gaitskell as party supremo.

20th – The government discloses its intention to develop a new nuclear weapon which will be launched from V-bombers.

21st – New five pound notes go into circulation, displaying Britannia without her helmet.

22nd – Unemployment statistics reveal the highest amount since 1947 – namely 878,356. Also on this day, British retail businessman, John Lewis, dies at the age of 77.

MARCH

3rd – Five weeks after disappearing in Beirut, where he worked as a foreign correspondent, Kim Philby (the so-called 'third man') makes contact with his wife via cable. It is increasingly likely that he has defected to the Russians.

7th – Two journalists (one from the *Daily Mail* and the other from the *Daily Sketch*) start their prison terms for declining to reveal their sources.

15th – As scandal rumours start brewing, John Profumo – the Secretary of State for War – offers his resignation, which is not accepted.

16th – William Henry Beveridge dies, aged eighty-four. Beveridge gives his name to a report published in 1942, which laid foundations for the post-war welfare state.

18th – Ted Dexter captains the England cricket team to a 3–0 whitewash of New Zealand, courtesy of a seven-wicket victory in the third test at Christchurch.

21st – London's first automatically controlled underground trains appear on the tube.

22nd – John Profumo informs the House of Commons that there was "no impropriety whatever" in his association with 21-year-old model, Christine Keeler. Keeler's 'liaison' with a Soviet diplomat has only served to increase speculation about whether or not Profumo or anyone else is compromised with their link with Miss Keeler.

25th – Captain Terence O'Neill succeeds Basil Brooke as the Unionist Prime Minister of Northern Ireland.

26th – Mounted police are required to scatter four thousand unemployed protesters, who have converged outside the Palace of Westminster.

27th – A report entitled 'The Reshaping of British Railways' is published. The 'author', Dr. Beeching, will not win any popularity contests with his recommendations that more than two thousand railway stations should close, with a loss of almost seventy thousand jobs. Beeching's 'axe' is sure to provoke a political storm.

29th – The Conservative government finally relinquishes its support for the ten-year-old Central African Federation, as Northern Rhodesia prepares to break away.

30th – Ayala claims first place in the Aintree Grand National for owner, Mr. P.Raymond, who had paid a mere forty guineas for the horse four months earlier.

APRIL

3rd – Tottenham Hotspur's Cliff Jones helps himself to a hat-trick, as Wales overcome Northern Ireland 4-1 at Windsor Park, Belfast, in a home international contest.

5th – Berkeley and Bradwell civil nuclear power stations are opened.

7th – Britain signs an agreement to purchase one hundred Polaris missiles from 'Uncle Sam'.

9th – President Kennedy confers honorary American citizenship on Sir Winston Churchill, whose own late mother, Jennie Churchill, had been an American citizen.

15th – Seventy thousand Aldermaston ban-the-bomb protesters arrive in London to demonstrate against Britain's nuclear programme.

17th – Twenty Campaign for Nuclear Disarmament activists are arrested by Special Branch. Their apparent involvement in 'Spies for Peace', which discloses secret military information has prompted a response from the law. Another rather different spy, Greville Wynne, is charged in Moscow with espionage.

24th – Mandy Rice-Davies, a model and associate of Christine Keeler, is arrested as she prepares to leave the country, as rumours of a scandal persist. Also on this day, Princess Alexandria marries Angus Ogilvy, a 34-year-old city of London banker, at Westminster Abbey, in a ceremony attended by two thousand guests.

25th – The First Lord of the Admiralty, Lord Carrington, and his deputy, Tom Galbraith, have been cleared of blame by a judicial tribunal investigating the circumstances surrounding the espionage activities of the homosexual Admiralty clerk, William Vassall.

MAY

1st – Sir Winston Churchill announces that he will stand down at the next general election, expected next year. "My accident last year has decreased my mobility", he stated. Britain's larger-than-life statesman is now a reluctant passenger in a collapsible wheelchair.

7th – Trial proceedings begin for spy duo, Greville Wynne and his associate Oleg Penkovsky, in Moscow, who are each accused of leaking sensitive Russian information.

8th – Comedian Max Miller dies at the age of 67.

11th – At the conclusion of their four-day trial, Wynne and Penkovsky receive brutal sentences. The latter is to be executed, while the former faces three years in prison and another five in a labour camp for their espionage.

15th – Rotterdam is the venue for the first triumph by a British club in a European football competition, as Tottenham Hotspur thrash Atletico Madrid 5–1 in the Cup Winners' Cup final. Meanwhile in Scotland, the FA Cup replay is settled decisively in favour of Glasgow Rangers, who run out 3–0 comfortable winners against bitter rivals Glasgow Celtic, in front of 120,000 supporters at Hampden Park.

22nd – Lord Milford, Britain's first communist peer, takes his seat in the House of Lords. Also on this day, Wembley stadium plays host to the European Cup final, during which 45,000 watch AC Milan defeat Benfica 2–1. Benfica's goalscorer, Eusebio, would endure more heartache at this venue in three year's time.

25th – Matt Busby's Manchester United atone for a mediocre league season, by overcoming Leicester City 3–1 in the FA Cup final, courtesy of a double from Scotsman, David Herd, and a goal from his fellow international, Denis Law.

27th – The Home Secretary causes controversy when he confesses that he failed to reveal the truth about the deportation of Chief Enharo. Meanwhile, Aston Villa are held at home to a goal-less draw, thereby enabling their opponents and neighbours, Birmingham City, to win the football League Cup 3–1 on aggregate.

29th – French jockey, Yves Saint-Martin, rides Relko to victory in the Epsom Derby, to the delight of its owner Monsieur M. Dupre.

30th – Anthony Wedgwood Benn's hopes of sitting in the House of Commons have been boosted by publication of the Peerage Bill, which will enable Viscount Stansgate and any other elected peers to renounce their peerages.

JUNE

4th – Denis Law records another hat-trick for Scotland, but his three goals fail to prevent Norway winning 4–3 in Bergen.

5th – Bobby Charlton emulates his Manchester United team-mate by scoring a hat-trick, as England demolish Switzerland 8–1 in Basle. Meanwhile at Westminster, a political volcano erupts, as John Profumo resigns his ministerial position, when it becomes clear that his earlier assertion of "no impropriety" is contestable. The government braces itself for further scandal.

9th – Scottish farmer, Jim Clark, drives his Lotus Climax to victory in the Belgian Grand Prix.

10th – Fifty-year-old Dr. Stephen Ward, an artist and osteopath, appears in court, charged with living off immoral earnings. Despite having friends in high places, Ward's dubious private life seems sure to land him in serious trouble, as the knives are out for any individual who has undermined the government.

17th – Harold Macmillan has to ride out a storm of criticism, during a House of Commons debate on the so-called 'Profumo affair'. Revelations of a different scandal emerge from Buckingham Palace, when it is confirmed that fourteen-year-old Prince Charles purchased a cherry brandy from a hotel bar.

18th – Wembley provides the setting for another sporting occasion, when Cassius Clay, the heavyweight champion of the world, defends his boxing crown against local challenger, Henry Cooper. Clay fulfils his boast that he would win in five rounds, but not before Cooper had floored him in the fourth round.

19th – Britain's first 'home-grown' oral contraceptive is now available on national health service prescription.

20th – Labour Party candidate, Merlyn Rees, emerges triumphant from a Leeds by-election for parliament, cashing in on growing Conservative unpopularity, as public disquiet about a scandal-stricken administration escalates.

27th – President Kennedy pays a visit to his ancestral home in the county of Wexford.

30th – A back-bench Conservative rebellion in the House of Commons has served to underline the lack of confidence within the Prime Minister's own party of his government's handling of the Profumo scandal and its implications for national security.

JULY

1st – One of the worst-kept secrets was 'revealed' today, when the government confirmed that former Foreign Office employee Kim Philby was indeed the 'third man' in the spy ring of Guy Burgess and Donald MacLean.

3rd – A court in Nice in the south of France overturns Somerset Maugham's attempted adoption of his secretary as his son. Also on this day, the government announces the introduction of continental road traffic signs.

4th – John Silkin, representing the Labour Party, is elected to parliament, after victory in a by-election in the London constituency of Deptford.

5th – American Charles 'Chuck' McKinley overcomes the challenge of Australia's Fred Stolle to win the final of the men's singles tournament at Wimbledon.

7th – Twenty-year-old Margaret Smith defeats California teenager Billie Jean Moffitt, 6–3 6–4 to become the first Australian woman to win the ladies' singles at Wimbledon.

9th – The visit of the King and Queen of Greece to London prompts violent demonstrations, during which 94 people are arrested.

14th – An announcement is made by the British Broadcasting Corporation that the television panel game, 'What's My Line?', is to be finished.

15th – Guiseppe Martelli, a nuclear physicist, is cleared by a London court of a charge that he had been spying for the Soviet Union.

16th – A new ministry, entitled the Ministry of Defence, is proposed by the Conservative government.

22nd – Trial proceedings against Stephen Ward begin. Meanwhile, the recent revelations of exploitation and intimidation of tenants by slum landlords, such as Peter Rachman, have obliged the government to create an independent commission of inquiry. Also on this day, sculptor Frank Dobson dies at the age of 74.

25th – Britain, Soviet Russia, and the United States of America reach agreement on a partial nuclear test ban treaty.

26th – A new speed limit of fifty miles per hour is introduced to the United Kingdom, but to what extent it is being observed is open to question.

29th – Having fled to the Soviet Union, British traitor, Kim Philby, is awarded Soviet citizenship, as a reward for his services to Russia.

31st – The Peerage Bill receives Royal Assent, thereby enabling Viscount Stansgate to renounce his title in favour of plain old Anthony Wedgwood Benn. Also on this day, Dr. Stephen Ward is taken to hospital, after he was discovered unconscious in a friend's flat, following an overdose of sleeping tablets. Beside him were twelve letters, giving rise to rumours of a suicide bid. In spite of this trauma, Ward is still found guilty on two charges of living on immoral earnings.

AUGUST

1st – Under the terms of the Criminal Justice Act, 1961, the minimum age for detention in prison is raised to seventeen.

3rd – Dr. Stephen Ward dies from his sleeping pills overdose.

7th – Scotland Yard intends to re-examine the case leading to Dr. Ward's conviction, after key witnesses, Vicky Barrett and Ronna Ricardo admit that their evidence and court statements were untrue.

8th – A temporary thaw in the cold war is achieved, when the Soviet Union, Britain, and the United States sign the Moscow treaty, which forbids nuclear weapon tests in the atmosphere, outer space, and under the sea. Britain's Foreign Secretary, Lord Home, claims the treaty is a "great occasion for us all". Meanwhile, in the United Kingdom, a gang of at least fifteen armed men ambush the Glasgow to London mail train at Cheddington, Buckinghamshire, and seize 120 mailbags, containing approximately two and a half million pounds. Also on this day, a government doctor claims that sex change operations will never be possible.

9th – The Post Office reveals that £2.6 million was stolen in the 'great train robbery'. Also on this day, ITV broadcasts the first showing of a new popular music programme, entitled 'Ready Steady Go!'.

13th – The hide-out of the 'great train robbers', Leatherdale Farm, is uncovered by the police.

15th – Three Bristol soccer players are banned for life by the Football Association, after they confess to accepting bribes in order to lose football matches.

20th – The television news in Wales is read out by a female broadcaster for the first time.

22nd – Charlie Wilson is charged for his role in the 'great train robbery'. Also on this day, the first Viscount Nuffield (born William Richard Morris) dies at the age of eighty-five. Nuffield, the British motor-car manufacturer and philanthropist, provided large sums for the advancement of medicine in the University of Oxford, for Nuffield College, and in 1943 established the Nuffield Foundation, endowing it with ten million pounds.

26th – England cricket team succumb to an eight wickets test defeat at The Oval to the West Indies, thus losing the test series to the tourists by three tests to one.

SEPTEMBER

1st – Notorious British spy, Guy Burgess, is reported in Moscow as having died several days ago in obscurity.

5th – The infamous model, Christine Keeler, is seized by police and charged with perjury.

7th – Sussex defeat Worcestershire in English cricket's first one-day final, to lift the inaugural Gillette Cup.

9th – Scotland's Jim Clark wins the Formula One drivers' world championship on the back of seven Grand Prix victories, not to mention a second in the Indianapolis 500.

10th – American Express, the banking giant, launches its British credit card, five years after introducing one specifically for the United States of America.

12th – An aeroplane crashes in the French Pyrenees, causing the deaths of 36 British tourists.

16th – The new state of Malaysia (an amalgam of Malaya, North Borneo, Sarawak, and Singapore) is formed, which provokes an angry crowd of ten thousand demonstrators to burn Britain's embassy down in protest.

17th – An early warning ballistic missile station comes into operation at Flyingdales.

19th – New Zealand-born British caricaturist and political cartoonist, Sir David Alexander Cecil Low, dies, aged seventy-two. Low worked for *The Daily News, Evening Standard, Daily Herald,* and the *Manchester Guardian.* He was a master of caricature, as evidenced with his well-remembered Colonel Blimp.

20th – Princess Anne starts her first day at her new school – Benenden, in Kent.

26th – Many people scurry after the first copies of Lord Denning's report, which goes on sale in London. This inquiry into the Profumo scandal criticises the Macmillan government's hesitant response to the early revelations.

OCTOBER

1st – Harold Wilson, in his inaugural address as party leader to the Labour Conference at Scarborough, on the Yorkshire coast, predicts a new wave of "white heat" technology, stating that "we are redefining our socialism in terms of the scientific revolution."

6th – Neo-fascist Colin Jordan's wedding celebrations are gate-crashed by one thousand protesters who hurl apples and eggs at him.

10th – Ill health has prompted Harold Macmillan to announce an end to his premiership, after six and a half eventful years in office.

18th – Against all expectations, the Foreign Secretary, the fourteenth Earl Of Home, is appointed as the new Conservative Party leader and Prime Minister. Home 'emerges' as the supremo, after more obvious choices, such as Rab Butler, Lord Hailsham, and Reginald Maudling are black-balled by the Tory 'magic circle'.

20th – Lord Home selects his first cabinet team, but not before Iain Macleod and Enoch Powell resign their posts, claiming that they have no confidence in him.

22nd – The Old Vic theatre in London provides the venue for the National Theatre Company's first performance, with Peter O'Toole playing the role of Shakespeare's Hamlet, directed by Laurence Olivier.

23rd – The new Prime Minister renounces his six titles and re-invents himself as Sir Alec Douglas-Home. Also on this day, the Robbins report on higher education is published, which calls for six new universities, as well as university status to be accorded to ten colleges of advanced technology.

NOVEMBER

4th – The Royal Variety performance at the Prince of Wales Theatre includes the new pop music sensations, The Beatles. They perform four songs (including their number one singles 'From Me To You' and 'She Loves You'), but the whole event is remembered for John Lennon's cheeky suggestion that while those in the cheaper seats should clap their hands, the rest should rattle their jewellery!

7th – Gaining revenge for a narrow defeat five months earlier, Scotland's football team demolish Norway to the tune of six goals to one, with ace marksman Denis Law helping himself to his second successive hat-trick against the Scandinavians.

8th – The new Prime Minister finds himself a seat in the House of Commons, after successfully contesting the Kinross by-election in west Perthshire, Scotland.

13th – The British Broadcasting Corporation's board of governors decides to pull the plug on the satirical, anti-establishment 'That Was The Week That Was'.

18th – The Dartford-Purfleet tunnel is opened, linking the counties of Essex and Kent, under the river Thames.

20th – Wembley stadium's first floodlight fixture is marked by England putting Northern Ireland to the sword by a staggering 8-3. Chief executioners are Tottenham Hotspur's Jimmy Greaves who scores four goals, while Southampton's Terry Paine weighs in with a mere three goals. Northern Ireland's 'busy' goal-keeper, Harry Gregg (a survivor of the Munich disaster of 1958), is never selected again for his country, nor is Billy Bingham allowed to add to this, his fifty-sixth cap. Also on this day, Viscount Hailsham re-invents himself as Quinton Hogg, having followed his party leader and renounced his peerage.

22nd – On a day when the United States of America loses its President, novelist Aldous Leonard Huxley dies at the age of 69. His work included 'Brave New World' (1932), 'Eyeless In Gaza' (1936), and 'The Doors of Perception' (1954).

25th – The Duke of Edinburgh represents his wife at the funeral ceremony of John F.Kennedy, the assassinated American President.

DECEMBER

3rd – The Valiant, Britain's second nuclear submarine, is launched.

5th – Following in the footsteps of Sir Alec Douglas-Home, Quinton Hogg finds himself a seat in the House of Commons, via a by-election triumph.

6th – 21-year-old Christine Keeler is sentenced to nine months' imprisonment at the Old Bailey, having pleaded guilty to perjury and conspiracy to pervert the course of justice, following her deceit during the trial of an ex-boyfriend, Aloysius 'Lucky' Gordon, who was convicted of assaulting her.

10th – A grenade is thrown into a group of local government ministers and British diplomats at Aden airport, killing an Indian woman and injuring, amongst others, the British High Commissioner, Sir Kennedy Trevaskis. On the same day, Britons Alan Hodgkin and Andrew Huxley are recipients of Nobel prizes for physiology and medicine. Meanwhile, Zanzibar becomes independent within the British Commonwealth.

12th – Kenya becomes the 34th African territory to become independent, after Prince Philip hands Kenya's instruments of independence to Jomo Kenyatta.

27th – 'That Was The Week That Was' or 'TW3' is broadcast for the last time, to the immense relief of BBC officials, nervous at the show's willingness to pour scorn on anyone in authority.

THE NUMBER-ONE HIT SINGLES OF 1963

The Next Time by *Cliff Richard and The Shadows*
Dance On by *The Shadows*
Diamonds by *Jet Harris and Tony Meehan*
Wayward Wind by *Frank Ifield*
Summer Holiday by *Cliff Richard and The Shadows*
Foot Tapper by *The Shadows*
How Do You Do It? by *Gerry and The Pacemakers*
From Me To You by *The Beatles*
I Like It by *Gerry and The Pacemakers*
Confessin' by *Frank Ifield*
(You're The) Devil In Disguise by *Elvis Presley*
Sweets For My Sweet by *The Searchers*
Bad To Me by *Billy J Kramer and The Dakotas*
She Loves You by *The Beatles*
Do You Love Me? by *Brian Poole and The Tremeloes*
You'll Never Walk Alone by *Gerry and The Pacemakers*
I Want To Hold Your Hand by *The Beatles*

1964

JANUARY

1st – The BBC broadcasts the first-ever edition of a new popular music programme, called 'Top Of The Pops'. Performers on the first show include The Rolling Stones, Dusty Springfield, and the Dave Clark Five.

5th – The London Underground has the first ticket collecting machine installed.

13th – The British fashion designer, Mary Quant, today criticised Paris fashion, describing it as "out of date". Quant's fashion vision is directed at young people who "are tired of wearing essentially the same as their mothers".

17th – Statistics revealed by the Television Audience Measurement organisation indicate that the comedy, 'Steptoe and Son', is Britain's most popular television programme, with no fewer than approximately 25 million viewers.

20th – The trial proceedings of the so-called 'great train robbers' begin.

21st – Figures published by the government reveal that the average weekly wage in Britain currently stands at £16.14s.11d.

23rd – Cecil King states his intention to re-launch the *Daily Herald* as 'The Sun' newspaper. Meanwhile, British forces fly into Uganda to quell an army uprising by troops unhappy at their inadequate pay.

26th – It is announced that the school-leaving age is to be raised to sixteen in the academic year 1970 to 1971.

28th – Talks in London about the future of Cyprus are disrupted when Turkish delegates walk out in protest.

FEBRUARY

6th – It is revealed that Britain and France have reached agreement on a rail Channel Tunnel, at a projected cost of £160 million.

8th – Having vowed not to tour the United States until they reach number one in the American charts, the Beatles fly into Kennedy Airport, New York to a tumultuous reception. With 'I Want To Hold Your Hand' sitting on top of the singles charts, the Beatles keep their promise.

9th – Fast becoming one of Britain's leading exports, the 'Fab Four' perform on the hugely popular Ed Sullivan Show, watched by seventy-three million viewers.

10th – The eighteenth-century novel, 'Fanny Hill' (by John Cleland) is pronounced obscene by a magistrate in London, who subsequently orders all copies of this book to be seized and confiscated.

19th – One thousand, five hundred British soldiers are flown to the Mediterranean island of Cyprus on peace-keeping duties. Meanwhile, actress Britt Ekland becomes comedian Peter Sellers' second wife.

21st – For the first time since the Second World War, ten pounds bank-notes are put into circulation in the United Kingdom.

23rd – The Beatles arrive back in Britain to a hero's reception by the fans.

26th – The government declares its intention to create a fleet of five Polaris submarines.

27th – The Bank of England's lending rate is increased to five per cent.

29th – Princess Alexandra gives birth to a boy, named James Robert Bruce.

MARCH

3rd – Following soon after the 'Beeching Axe', a mass closure of railway lines is proposed by the government.

9th – British soldiers serving in Cyprus become involved in the hostilities between the Greek and Turkish communities.

10th – The Queen gives birth to a fourth child – a boy, who is named as Edward Antony Richard Lewis.

11th – The British embassy in Cambodia is destroyed during demonstrations against the United States and Britain.

15th – Richard Burton and Elizabeth Taylor marry in Montreal, Canada.

16th – British forces come under fire in the Cypriot town of Ktima, even though they had seemingly arranged a ceasefire.

19th – A new government white paper is published, which seeks to address the issue of London being suffocated by too many people. Amongst other things, it is recommended that six suburban dormitory towns be expanded.

20th – Irish writer, Brendan Behan, dies at the age of forty-one. A former member of the Irish Republican Army, his works included 'The Quare Fellow', 'The Hostage', and the autobiographical 'Borstal Boy'.

21st – After four failed attempts, Team Spirit (owned by Mr J Goodman) wins the Aintree Grand National steeplechase.

27th – At the end of a fifty-one day trial at the Buckinghamshire Assizes, ten participants in the 'great train robbery' are found guilty. Nine further suspects await trial.

28th – The pirate radio station, Radio Caroline, starts broadcasting from a vessel in the North Sea.

30th – Clacton beach provides the reluctant venue for clashes between gangs of Mods and Rockers.

31st – The former cabinet office of the Admiralty is abolished, as the new Ministry of Defence assumes its duties.

APRIL

8th – Further disturbances between Mods and Rockers result in thirty arrests in London.

9th –Labour scores a morale-boosting victory in the inaugural Greater London Council, winning 64 seats against the Conservatives' return of 36 seats.

10th – Former Prime Minister, Harold Macmillan, declines the offer of an earldom and membership of the Order of the Garter.

14th – Consumers of alcohol and tobacco are less than amused by the budget, which raises the price of a pint of beer to 2/1, while a packet of cigarettes now increases to 4/10.

15th – Ronald Biggs and eleven accomplices are found guilty for their participation in the so-called 'great train robbery'. Also on this day, Leicester City hold Stoke City to a 1–1 draw, in the first leg of the football League Cup final.

16th – Twelve suspects in the great train robbery are sentenced to a collective total of 307 years' imprisonment.

20th – Queen Elizabeth's third son is registered as Edward.

21st – BBC2 takes to the air for the first time. The first broadcast is 'PlaySchool'.

22nd – A 3–2 victory renders Leicester City the third Midlands football team to win the League Cup in only its fourth year. England international goal-keeper, Gordon Banks, collects a winner's medal against a club that he would later play for. Also on this day, British spy, Greville Wynne, is exchanged at a Berlin border checkpoint for Russian spy, Gordon Lonsdale.

29th – Schools in Aberdeen are temporarily shut, as 136 cases of typhoid are reported in the 'granite city'.

MAY

1st – Princess Margaret gives birth to a daughter: Lady Sarah Frances Elizabeth.

2nd – Viscountess Astor (born Nancy Witcher Langhorne) dies at the age of eighty-four. An American by birth, she was the first woman to sit in the House of Commons. Meanwhile at Wembley stadium, West Ham United win the FA Cup for the first time, courtesy of a 3–2 victory against Preston North End. Among the scorers is Geoff Hurst, who would develop a talent for scoring in Wembley cup finals!

3rd – After reports of the beheading of two British soldiers by Yemeni rebels, more British reinforcements are flown into trouble-torn Aden.

7th – The omens for the Conservative government are not good, after the Labour Party makes substantial gains in the local government elections.

10th – British soldiers in the United Nations' peace-keeping force are flown home from Cyprus.

12th – Another pirate radio station begins broadcasting beyond the east coast of England. It is called Radio Atlanta, transmitting on 200.6 medium wave.

18th – British tea and rubber estates are seized by the government of Indonesia. Also on this day, gangs of Rockers and Mods create further mischief at several seaside resorts. There are seventy-six arrests in

Brighton, and fifty-one youths are arrested in Margate. The orgy of violence also afflicts Bournemouth, Clacton, and Southend, not to mention the coast of county Durham.

21st – The Beatles are Britain's most popular tourist attraction, according to the findings of a British Broadcasting Corporation survey.

22nd – A state of emergency is declared in British Guiana, as British soldiers fly out to restore law and order there.

27th – Bad memories of England's humiliating defeat at the hands of the USA soccer team in the 1950 World Cup finals are exorcised when New York witnesses a 10–0 massacre of 'Uncle Sam'. England's Hunt and Pickering each record hat-tricks, ten days after Byrne had scored a hat-trick in a victory in Lisbon over Portugal.

JUNE

3rd – Santa Claus triumphs in the Epsom Derby, providing jockey, Scobie Breasley, with his first success, at the thirteenth time of trying.

4th – Britain's Blue Streak rocket makes its first flight into space, having been launched from the Woomera Range in Australia.

8th – The notorious Christine Keeler ends her stint in prison, after six months of incarceration.

9th – British newspaper owner (and politician) the first Baron Beaverbrook dies, aged eighty-five, from cancer. Born a Canadian, under the name of William Maxwell Aitken, he gave energetic service as the Minister of Aircraft Production during the Second World War. He also controlled the *Daily Express, Sunday Express,* and *Evening Standard.*

12th – Fresh from filming 'A Hard Day's Night', the Beatles arrive in Adelaide, South Australia, to be greeted by an estimated three hundred thousand fans.

22nd – Yachtsman Francis Chichester sets a new transatlantic record by crossing 'the big pond' in less than thirty days.

JULY

2nd – Radio Atlanta and Radio Caroline merge into one national pirate radio station. Also on this day, the Ulster Folk Museum opens its doors for the first time at Cultra, in county Down, Northern Ireland.

3rd – Australia's Roy Emerson overcomes the challenge of Fred Stolle to win the Men's Singles at Wimbledon, while the Women's Singles is won for a third time by Brazil's Maria Bueno, who defeats the reigning champion, Margaret Smith of Australia.

6th – The King's African Rifles perform 'A Scottish Soldier' as Nyasaland becomes the new independent state of Malawi. The country's first Prime Minister states: "I want nothing but friendship between Britons and Malawians." Meanwhile, the London Pavilion cinema is the venue for the premiere of 'A Hard Day's Night' by the 'moptops', attended by Princess Margaret, amongst others.

10th – On the day that the album and single, 'A Hard Day's Night', are released in the United Kingdom, an estimated 150,000 Liverpudlians welcome the Beatles back to their home city. Three hundred are injured in this latest bout of 'Beatlemania'.

13th – The Appeal Court in London overturns 25-year prison sentences imposed on two of the great train robbers.

17th – Donald Campbell breaks the land-speed record on Lake Eyre, whilst 'travelling' at a mere 403.1 miles per hour.

21st – Tottenham Hotspur's highly-rated inside-right, John White, is killed by a flash of lightning, after sheltering under a tree on a golf course in Enfield, in north London. White won twenty-two caps for Scotland, scoring three goals, including one on his debut, in a 3–2 win over West Germany.

27th – Sir Winston Churchill makes his last appearance in the House of Commons, bringing to a close a hugely eventful parliamentary career, dating back to 1900.

28th – Party political differences were elbowed aside, as the House of Commons passed a motion, recording the admiration and gratitude of parliament to Sir Winston Churchill, for his courageous services to Britain and the world.

29th – The first Brook Advisory Clinic opens its doors to provide family planning advice to unmarried couples.

AUGUST

2nd - More fighting between Mods and Rockers prompts police reinforcements to be flown to Hastings, on the Sussex coast.

12th – Charlie Wilson, one of the convicted great train robbers, succeeds in escaping from prison. Also on this day, Ian Fleming (creator of James Bond), dies of a heart attack, at the age of fifty-six. Before penning his 007 stories, Fleming, an old Etonian, had been a journalist and a banker.

20th – A new lighter, portable television set is previewed in London. This new, smaller television is envisaged as a second set for families who are obliged to watch only one station, when they might want to see something else.

21st – The 'permissive society' had not yet arrived, when three women are found guilty of indecency, on account of wearing 'topless' dresses.

30th – The British island of Diego Garcia, in the Indian Ocean, is reportedly on a United States' shopping list for a military base.

SEPTEMBER

3rd – Reginald Maudling, Britain's Chancellor of the Exchequer, attends a two-hour meeting in Kuala Lumpur, after which it is decided that Britain, Australia, and New Zealand will support Malaysian troops against Indonesian aggression.

4th – The Forth Road Bridge is opened in Scotland on the 'fourth', thereby becoming the largest suspension bridge in Europe.

6th – New Rhodesian Prime Minister, Ian Smith, arrives in London, for discussions on a possible independence for Southern Rhodesia.

15th – Sir Alec Douglas-Home announces his government's intention to go to the polls and seek re-election in a national contest, scheduled for mid-October. Meanwhile, the Daily Herald ceases to function, to be replaced by The Sun newspaper.

18th – Irish playwright, Sean O'Casey, dies at the age of eighty-four. His works included 'The Shadow of a Gunman' (1923), 'Juno and the Paycock' (1924), and 'The Plough and the Stars' (1926).

21st – The Mediterranean island of Malta becomes independent within the British Commonwealth, after 164 years of British rule.

27th – Britain's supersonic tactical strike aeroplane, the TSR-2, makes its maiden flight.

28th – Survey results reveal that Radio Caroline is more popular than BBC Radio.

OCTOBER

3rd – Tottenham Hotspur's Jimmy Greaves registers his second successive hat-trick against Northern Ireland, as England win narrowly at Windsor Park, 4–3.

14th – Mary Rand, who failed to match expectations at the Rome Olympics, collects the first Olympic gold medal ever achieved by a British female athlete, with a world record in the long jump. Her achievement is later matched by Ann Packer, who wins the 800 metres, while Welshman Lyn Davies secures the long jump double gold for Britain, at the Tokyo Olympics.

15th – The Conservative Party braces itself for a predicted defeat, as Britain's electorate go to their respective polling stations to cast their votes.

16th – Harold Wilson is invited to form a new Labour government, following his party's narrowest of general election victories. A wafer-thin majority of four seats has enabled Labour to end thirteen years of Conservative government. Whilst the two major parties won 620 seats between them, the once-mighty Liberal Party could only return nine members to parliament.

17th – New Prime Minister, Harold Wilson, announces the personnel who will form the Labour cabinet. Prominent ministers include James Callaghan, Barbara Castle, Richard Crossman, Denis Healey, and Roy Jenkins, as well as George Brown.

26th – The new premier warns of a potential economic crisis, and therefore the new government proposes a fifteen per cent import surcharge and an export tax rebate to cope with a balance of payment crisis.

27th – Harold Wilson warns white Southern Rhodesia that the threat of a unilateral declaration of independence amounts to an act of treason. Unimpressed, Ian Smith retorts that Wilson's remarks are "blackmail and intimidation".

28th – Rioting takes place in nationalist areas of Belfast, after an Irish republic tricolour flag is taken down by the Royal Ulster Constabulary.

29th – Professor Dorothy Crowfoot Hodgkin of Oxford University is nominated for the 1964 Nobel Prize for Chemistry, previously won in 1911 by no less than Marie Curie.

31st – The end of an era occurs at the naughty Windmill Theatre, which gives its farewell performance of the 'Windmill Girls', after a stint of thirty-two years.

NOVEMBER

9th – Film star, Judy Garland, gives a concert in London jointly with her daughter, Liza Minnelli.

11th – The Labour government increases income tax by six per cent, in order to finance larger old age pensions.

17th – The government bans the export of arms to the apartheid regime of South Africa.

23rd – The Bank of England's lending rate increases to seven per cent.

25th – The recent slide in the value of sterling has prompted the new government to accept a humiliating loan of £1,080 million, funded by eleven different nations.

30th – Sir Winston Churchill 'celebrates' his ninetieth (and last) birthday.

DECEMBER

1st – Professor John Burdon Sanderson Haldane dies at the age of seventy-two. A biologist and geneticist, Haldane was renowned not just for his work in mathematical evolutionary theory, but also for explaining science to the layman.

6th – St. Paul's Cathedral in London provides the setting for a sermon from guest preacher, the Nobel Prize-winner, Martin Luther King.

8th – British businessman, Lord Marks, dies at the age of seventy-six.

9th – Dame Edith Sitwell dies, aged 77. This poet was regarded as a great experimenter in verse forms, and her best-known poems were probably 'Façade' (set to music by William Walton), 'Gold Coast Customs', and 'Still Falls The Rain'.

10th – Dorothy Hodgkin of the United Kingdom is among the recipients of a Nobel Prize, at the annual ceremony in Stockholm, Sweden.

18th – British academic, David Kitson, is imprisoned by the apartheid regime of South Africa, for alleged "revolutionary conspiracy".

20th – Rebels in the Congo massacre fifteen missionaries from the United Kingdom.

21st – The likelihood of any convicted murderer facing the death penalty in the future is all but wiped out, after the House of Commons emphatically voted in favour of the abolition of capital punishment, by 355 votes to 170. It is anticipated that the House of Lords will reluctantly accept the decision of the Commons.

23rd – Lord Beeching, the notorious head of British Railways, is himself 'axed' by the new government.

29th – The infamous Kray brothers are reportedly linked to a shooting incident, in the east end of London.

31st – Donald Campbell breaks the world water-speed record, with a speed of 276.33 miles per hour, recorded on Lake Dumbleyung.

THE NUMBER-ONE HIT SINGLES OF 1964

Glad All Over by *The Dave Clark Five*
Needles And Pins by *The Searchers*
Diane by *The Bachelors*
Anyone Who Had A Heart by *Cilla Black*
Little Children by *Billy J Kramer and the Dakotas*
Can't Buy Me Love by *The Beatles*
World Without Love by *Peter and Gordon*
Don't Throw Your Love Away by *The Searchers*
Juliet by *The Four Pennies*
You're My World by *Cilla Black*
It's Over by *Roy Orbison*
House Of The Rising Sun by *The Animals*
It's All Over Now by *The Rolling Stones*
A Hard Day's Night by *The Beatles*
Do Wah Diddy Diddy by *Manfred Mann*
Have I The Right? by *The Honeycombs*
You Really Got Me by *The Kinks*
I'm Into Something Good by *Herman's Hermits*
Oh Pretty Woman by *Roy Orbison*
Always Something There To Remind Me by *Sandie Shaw*
Baby Love by *The Supremes*
Little Red Rooster by *The Rolling Stones*
I Feel Fine by *The Beatles*

1965

JANUARY

1st – The New Year's Honours List includes England international footballer Stanley Matthews, who becomes the first professional soccer player to ever be knighted.

7th – The Kray twins (Reggie and Ronnie) are remanded in custody, accused of demanding money with menaces. On the same day, it is reported that a two-week package holiday to Spain's Costa del Sol costs a mere £66. 16*s*. –*d*., while one to Greece could cost as little as £93. 17*s*. –*d*.

8th – Pop singer Adam Faith cancels proposed concerts in South Africa, after he is denied permission to perform in front of multi-racial audiences.

15th – Ninety-year-old Sir Winston Churchill is seriously ill, following another stroke. Meanwhile in Belfast, the Taoiseach, Sean Lemass, arrives to meet his northern counterpart, Terence O'Neill, in an attempt to de-frost the 'cold war' between north and south. It is after all, the first time on Irish soil that the Prime Ministers of north and south have met since partition. Also on this day, it is revealed that the child's body found five weeks ago in a coffin in Stepney, east London, is none other than a certain Lady Anne Mowbray, who lived briefly from 1472 to 1481. Her remains are subsequently re-interred in Westminster Abbey.

19th – Harold Wilson informs France that Britain intends to persevere with the Concorde project, in spite of escalating costs.

21st – Recently appointed as Foreign Secretary, Labour's Patrick Gordon Walker is defeated in a by-election at Leyton, in east London. Having already failed to win a parliamentary seat at the recent general election, his position as a cabinet minister looks increasingly untenable.

22nd – As a consequence of his recent by-election humiliation, Patrick Gordon Walker resigns, and passes the Foreign Secretary baton on to Michael Stewart.

24th – Sir Winston Leonard Spencer Churchill dies, after an extraordinary 'innings' of ninety years. Churchill firmly believed he would follow his famous father Randolph to an early grave, but after death-defying escapades in his early years, Churchill developed into a high-profile politician, who served both Liberal and Conservative cabinets in a variety of positions. His own 'immortality' was guaranteed, after he was thrust into the role of Prime Minister, when he dared to defy the seemingly unstoppable German war machine. The rest is history!

25th – Various Members of Parliament pay their respective tributes to the departed Churchill in the House of Commons.

27th – Thousands of people file past Sir Winston Churchill, as his lying-in-state begins at Westminster Hall, in the heart of the Houses of Parliament.

30th – Churchill is buried in a village ceremony near his family's home, at Blenheim Palace. The humble graveside ceremony is in marked contrast to his state funeral service at St. Paul's Cathedral, which is watched on television by an estimated 350 million Europeans.

FEBRUARY

1st – A reported two hundred thousand people greet the arrival of the Queen in Addis Ababa, Ethiopia.

3rd – General Franco's Spanish forces are reportedly squeezing the British colony of Gibraltar, with a creeping blockade, in an attempt to pressurise Britain in to surrendering sovereignty of the island to Spain.

4th – The Conservative candidate, Anthony Barber, wins the by-election in Altrincham, Cheshire.

8th – New health minister, Kenneth Robinson, announces that the advertising of cigarettes is to be banned on television, which is regarded as an effective outlet for targeting young people.

9th – Northern Ireland's Prime Minister, Terence O'Neill, becomes the first premier from 'the north' to visit Dublin since 1921, as Sean Lemass returns the compliment, after his recent visit to 'the six counties'.

11th – The wedding takes place of Liverpudlian hairdresser, Maureen Cox, and a Mr. Richard Starkey, also of Liverpool. The wedding might be expected to be a low profile one, but for the fact that the groom is Beatles' drummer Ringo Starr.

16th – British Rail announces its intentions to cut the rail network by fifty per cent, as proposed in the controversial Beeching report.

17th - The British colony of Gambia becomes Africa's smallest independent state and the 21st member of the British Commonwealth.

22nd – For the first time, the TSR-2 flies faster than the speed of sound.

23rd – A price war in the spirits trade is anticipated, as Distillers sell scotch whisky at a mere 7/- a bottle. Meanwhile, the government pledges support to the United Nations' initiative to create a permanent peace-keeping force of up to six battalions. Also on this day, the British half of Laurel and Hardy dies at the age of 74. Stan Laurel, born Arthur Stanley Jefferson, was raised in Lancashire, before migrating across the Atlantic Ocean, where he found fame in the durable partnership of Laurel and Hardy. The accident-prone duo suffered mishaps in more than two hundred films.

25th – Rumblings of discontent about the 'magic circle' process which enabled Harold Macmillan and then Alec Douglas-Home to emerge unexpectedly as Conservative Prime Ministers has obliged the party to declare that future leaders of the Tories will be elected by Conservative Members of Parliament. Also on this day, Dr.Heenan, the Archbishop of Westminster, is created a cardinal.

26th – The whisky price war spreads to the wine trade, where a bottle of wine now retails for as little as 5/6d. per bottle.

MARCH

2nd – It is reported that Patrick McGoohan (who stars as The Prisoner) and Roger Moore (a.k.a. The Saint) are Britain's top earning actors, collecting a cool £2,000 per week in wages.

4th – David Attenborough is appointed as head of the infant BBC Two.

6th – Baron Morrison of Lambeth dies, aged 77. Born Herbert Stanley Morrison, he became a key figure in the Labour Party, serving as war-time Home Secretary, before becoming Deputy Prime Minister from 1945 to 1951.

7th – Regent's Park's latest attraction, Goldie (the Golden Eagle), enjoys his tenth day of freedom, having escaped from London Zoo. Thousands of people give up their Sunday to pay a visit to the bird of prey that is 'on the run'.

9th – Court proceedings start in the trial of Reggie and Ronnie Kray.

10th – Another jailbird, Goldie, is re-interned at London Zoo, after his re-capture.

14th – A grenade attack on an army post in Aden causes the death of a British soldier.

24th – 26-year-old Liberal Party candidate, David Steel, wins the by-election of Roxburgh, Selkirk and Peebles in the Scottish borders, thereby becoming the youngest member of parliament.

27th – Jay Trump, owned by Mrs M Stephenson, wins the Aintree Grand National race.

28th – Mary, the Princess Royal (alternatively titled the Countess of Harewood) dies, after collapsing while walking in the grounds of her home. The 67-year-old was the only daughter of King George V and Queen Mary.

APRIL

2nd – Harold Wilson has talks in Paris with President de Gaulle, concerning the escalating conflict in Vietnam, in former French Indo-china.

5th – Charismatic young Scottish manager, Tommy Docherty, watches his Chelsea team secure a 0–0 draw at Filbert Street, which ensures that the west Londoners would win the football League Cup, 3–2 on aggregate, against the holders, Leicester City. The two goal-keepers who achieved clean sheets were none other than Gordon Banks and his future England understudy, Peter Bonetti.

6th – Reggie and Ronnie Kray are acquitted at the Old Bailey of orchestrating a protection racket. Also on this day, the first Labour budget for fourteen years imposes 1d. on a pint of beer and 4/– on a bottle of whisky. Meanwhile, in Hollywood there are notable successes for Britain, with Julie Andrews winning an Oscar, while the film 'My Fair Lady' proves equally successful.

7th – The Home Secretary declares that incitement to racial hatred will become illegal.

9th – Eric Lubbock, made famous by his by-election triumph in Orpington, sets his political career to the side as he returns to the more civilised pursuit of boxing, after an absence of thirteen years. The verbal sparring of the House of Commons proves no preparation, and the Liberal is floored in only two minutes.

18th – Fifty-six arrests take place in Brighton on Easter Sunday, as Britain's seaside resorts brace themselves for further confrontations between Mods and Rockers on the Monday bank holiday.

19th – Fresh from his not guilty verdict, alleged gangster (and homosexual) Reggie Kray gets married. Wedding telegrams are received from such well-wishers as Judy Garland and fellow-actress, Barbara Windsor.

21st – British physicist, Sir Edward Victor Appleton, dies at the age of seventy-two. Appleton was awarded the 1947 Nobel Prize in physics, for the discovery of the Appleton layer of ionosphere, which reflects radio waves.

23rd – The 250-mile Pennine Way is opened. It is hailed as Britain's first long-distance footpath, extending from Edale in Derbyshire to Kirk Yetholm in Roxburghshire, in the Scottish borders.

28th – Harold Wilson becomes the first Labour premier to visit the Pope , in Rome.

MAY

1st – The FA Cup final bursts into life after extra-time is required to break the deadlock. First, England international, Roger Hunt, opens the scoring for Liverpool, but then Billy Bremner equalises for Leeds United, only for his fellow-Scotsman Ian St. John to grab a late winner, which provides Bill Shankly's club with their first-ever FA Cup success.

2nd – Scotland Yard swallows its pride and acknowledges that it needs help from anyone in the world who can provide information on the whereabouts of three elusive train robbers.

6th – The Labour government secures a narrow majority of four votes, after a debate in the House of Commons on the sensitive issue of steel nationalisation.

14th – The late John F Kennedy's widow Jackie and their children, Caroline and John, visit Runnymede, the site of the Magna Carta signature, to witness the Queen dedicate an acre of wood and grassland to the assassinated President.

17th – 31 coal-miners are killed in a Welsh colliery disaster.

19th – West Ham United follow in the footsteps of Tottenham Hotspur, by securing victory in a European Cup Winners' Cup final, when they overcome 1860 Munich by two goals to nil. Three of the cup winners (Geoff Hurst, Bobby Moore, and Martin Peters) would return to the same venue of Wembley to record an even more historic triumph over German opposition a year later!

21st – Sir Geoffrey De Havilland dies, aged eighty-two. This British aircraft designer built his first aeroplane in 1908, later becoming director of the company that bears his name, and which produced the likes of the Mosquito and the Tiger Moth.

24th – The Labour administration announce that Britain will be switching to the metric system.

27th – The Queen, accompanied by her husband, paying their first visit by a British monarch to Germany since the First World War, is driven through West Berlin to witness the controversial Berlin Wall. West Berlin's mayor, Willy Brandt, and West German chancellor, Ludwig Erhard, act as hosts.

31st – Britain's racing driver, Jim Clark, scores a notable first, as he becomes the first non-American to secure victory in the Indianapolis 500.

JUNE

2nd – It takes a casting vote from the Speaker of the House of Commons to enable a bill to be passed, which imposes a Corporation Tax on company profits.

6th – An estimated fifty island crofters protest at the first Sunday ferry crossing from the Scottish mainland to the Isle of Skye. The demonstrators regard the Sunday boat service as a "desecration of the biblical Sabbath".

7th – Major Squires, a British army officer who vanished from Berlin in 1947, is now reportedly working for the Soviet Union.

10th – A service at St. Paul's Cathedral commemorates the 750th anniversary of the signing of the Magna Carta by King John in 1215.

11th – 'Dixon of Dock Green' actor Jack Warner is among the recipients of an OBE in the Queen's Birthday Honours. His thunder is somewhat stolen by the award of MBEs to the chart-topping Beatles.

14th – Two OBEs return their honours to the Queen in disgust at the honours to be bestowed by Her Majesty on the Beatles.

15th – A total of nine people have sent their honours back to Buckingham Palace, as outrage prevails against the awards to the Beatles, described by one OBE holder as "vulgar nincompoops".

18th – The government pledges its determination to curb drink-driving, by proposing the introduction of a legal alcohol blood limit for motorists.

20th – Harold Wilson's Commonwealth peace mission to Vietnam is scorned at by the Chinese authorities in Peking.

23rd – The Soviet Union joins China and North Vietnam in condemning Wilson's peace mission, which had originally received approval from the Commonwealth leaders.

25th – The Commonwealth Conference in London comes to a conclusion, with evident disharmony over the twin problems of Rhodesia and the Vietnam conflict.

27th – Fresh from his triumph at the Indianapolis 500, Jim Clark is greeted by the chequered flag, as he races to success in the French Grand Prix.

JULY

3rd – In the Wimbledon All-England tennis tournament, Margaret Smith obtains revenge by defeating Maria Bueno, the defending champion, to secure her second ladies' singles title. Her fellow-Australian, Roy Emerson, overcomes Fred Stolle to achieve victory in the men's singles final.

14th – Adlai Stevenson, a twice defeated American presidential election candidate, collapses in a London street, and dies from a heart attack, aged 65.

20th – Against expectations, the House of Lords approves of the desire of the House of Commons to abolish the death penalty, by a comfortable 100 majority.

22nd – London's population are alarmed to hear that 1964 was the worst year in the twentieth century for incidences of criminal activity in the city. Also on this day, Sir Alec Douglas-Home announces an end to his brief tenure as leader of the Conservative Party. A leadership contest is expected soon.

23rd – 28-year-old university lecturer, Gerald Brooke, is sentenced by a Moscow court to a five-year prison term, as a consequence of smuggling pamphlets into the Soviet Union, during a holiday there. Brooke pleaded guilty to anti-Russian activities.

24th – Freddie Mills, a former light-heavyweight boxing world champion, is found dead in a car in central London's Soho district, having apparently been shot. He was forty-three years old.

26th – The expected onset of international direct dialling has prompted the GPO to state that it is switching to numbers-only telephones.

27th – Edward Heath, at the age of forty-nine, is elected the new Conservative Party leader, having surprisingly defeated the apparent favourite, Reginald Maudling, by 150 votes to 133. A third candidate, Enoch Powell, could only attract fifteen votes. Heath is entrusted with the task of undermining a government, whose room for manoeuvre is restricted by a wafer-thin majority.

29th – The Beatles' second film 'Help!' has its royal world charity premiere at the London Pavilion.

30th – Published broadcasting statistics reveal that ITV's Coronation Street is the most watched weekly television show.

AUGUST

1st – Jim Clark clinches the Formula One world drivers' championship, after completing the German Grand Prix. On the same day, radio and television licenses are increased.

3rd – The Queen's Award to Industry for export and technological achievement is created as an incentive to British businessmen and women.

9th – Britain accepts the new state of Singapore, after she breaks away from Malaysia.

10th – Blackpool is the venue for a remarkable world record in which twelve-year-old South African, Kim Muir, swims the 110 yards backstroke in only 68.7 seconds. Also on this day, Buckingham Palace nullifies the OBE that had previously been granted to the now disgraced traitor, Kim Philby.

12th – Sixty-year-old Judge Elizabeth Lane becomes the country's first female High Court judge. Judge Lane had previously been appointed the first female county court judge and the first female divorce commissioner.

15th – The Beatles perform to no fewer than a reported fifty-five thousand screaming fans at Shea Stadium in New York.

18th – Rolling Stones lead vocalist Mick Jagger performs the function of best man at the wedding ceremony of photographer David Bailey and French actress Catherine Deneuve.

19th – The Home Secretary orders the establishment of an enquiry into the murder case of Timothy John Evans, who was hanged in 1950 after the guilty verdict.

21st – Keith Peacock of Charlton Athletic makes English footballing history, when he becomes the first substitute to 'come off the bench' in a league match.

27th – A 'superpowers summit' takes place at Perugia Way, Beverley Hills, when Elvis Presley, the 'king of rock'n'roll' plays host to the new pretenders, the Beatles. The meeting is far from comfortable, not least because the four guests were so in awe of 'the King' that they were uncharacteristically quiet.

SEPTEMBER

2nd – The Labour government's parliamentary majority is reduced to a precarious two seats, following the death of Sir Harry Hylton-Foster, the Speaker of the House of Commons.

16th – Coronation Street celebrates its tenth anniversary on ITV, drawing favourable comments from the Prime Minister, who declares his enjoyment of the show.

19th – A Gallup opinion poll, commissioned by ABC Television, reveals that church attending is on the decline, while television viewing is on an upward curve.

21st – It is reported that British Petroleum has struck oil in the North Sea.

25th – British Foreign Office minister, George Thomson, is snubbed by Egypt's President Nasser, who cancels a proposed meeting, allegedly as a protest against Britain's suspension of the constitution in strife-torn Aden.

27th – British officials at the United Nations are less than amused to hear the Argentine foreign minister re-assert his country's claim to sovereignty of the disputed Falkland Islands.

28th – The Prime Minister informs his party conference at Blackpool that Labour would sooner contest another general election than enter into a parliamentary pact with the Liberal Party.

29th – Aston Martin reveals its first four-seater motor vehicle, namely the DB6.

30th – Judge Elizabeth Lane is officially sworn in as the first woman judge in Britain. Meanwhile, the record company, EMI, starts to distribute its artists' albums via three thousand grocers' stores, at a cost of 12/6d. each.

OCTOBER

6th – New Conservative Party leader, Edward Heath, pledges his intention to take Britain into the 'Common Market', when his party are returned to government.

7th – Harold Wilson opens access to London's newest skyscraper, the 620 foot Post Office Tower, which boasts a revolving circular restaurant. Even Tony Benn, the Postmaster-General, is enthusiastic, describing the tower as the Big Ben of the twentieth century.

14th – The Labour administration's support for the American war effort in Vietnam prompts Bertrand Russell to tear up his party membership card in disgust.

17th – A corpse discovered in a shallow grave in the Pennines is confirmed as that of a missing youngster, Lesley Anne Downey.

21st – A young boy's dead body is found by police, searching in the Pennines.

26th – The Queen writes to Rhodesia's premier, Ian Smith, expressing her desire that a peaceful, negotiated settlement can arrest his country's continuing crisis. Meanwhile at Buckingham Palace, Her Majesty has the dubious pleasure of handing the Beatles their MBE 'gongs'. The Fab Four cope with the ceremony by smoking marijuana in the palace's toilets!

27th – 36 people lose their lives, after an aeroplane suffers a crash landing at Heathrow Airport.

28th – A massive police presence is required outside Cheshire courthouse, as child murder suspects, Ian Brady and Myra Hindley, arrive for a hearing. While the search for possible further dead children intensifies, the Murder (Abolition of the Death Penalty) Bill ironically completes its final parliamentary stages.

29th – Harold Wilson's visit to Ian Smith in Rhodesia fails to pay dividends, as his host declines to climb down from his threat of self-enacted independence.

31st – Cork's opera house re-opens, having originally been damaged in a blaze, ten years earlier.

NOVEMBER

1st – Britain is on the receiving end of hurricane-force winds, which not only wreak considerable damage, but account for the deaths of seven people.

5th – The new craze for mini-skirts obliges new Customs regulations aimed at women who purchase children's sizes, to avoid taxes.

8th – The new British colony of the British Indian Ocean Territory is created. Also on this day, the Race Relations Bill and the Murder Bill become law.

9th – The Prime Minister abandons his government's proposals for steel nationalisation.

11th – Rhodesia's Prime Minister lights a fuse, when he broadcasts the anticipated Unilateral Declaration of Independence at 11am on Armistice Day. Incensed by Ian Smith's bold move, the British government denounces the new rebel regime as illegal, and threatens to respond with economic sanctions.

12th – Britain's Governor of Rhodesia, Sir Humphrey Gibbs, refuses to obey Ian Smith's order to resign from his 'obsolete' post.

16th – As a war of words between London and Salisbury, Rhodesia intensifies, Britain's parliament rushes through emergency legislation, which allows for the imposition of economic sanctions against the infant, break-away state. Royal Assent is immediately granted to this Southern Rhodesia Bill. Also on this day, Ireland's first Taoiseach, William Thomas Cosgrave, dies, aged eighty-five. 'WT' served as President of the Executive Council (or Prime Minister) from 1922 to 1932.

18th – Provisional timetables for flights on the new Concorde are made available. Flights from London to New York are scheduled for three hours, while Concorde journeys from London to Tokyo are expected to last thirteen hours.

22nd – The government-imposed enquiry of investigation into the questionable murder conviction of Timothy John Evans begins.

24th – An experimental new road traffic speed limit of seventy miles per hour on Britain's motorways is introduced by the government.

29th – 'Clean Up TV' campaigner, Mrs. Mary Whitehouse, launches a new pressure group, entitled The National Viewers' and Listeners' Association. Mrs. Whitehouse claims that she has an army of half a million television viewers willing to support her scrutiny of perceived immorality and bad taste broadcasts on television and radio.

DECEMBER

1st – Harold Wilson confirms that Royal Air Force Javelins, arriving in Zambia, are intended to provide military assistance. He also claims that Rhodesia may soon have tougher sanctions imposed on the breakaway regime.

14th – An Anglo-Irish trade agreement is signed, providing evidence of improving relations between Britain and the Republic of Ireland.

15th – London Zoo's reluctant resident, Goldie (the golden eagle), achieves a second successful jailbreak of this year.

16th – British writer, William Somerset Maugham, dies at the age of ninety-one, having been taken ill at the Villa Mauresque, his luxurious home at Cap Ferrat. Born in Paris in the same year as Sir Winston Churchill, he wrote 'Liza of Lambeth' and 'Of Human Bondage'.

17th – The Labour administration takes the drastic step of imposing an oil embargo on the rogue state of Rhodesia, although Edward Heath, the Leader of the Opposition, expresses his reservations. Also on this day, new forms of service for the Anglican Church are published.

21st – Plans for a Road Safety Bill are announced. The proposed legislation features provisions for random breath-tests and legal blood alcohol limits.

22nd – Barbara Castle is appointed as Minister of Transport in a cabinet re-shuffle. Also on this day, Richard Frederick Dimbleby, British broadcaster, dies, at the age of fifty-two, from cancer. Dimbleby was the BBC's first war correspondent, and he later presented current affairs television programmes. Meanwhile, the seventy miles per hour speed restriction on British roads comes into force.

27th – The giant Sea Gem oil rig, forty miles east of Grimsby, collapses. Thirteen of the thirty-two men on board drown in the icy North Sea, as a consequence. Meanwhile in Rhodesia, petrol rationing is introduced, as sanctions begin to bite.

28th – The nine hundredth anniversary of Westminster Abbey is celebrated.

THE NUMBER-ONE HIT SINGLES OF 1965

Yeh Yeh by *Georgie Flame and the Blue Flames*
Go Now by *The Moody Blues*
You've Lost That Lovin' Feelin' by *The Righteous Brothers*
Tired Of Waiting For You by *The Kinks*
I'll Never Find Another You by *The Seekers*
It's Not Unusual by *Tom Jones*
The Last Time by *The Rolling Stones*
Concrete And Clay by *Unit Four Plus Two*
The Minute You're Gone by *Cliff Richard*
Ticket To Ride by *The Beatles*
King Of The Road by *Roger Miller*
Where Are You Now, My Love? by *Jackie Trent*
Long Live Love by *Sandie Shaw*

Crying In The Chapel by *Elvis Presley*
I'm Alive by *The Hollies*
Mr. Tambourine Man by *The Byrds*
Help! by *The Beatles*
I Got You Babe by *Sonny and Cher*
(I Can't Get No) Satisfaction by *The Rolling Stones*
Make It Easy On Yourself by *The Walker Brothers*
Tears by *Ken Dodd*
Get Off Of My Cloud by *The Rolling Stones*
The Carnival Is Over by *The Seekers*
Day Tripper/We Can Work It Out by *The Beatles*

1966

JANUARY

4th – A memorial service at Westminster Abbey for the late Richard Dimbleby is attended by four thousand guests.

7th – It is announced that Britain will collaborate with Australia and Canada in drought relief operations in central Africa – including Rhodesia.

12th – Three visiting Labour Members of Parliament are given a rough reception by approximately four hundred white Rhodesians in their capital, Salisbury. Meanwhile, Britain's Prime Minister finds himself in a verbal tennis match with his Sierra Leone counterpart, who urges Britain to engage militarily against Rhodesia. Harold Wilson explains to the assembled Commonwealth conference in Lagos the impracticability of this suggestion.

13th – After being rough-handled in a Salisbury banqueting hall, the three 'fact-finding' Labour MPs' mission in Rhodesia abruptly ends in expulsion. They ought to be relieved, after their ordeal the previous day.

17th – Bread consumers' eyebrows are raised, after leading bakers increase the cost of a standard loaf by one penny – to 1/3d halfpenny.

20th – A death sentence imposed on a Rhodesian black is nullified by the Queen, who commutes the death penalty.

21st – The Smith regime in Rhodesia snubs its monarch and provokes further wrath by ignoring the Royal Prerogative of commuting death sentences.

28th – The Pedestrians' Association express their satisfaction when the bill permitting random breath tests is published. Among its contents is the restriction of a maximum eighty milligrams of alcohol in 100cc of blood. Many motorists are less amused by the new provisions.

31st – Virtually all trade between Britain and Rhodesia is curtailed by order of the British government's Board of Trade.

FEBRUARY

1st – The Wilson government increases its squeeze on lending by banks.

3rd – The Companies Bill is published in parliament. Its provisions include the stipulation that businesses will have to declare their donations to any of the political parties.

8th – Forty-three year-old entrepreneur, Freddie Laker, establishes a cut-price airline service that will target the growing number of passengers taking 'package holidays'. Also on this day, ban-the-bomb protesters picket the National Film Theatre, which is screening the banned drama, 'The War Game', about a Hydrogen bomb attack on Britain.

9th – The Labour administration announces its proposal to create a prototype fast-breeder reactor at Dounreay, on the north coast of Scotland.

10th – The brewers, Watneys, place an extra penny on the pint of bitter, which will now retail at 1/8d. Meanwhile, actor Jack Hawkins leaves hospital, two and a half weeks after undergoing an operation to combat cancer of the throat.

17th – The British government expresses its disapproval to the apartheid regime of South Africa, which is reportedly supplying petrol to its white supremacy ally, Rhodesia.

19th – Christopher Mayhew stands down as Navy Minister in dismay over the Labour government's "dangerously mistaken" defence policies.

27th – Shell Oil announces it has struck oil in the Trucial State of Muscat and Oman.

28th – Hampered by the slenderest of parliamentary majorities, Harold Wilson takes the bold step of scheduling another general election for Thursday 31st of March, in the hope of obtaining a more emphatic mandate for his government.

MARCH

1st – Jim Callaghan, the Chancellor of the Exchequer, announces that Britain will switch to decimal currency in 1971.

3rd – The British Broadcasting Corporation promises colour broadcasts on television for next year.

4th – Both Britain and the United States accept the existence of the state of Ghana, which severs ties with Guinea.

5th – A British Boeing 707 crashes into Mount Fuji, Japan, causing the deaths of 124 people.

7th – The Wilson administration pledges its desire to establish a new Ministry of Social Security, to replace National Assistance.

8th – The Nelson Pillar in O'Connell Street, Dublin, is demolished by an I.R.A bomb.

15th – The Royal Air Force is given a base on Madagascar, from which it can patrol the African coast for anyone violating the sanctions imposed on Rhodesia.

17th – Arkle stakes its claim to be the greatest steeplechaser in racing history, by storming to a thirty-length triumph in the Cheltenham Gold Cup. This victory completes a hat-trick of consecutive wins in this prestigious race for the Duchess of Westminster's popular horse.

20th – Panic ensues as the Jules Rimet Trophy, otherwise known as the football World Cup, disappears from Westminster Central Hall.

23rd – In what would prove to be the last two-legged League Cup final, West Bromwich Albion 'hammer' West Ham United 4–1, thereby becoming the fourth different Midlands football club in six years to lift the English League Cup, courtesy of a 5–3 aggregate total. Meanwhile, in Rome, Dr. Ramsey visits the Vatican, thus representing the first meeting between the Archbishop of Canterbury and the Pope in an official capacity for more than four hundred years. Devout Protestants are less than amused with this perceived step towards ecumenism.

26th – Anglo, owned by Mr. S Levy, triumphs at the Aintree Grand National steeplechase.

27th – A chance discovery in a south London garden by the dog of Mr. David Corbett has re-located the missing Jules Rimet Trophy. The victorious captain of the next football World Cup team will have this coveted piece of silverware to lift, courtesy of the endeavours of a mongrel called Pickles.

31st – Voting takes place in the general election.

APRIL

1st – Harold Wilson's calculated gamble of going to the electorate, one and a half years into his government's term of office, has paid off handsomely. The Labour Party's bid to re-govern Britain has been endorsed to such an extent that it now commands a comfortable House of Commons majority of ninety-six, after all the constituency results have been declared. Also on this day, the British Airports Authority is established.

2nd – Cecil Scott Forester, born Cecil Smith, dies at the age of 66. This English novelist made his name as the author of the Captain Hornblower series and 'The African Queen' (1935).

5th – The Shell company admit that a recent North Sea oil discovery, off the coast of Great Yarmouth, is of "considerable importance".

8th – The number of illegitimate births in England and Wales has almost doubled in the last ten years, according to newly-published statistics.

10th – English satirical writer, Evelyn Arthur St. John Waugh, dies at the age of sixty-two. Waugh was the author of such works as 'Brideshead Revisited', 'Vile Bodies', and 'A Little Learning'. Meanwhile in Ireland, Irish republicans commemorate the fiftieth anniversary of the Easter Rising.

14th – The Sussex Downs are recognised as an Area of Outstanding Natural Beauty.

19th – Ian Brady and Myra Hindley, the accused 'Moors Murderers', go on trial at the Old Bailey. Also on this day, Edward Heath re-shuffles his shadow cabinet, which is bad news for Ernest Marples and Selwyn Lloyd, who are both shown the exit door.

21st – The State Opening of the new parliament is broadcast on television for the very first time.

25th – Lord Cromer is replaced as Governor of the Bank of England by Leslie O'Brien.

30th – Hoverlloyd commence the first regular hovercraft service across the English Channel, between the ports of Ramsgate and Calais.

MAY

1st – British driver John Surtees triumphs in the Syracuse Grand Prix in Sicily.

4th – It is announced that dentists and doctors will be awarded pay increases of between ten and 35 per cent. The 'average' General Practitioner's annual salary is now £4,000.

6th – 24-year-old Myra Hindley and 28-year-old Ian Brady are sentenced to life imprisonment, following their conviction for the murders of Lesley Anne Downey (10 years of age), Edward Evans (seventeen), and John Kilbride (aged twelve). It was Hindley's brother-in-law, David Smith, who initially informed the police, who are still searching the Pennine moors for more child victims.

14th – The FA Cup trophy will be making a short journey across Stanley Park, from Anfield to Goodison Park, after Everton's 3-2 victory today in the final against the Owls of Sheffield Wednesday. It was the Toffees' first FA Cup triumph since 1933.

17th – Barbara Castle, Labour's Transport Minister, states that the experimental speed limit of seventy miles per hour will continue until 1967. Also on this day, former world middleweight boxing champion, Randolph Turpin, is found dead in his Leamington Spa flat, having apparently been shot dead.

18th – Roy Jenkins, the Home Secretary, declares that the number of different police forces in England and Wales will be reduced by 68. Meanwhile, Britain begins talks with General Franco's Spain on the constitutional future of Gibraltar.

21st – Cassius Clay defeats Henry Cooper for a second time, to remain the world heavyweight boxing champion. Cooper's valiant challenge lasted this time until Round Six.

22nd – Scottish grand prix driver, Jackie Stewart, comes first in the Monaco Grand Prix.

23rd – The seamen's strike has prompted the government to announce a state of emergency to ensure the maintenance of essential services and supplies.

25th – Scobie Breasley scores his second success in three years in the Epsom Derby, as he pilots Lady Zia Wernher's Charlottetown to victory.

26th – An enquiry into the seamen's industrial dispute is ordered by the government. Also on this day, British Guiana becomes the independent Caribbean state of Guyana.

30th – Fresh from his triumph in Monaco, Jackie Stewart appears to be racing to certain victory in the Indianapolis 500, but when his car comes to a halt, with eight laps remaining, his fellow British competitors, Jim Clark and Graham Hill, battle it out for first place. Eventually it is Hill, the 1962 world drivers' champion, who emerges as the winner, becoming the first participant to win this prestigious American contest on their debut appearance.

JUNE

1st – The Automobile Association announces the first rise in its annual subscription fee, since it was established in 1905, from two to three guineas. Also on this day, it is claimed that Philips Petroleum has made the richest gas strike so far in the North Sea. Meanwhile, popular American singer-songwriter, Bob Dylan, receives a mixed reception during his Royal Albert Hall performance. A number of purists of folk music were dismayed when Dylan and accompanying musicians, The Band, abandon the traditional acoustic guitar for an electric one, leading to shouts of 'Judas' from one or two musical luddites.

2nd – Eighty-three-year-old Eamon de Valera is re-elected for another seven years as the President of the Republic of Ireland. 'Dev' defeated his nearest challenger, Tom O'Higgins, by a slender margin of ten thousand votes. Also on this day, Philips Petroleum reveal that a gas flow of "up to seventeen million cubic feet a day" has been achieved, eighty miles off the Humberside coast. Consequently, it is reckoned that all British gas will soon be natural.

6th – Northern Ireland's Prime Minister, Captain Terence O'Neill, cuts short a visit to Paris, and returns home to impose a ban on the loyalist paramilitary organisation, the Ulster Volunteer Force. This drastic action has been implemented in response to the murder of a young Roman Catholic in Belfast. Meanwhile, the British Broadcasting Corporation's latest comedy offering, 'Til Death Us Do Part', featuring the bigoted Alf Garnett, makes its screen debut. Also on this day, England cricket team suffer a humiliating innings defeat at Old Trafford against the West Indies. The tourists wrap up victory inside three days, courtesy of the bowling of Gibbs and the all-round efforts of Sobers.

8th – Certain members of the Conservative Party are in uproar at 'Til Death Us Do Part', which included a line which suggested that Edward Heath is a "grammar school twit."

11th – The Queen's birthday honours list awards OBEs to such celebrities as the comedy actor, Peter Sellers, and the fashion designer, Mary Quant.

14th – Walter McGowan defeats Salvatore Burruni of Italy, to become the world flyweight boxing champion.

20th – James White is sentenced to eighteen years in prison for his involvement in the 'great train robbery'.

27th – Arthur Schloss Waley dies at the age of seventy-six. Waley was a British poet and Oriental scholar, who was best known for his translations of Chinese and Japanese verse.

28th – Harold Wilson reveals the names of Marxist extremists who, he alleges, are exploiting the seamen's dispute in order to gain power in the National Union of Seamen.

29th – Barclay's Bank proudly reveal the introduction of Britain's first credit card, called the Barclaycard. Seamen meanwhile announce that they will abandon their strike on Friday the first of July. Also on this day, on the second leg of England football team's four-match tour of northern and eastern Europe, the prolific Jimmy Greaves finds the back of the net four times, as Alf Ramsey's team demolish Norway 6–1 in Oslo. In spite of this emphatic triumph on the eve of the World Cup finals, experienced duo of Flowers and goal-keeper Springett would never play for England again, having amassed eighty-two caps between them.

JULY

2nd – There are two new winners of the singles' titles at the All-England Club, as Billie Jean King defeats three-times ladies' champion, Maria Bueno, and the men's final is decided in favour of Spain's Manuel Santana, who prevents Dennis Ralston from achieving an American double at Wimbledon.

3rd – The Minister of Technology, Frank Cousins, resigns from the government in protest at its prices and incomes policy. His replacement will be Anthony Wedgwood Benn. Also on this day, more than thirty people are arrested in Grosvenor Square, London, during a demonstration against the Vietnam War.

4th – The Labour administration publishes its Prices And Incomes Bill. Meanwhile, two people are arrested, after disrupting the visit of the Queen and her husband to Northern Ireland. First, a beer bottle and then a concrete block were hurled at the monarch's car. Nobody was injured, except the car bonnet.

9th – American golfing maestro, Jack Nicklaus, wins the British Open for the first time. Nicklaus tames the Muirfield golf course with a winning total of 282 shots.

11th – BMC and the Jaguar motor company reveal their intention to merge under the proposed name of British Motor Holdings. Also on this day, England football team are held to a scoreless draw by the uncompromising Uruguayans in their opening match of the World Cup finals. This stalemate ends a sequence of seven successive victories for Alf Ramsey's team, who become the first England team to fail to score in a Wembley international since 1938!

14th – The bank rate increases from six to seven per cent. Meanwhile, Gwynfor Evans, representing the Welsh Nationalists, gains the vacant parliamentary seat of Carmarthen in a by-election from the previous occupants, the Labour Party.

17th – Harold Wilson, in the company of the Soviet premier, Alexei Kosygin, attends an industrial fair in Moscow, during a tour of Russia.

20th – Protestant extremist, the Reverend Ian Paisley, is imprisoned in Northern Ireland, for breaching the peace at a church assembly in June. Also on this day, the prospect of turmoil in the labour movement looms, as the Prime Minister, fresh from his Russian expedition, announces a raft of measures aimed at halting Britain's escalating inflation. The package includes a six-month freeze on wages, salaries, and prices, while other controversial moves include cuts in holiday currency allowances, more hire purchase restraints, and purchase tax increases. While the British public braces itself for this unpleasant economic medicine, there is some relief on the football field, as a Roger Hunt double sinks France 2–0 in England's final group match. The hosts now have the small matter of a quarter-final in three days' time against Argentina.

21st – The first-ever Welsh Nationalist Member of Parliament, Gwynfor Evans, is sworn in without the anticipated fuss over whether the ceremony would be performed in English or Welsh. In the event, English was used, while the Speaker of the House of Commons declined a request for the use of Welsh.

22nd – Eleven people are killed in Wales when a pleasure boat crashes on the River Mawddach, Merionethshire.

27th – The Trades Union Congress's general council agrees to accept the government's wage standstill.

28th – Seventy-year-old Florence Nagle becomes the first woman in Britain to be granted a licence to train racehorses, after a lengthy twenty-year campaign.

30th – A Geoff Hurst hat-trick ensures that England become the third footballing nation to win the World Cup as hosts. Hurst's West Ham United team-mate, Martin Peters, also scores as Alf Ramsey's team overcome previous champions, West Germany, 4–2 in a two-hour epic. The losers are aggrieved by the controversial award of a goal by a Russian linesman. Nevertheless, Bobby Moore ascends the famous Wembley steps to lift the greatest prize in football.

AUGUST

1st – More than thirty people are feared dead, off the Cornwall coast, having been aboard the pleasure boat, Darlwyne.

4th – Not for the first time, the terrible twins, Reggie and Ronnie Kray are arrested by the police, who are investigating a murder. Also on this day, Sir Edmund Compton is named as Britain's first Parliamentary Commissioner or 'Ombudsman'.

10th – It is announced that the public inspection of Cabinet and other official documents is to be permitted, after a gap of thirty years has elapsed, instead of the present fifty years. Meanwhile, George Brown is rewarded for reluctantly biting his lip during the revelation of the tough economic measures by being appointed as Foreign Secretary, in place of Michael Stewart, in a cabinet re-shuffle.

12th – Three policemen who may have intercepted a prison breakout from Wormwood Scrubs in west London, are shot dead. Of some consolation is the fact that detectives are in possession of the murder gang's car registration number.

15th – John Whitney is charged in connection with the west London murders.

17th – John Duddy is arrested in Glasgow, also suspected of involvement in the murders.

22nd – Proposals are revealed for the construction in London's west end of Centre Point, which on completion will be a 385-foot, 34-floor skyscraper.

23rd – The Cotswolds are officially recognised as an Area of Outstanding Natural Beauty.

27th – Francis Chichester departs from Plymouth on his latest adventure, namely a solo round-the-world voyage.

29th – Perhaps unnerved by bad experiences on tour in the Philippines, as well as incurring the wrath of the Ku Klux Klan and the American bible belt, the Beatles perform their last-ever official concert at Candlestick Park, San Francisco. The 'fab four' now intend to concentrate on recording in the studio, in preference to the dubious pleasure of performing to screaming fans.

31st – A British airliner crashes in Yugoslavia, causing the death of more than ninety people.

SEPTEMBER

2nd – Yorkshire clinch the cricket County Championship title for the fifth time in the last eight seasons.

5th – The selective Employment Tax comes into force in the United Kingdom.

8th – The new Severn road bridge opens for business.

10th – 'Oliver!', the longest-running musical in London's west end, finishes a run of six years and three months. Also on this day, it is announced that free post-primary education will be introduced next year in the Republic of Ireland.

15th – A German submarine, entitled the *Hai*, sinks off Dogger Bank. Meanwhile, at the Cumbrian port of Barrow, Queen Elizabeth, the

Queen Mother, launches HMS *Resolution*, Britain's first Polaris nuclear submarine.

25th – Circus owner, William George "Billy" Smart, dies at the age of seventy-three.

27th – The motor vehicle company, BMC, announces more than eleven thousand redundancies to take effect in mid-November. In the meantime, a mere seven thousand employees are laid off.

29th – Prince Philip's stay at the British Ambassador's residence in Buenos Aires, Argentina, is disturbed by gunfire, on a day when twenty Argentine nationalists stage an impromptu invasion of the Falkland Islands.

30th – Port Stanley's 'uninvited guests' who had arrived a day ago in a hijacked airliner surrender to a local Roman Catholic priest. Also on this day, Lord Thomson of Fleet adds his new acquisition, The Times, to his ownership of its sister newspaper, the Sunday Times.

OCTOBER

2nd – Twice World Champion, Jim Clark, steers his car to first place in the Formula One United States Grand Prix.

4th – The Prices And Incomes Act comes into effect, empowering the Wilson government to freeze wages and prices for the foreseeable future.

11th – The GPO announces that all British businesses and households will be allocated postcodes, starting with Croydon, in early November. Also on this day, Jensen reveals its latest models, the FF and the Interceptor.

18th – Timothy John Evans is granted a free pardon by the Queen. Regrettably, Evans was sent to the gallows sixteen years ago at the age of 25. It now appears that Evans, according to a High Court judge, was "probably innocent".

20th – More bad news is presented to the government, when they learn that the unemployment total has increased by one hundred thousand to almost 450,000.

21st – The coal-mining village of Aberfan is on the receiving end of an avalanche from a coal slag heap, which tragically kills 144 people, including 116 children.

22nd – Dr. Hewlett Johnson, known as the "Red Dean" of Canterbury, dies, aged ninety-two.

23rd – John Surtees is greeted by the chequered flag as he wins the Mexican Grand Prix. Nevertheless, the 1964 world champion fails to stop Australia's Jack Brabham from collecting his third drivers' world championship title.

27th – Harold Wilson states that he will provide no more personal recommendations for honours for political services rendered. Meanwhile, no fewer than eighty-two victims of the Aberfan disaster are buried in a mass grave.

29th – The British Army removes its restrictions on colour.

31st – Employees of the British Motor Corporation stage a strike in protest at the struggling company's job cuts.

NOVEMBER

7th – Figures published by the United States National Science Foundation indicate an alarming rise in the number of engineers and scientists migrating from Britain to the other side of the 'big pond'. While migration figures from other west European states are in decline, Britain is clearly suffering a brain drain.

9th – The car firm, Rootes, reveals the new Hillman Hunter. Also on this day, forty-nine year-old Jack Lynch, a former Gaelic sports player, succeeds Sean Lemass as the Taoiseach of the Republic of Ireland. Lynch's surprising emergence as Lemass's successor was achieved, following an endorsement by Fianna Fail over his nearest challenger, George Colley.

11th – The strike action at the British Motor Corporation factories comes to a halt.

13th – Twelve months after Ian Smith's Remembrance Sunday 'coup', his followers stage an Armistice Day protest outside 10 Downing Street.

20th – Four weeks after his daring escape from Wormwood Scrubs prison, George Blake, the convicted spy, is reported to be in East Berlin.

23rd – British Petroleum claims it has struck its best gas-producing areas yet in the North Sea, approximately forty miles east of the Humberside coast.

24th – The Labour administration is given more cause for concern, as the new unemployment figures reveal almost a further one hundred thousand people out of work.

25th – Warren Mitchell, who plays the part of ranting Alf Garnett in 'Til Death Us Do Part', is named as 1966's best actor on television.

30th – The Prime Minister advises the need for European economic growth to fend off American domination.

DECEMBER

2nd – The British and Rhodesian Prime Ministers hold a meeting on board Her Majesty's Ship *Tiger,* off the coast of Gibraltar. A working document is prepared in an attempt to clear the air.

5th – The former Minister of Technology, Frank Cousins, stands down as Labour's Member of Parliament for the midlands constituency of Nuneaton.

6th – "The fight goes on", declares Ian Smith, after he and his cabinet reject Britain's working document as "repugnant". Having dismissed Britain's calls for an end to Unilateral Declaration of Independence, the breakaway regime can expect further sanctions to be imposed against her.

12th – It is reported that the Gas Council-Amoco group has achieved another impressive North Sea gas strike.

16th – The United Nations Security Council votes in favour of the British resolution for mandatory sanctions (including an oil embargo) against Rhodesia.

20th – Harold Wilson states that the introduction of majority rule is a must, before a resolution of the Rhodesian crisis can be achieved.

21st – Lord Thomson's purchase of *The Times* is approved by the Monopolies Commission.

22nd – Rhodesia follows its neighbour, South Africa, by exiting the British Commonwealth.

THE NUMBER-ONE HIT SINGLES OF 1966

Keep On Running by *The Spencer Davis Group*
Michelle by *The Overlanders*
These Boots Are Made For Walkin' by *Nancy Sinatra*
The Sun Ain't Gonna Shine Anymore by *The Walker Brothers*
Somebody Help Me by *The Spencer Davis Group*
You Don't Have To Say You Love Me by *Dusty Springfield*
Pretty Flamingo by *Manfred Mann*
Paint It Black by *The Rolling Stones*
Strangers In The Night by *Frank Sinatra*
Paperback Writer by *The Beatles*
Sunny Afternoon by *The Kinks*
Get Away by *Georgie Fame and the Blue Flames*
Out Of Time by *Chris Farlowe and the Thunderbirds*
With A Girl Like You by *The Troggs*
Yellow Submarine/Eleanor Rigby by *The Beatles*
All Or Nothing by *The Small Faces*
Distant Drums by *Jim Reeves*
Reach Out, I'll Be There by *The Four Tops*
Good Vibrations by *The Beach Boys*
Green Green Grass Of Home by *Tom Jones*

1967

JANUARY

1st – England football team's World Cup triumph is recognised in the New Year Honours list as manager Alf Ramsey is granted a knighthood, while West Ham United centre-half Bobby Moore is awarded an OBE.

4th – The Ken Dodd Show, broadcast on the BBC, is revealed as the most popular Christmas television programme. Also on this day, Donald Malcolm Campbell, the son of Sir Malcolm Campbell, is killed at the age of 45, when his Bluebird somersaults over Coniston Water during another record-breaking attempt. He had previously set six new records on water and one on land.

7th – 'The Forsyte Saga' is broadcast for the first time on BBC1.

11th – 'Cathy Come Home', the controversial television play, is broadcast again. The drama has increased public awareness of the plight of homelessness among some young people. Meanwhile, the anti-abortion pressure group, the Society for the Protection of Unborn Children, is created. Also on this day, the last detachment of British troops leaves Sarawak, in east Malaysia.

12th – Canadian newspaper magnate Lord Thomson appoints Harold Evans as editor of *The Sunday Times,* and William Rees-Mogg as editor of *The Times.* A new town is proposed for rural Buckinghamshire, to be entitled Milton Keynes.

17th – Anthony Wedgwood Benn, the Technology Minister, announces that the American motor company, Chrysler, will be permitted to take over the Rootes car firm. Meanwhile, Jo Grimond stands down as Liberal Party leader, having steered Britain's struggling third political party since 1956.

18th – 34-year-old former Etonian, Jeremy Thorpe, succeeds Jo Grimond after a ballot of the Liberal Party's twelve members of parliament. There are however rumblings of discontent at grassroots level at how the new leader was chosen by so few MPs.

26th – The bank rate is reduced from seven to 6.5 per cent as the economy improves.

27th – Malta's Prime Minister, Borg Olivier, orders Britain to "get out" of his country. Also on this day, the seafaring adventurer Francis Chichester is awarded a knighthood.

31st – There is turmoil at the London School of Economics where radical students disrupt a meeting and demand the resignation of Rhodesian, Walter Adams, the head of the LSE. A porter dies as a result of the disturbance.

FEBRUARY

1st – Students demonstrate their disapproval of a government initiative to increase fees for overseas students.

5th – The Musicians' Union forbids the performing of the Rolling Stones' latest single, 'Let's Spend the Night Together', from Eamonn Andrews' television programme. A similar objection was raised by the Ed Sullivan Show, obliging Mick Jagger to mumble 'let's spend some time together' as a compromise. Meanwhile, former presenter of 'That Was The Week That Was', David Frost, grills insurance fraudster Dr. Emil Savundra, in a television interview. Frost eventually walks out on his guest, who refers to the victims of his sharp business practices as "peasants".

6th – Russian Prime Minister, Alexei Kosygin, arrives in London on an official visit. Also on this day, the newly-created Northern Ireland Civil Rights Association states its aims.

8th – British publisher, Sir Victor Gollancz, dies at the age of seventy-three.

10th – Dr. Emil Savundra, the notorious former chairman of the Fire, Auto, and Marine Insurance company is arrested and charged with fraud.

12th – Mike Burke and Dougal Haston become the first British mountaineers to successfully climb the north face of the Alps' Matterhorn during the winter. Also on this Sunday, police acting on an alleged tip-off from the *News Of The World* newspaper, arrive at Keith Richard's Redlands home, and proceed to arrest the Rolling Stones' guitarist and his song-writing partner, Mick Jagger, on drugs possession charges. Also present during the drug bust was female singer, Marianne Faithful, subsequently described as 'Miss X', naked but for a fur rug. Another guest, Beatles' guitarist, George Harrison, had left just before the police came.

13th – Agreement is reached on the need for a "hot line" of communication between 10 Downing Street and the Kremlin. Meanwhile, teenagers run riot at Heathrow Airport, as latest American pop sensations, The Monkees, arrive.

14th – Approximately one hundred members of the Labour parliamentary party vote their disapproval of the renewed bombing campaign by the United States in North Vietnam.

16th – British movies, 'Alfie', 'A Man for All Seasons', and 'Georgy Girl' scoop top honours at the Golden Globe film awards.

17th – A new parliamentary bill for birth control on the rates receives an unopposed second reading in the House of Commons.

20th – The closure of two cotton mills in Lancashire is announced by Viyella International.

23rd – More than thirty Labour members in the House of Commons abstain in a vote of censure of government increases in fees for overseas students.

26th – Police drug raids in the west country result in the arrests of approximately thirty people.

28th – Another Labour Party backbench rebellion occurs when more than sixty members of parliament refuse to support the government's Defence White Paper.

MARCH

1st – British soldiers are obliged to open fire on protesters, during street disturbances in Aden. Also on this day, Queen Elizabeth opens the Queen Elizabeth Hall and the Purcell Room. Meanwhile, at Westminster the Decimal Currency Bill is published.

4th – Defending champions, West Bromwich Albion, are defeated 3–2 in the League Cup's first Wembley final by Queen's Park Rangers. The west Londoners thus become the first Division Three team to win a Wembley final.

6th – The trial use of helicopters employed in the fight against crime is started.

13th – An all-night sit-in demonstration is staged by some students at the London School of Economics, protesting at the suspension of two students.

15th – Manny Shinwell stands down as chairman of Labour's parliamentary party.

16th – The bank rate is reduced from 6.5 to six per cent.

17th – A star-grading system for petroleum becomes operational.

19th – The *Torrey Canyon*, an oil tanker, runs aground off Land's End, with 120,000 tons of crude oil aboard. Meanwhile, thirteen student protesters call off their five-day hunger strike, after two student leaders are re-instated at the London School of Economics. The college of higher education remains in turmoil over its appointment of Rhodesian, Walter Adams, as the director of the LSE.

20th – Sir Francis Chichester sails round Cape Horn and proceeds via the Atlantic Ocean towards Britain.

24th – Oil from the *Torrey Canyon* starts to pollute the shores of the Cornish coast.

30th – The pollution threat posed by the *Torrey Canyon* has necessitated the drastic action of fighter aircraft bombing the tanker and setting the oil on fire, to curtail what has been described as the "greatest peacetime threat to Britain".

APRIL

1st – Britain's first Ombudsman, Sir Edmund Compton, starts his new appointment on April Fools' Day. He anticipates dealing with as many as seven thousand grievances per year.

3rd – Calder and Boyars is sent for trial for publishing the controversial 'Last Exit To Brooklyn'. Also on this day, British soldiers clash with more than one thousand Arab protesters in Aden. Three demonstrators are killed, and eleven soldiers are injured.

4th – The Labour administration claims that the risk of thrombosis, arising out of the contraceptive pill is "very slight", and not sufficient to merit a ban.

8th – Winning owner, Mr C Watkins, can scarcely believe his good fortune, as his apparent no-hoper Foinavon triumphs in the Aintree Grand National, at the remarkable odds of 100–1. The horse's victory was due in no small part to its jockey, John Buckingham, steering clear of a melee of horses at the 23rd fence, an innocuous obstacle which has since been christened 'the Foinavon fence'.

11th – Tom Stoppard's 'Rosencrantz and Guildenstern are dead' makes its debut appearance at the National Theatre.

12th – For the first time in a decade, the pound sterling achieves parity with the dollar.

14th – Results from yesterday's local government elections provide encouragement for the Conservative Party, which achieves a landslide victory in the GLC elections, as well as gaining control of a further nine county councils.

15th – New football world champions, England, suffer their first defeat, at the hands of the 'auld enemy', as Scotland humble them 3–2 on the hallowed turf of Wembley. The tartan army's goal heroes are Denis Law, Bobby Lennox, and Jim McCalliog.

26th – One of Pablo Picasso's works is sold in London for a staggering 532,000 dollars.

27th – The Home Secretary, Roy Jenkins, informs the House of Commons that he may reinforce race relations laws with new legislation.

MAY

1st – Ten criminals flee with approximately £700,000 in gold bars from a security van, in Britain's largest-ever bullion robbery.

2nd – Harold Wilson announces that Britain is going to re-apply for membership of the European Economic Community.

4th – The bank rate is reduced to five and a half per cent.

5th – Ariel 3, the first all-British satellite, is launched in the United States of America.

10th – The Road Safety Bill, which includes compulsory breath tests, becomes law.

14th – Liverpool's new Roman Catholic Cathedral of Christ the King is opened.

15th – Anti-British protesters march through Peking and ransack a British diplomat's home.

16th – It was a case of deja-vu, as President de Gaulle informs a press conference that he will not accept Britain's application to join the Common Market, until such "formidable obstacles" as Britain's special relationship with the United States are removed.

20th – The first-ever all-London FA Cup final is won by Tottenham Hotspur, who duly lift the prized possession for the third time in seven years. Among the recipients of winners' medals are Jimmy Greaves and Terry Venables, who help to inflict misery on their former club, Chelsea, who lose 2–1 in a one-sided final.

22nd – The diplomatic cold war between Britain and China intensifies, as the Peking authorities expel a British diplomat and close down the Shanghai consulate.

25th – Conservative Member of Parliament, Enoch Powell, describes Britain as "the sick man of Europe". Also on this day, Glasgow Celtic come from behind, to defeat Italy's Inter Milan 2–1, thereby becoming the first British football club to lift the coveted European Champions' Cup. Goals from Tommy Gemmell and then Steve Chalmers enable Jock Stein's 'Lisbon Lions' to make soccer history.

28th – 65-year-old Francis Chichester arrives back in Plymouth, after an epic four-month, 28,500-mile circumnavigation of the globe in his yacht. Congratulatory telegrams are received from both the monarch and her Prime Ministers. Meanwhile, more than half a million opponents of abortion have reportedly signed a petition, protesting against the Medical Termination of Pregnancy Bill.

30th – The actor, Claude Rains, dies at the age of 77.

JUNE

1st – The Beatles' long-awaited sequel to their 'Revolver' album, 'Sergeant Pepper's Lonely Hearts Club Band', is released by the Parlophone label of EMI records. Tracks such as 'A Day In The Life' and George Harrison's 'Within You, Without You' reveal that the fab four's new psychedelic music is a far cry from their material of 1963 to 1964. Not only do critics rave about the experimental new songs, but record buyers feast their eyes on a truly eye-catching album cover.

3rd – Almost ninety people are killed when a British airliner crashes at Perpignan in France. Also on this day of deaths, writer Arthur Mitchell Ransome dies at the age of eighty-three. As a journalist, he covered the Russian Revolution of 1917, before writing 'Swallows And Amazons' (1930) and 'Peter Duck' (1932). Meanwhile, Arthur William Tedder, the first Baron Tedder, dies at the age of seventy-six. This British air marshal reorganised the Middle East Air Force, before serving as deputy supreme commander under Eisenhower for the Allied invasion of Europe.

4th – Another air disaster follows scarcely twelve hours after the crash in the Pyrenees. This time, a British Midland Airways Argonaut from Majorca crash lands near Stockport in Cheshire, resulting in the deaths of almost eighty people. Also on this day, Jim Clark drives his new Lotus-Ford to victory in the Dutch Grand Prix.

7th – The Queen unveils a memorial plaque for her late grandmother, Queen Mary (1867-1953) at Marlborough House. It is no ordinary ceremony however, because the invited guests include the pariah couple of the Duke and Duchess of Windsor. This development marks a belated attempt by the Royal Family to heal old wounds, arising out of King Edward VIII's abdication in December 1936.

20th – Eighteen Britons are shot dead in a police mutiny in Aden.

26th – It is announced that Britain's membership application for the Common Market is to be referred by the Council of Ministers to the European Economic Community's commission.

27th – British banking's first cash-dispensing machine is introduced by Barclays Bank. Meanwhile, following their February drug bust, Rolling Stones duo Mick Jagger and Keith Richard are found guilty of possessing illegal substances.

29th – Mick Jagger is sentenced to three months' imprisonment, while his 'partner-in-crime' Keith Richard receives a one-year jail sentence. British pop's most notorious celebrities immediately launch an appeal.

30th – A period of severe economic restraint in Britain comes to a welcome end.

JULY

1st – BBC Two starts broadcasting in colour, which is good news for tennis fans, who are able to view the proceedings at Wimbledon in colour.

2nd – The Queen and Prince Philip preside as guests of honour over Canada's centenary celebrations in Ottawa.

3rd – A new regular, daily thirty-minute news programme, entitled News At Ten, is launched by ITV.

8th – John Newcombe becomes the seventh different Australian to win the men's singles at Wimbledon in the last fifteen years, when he overcomes Wilhelm Bungert. Meanwhile, in the ladies' event, defending champion, Billie Jean King, breaks British hearts by defeating Ann Jones in the final. Also on this day, actress Vivien Leigh dies from tuberculosis, at the age of fifty-three. Married to Laurence Olivier from 1937 to 1960, Leigh landed the plum role of Scarlett O'Hara in 'Gone With The Wind' (1939), and she also excelled herself as Blanche Dubois in 'A Streetcar Named Desire' (1951).

12th – Barbara Castle, the Transport Minister, states that the hitherto provisional seventy miles per hour speed limit is to be permanently enforced.

14th – The Decimal Currency Act becomes law, paving the way for the introduction of decimal currency in Britain in 1971. Meanwhile at Westminster, the House of Commons votes to legalise abortion a mere ten days after a bill to legalise homosexual acts between adult men is also approved.

16th – Eyebrows are raised as an estimated five thousand people attend a 'Legalise Pot 1967' demonstration in London's Hyde Park. Also on this day, two thousand Britons flee from the Biafra region of Nigeria, as trouble starts to brew.

17th – Britain's inaugural Anti-Litter Week is promoted by the Keep Britain Tidy group. Meanwhile, London's first supersonic boom test takes place.

18th – The announcement of defence cuts is criticised by Conservative MPs, who are hostile to the decision to gradually withdraw all of the armed forces from all areas east of the Suez Canal by the middle of the 1970s. The initiative, it is feared, will encourage the imperialist ambitions of China.

21st – Sherlock Holmes actor, Basil Rathbone, dies at the age of 75.

23rd – 29-year-old Durham cyclist, Tommy Simpson, collapses during the rigorous Tour de France event, and dies soon afterwards. World road-race champion in 1965, Simpson was the first Englishman to ever wear the prized yellow jersey.

25th – Margaret Herbison is replaced as Minister of Social Security by Judith Hart.

27th – The Sexual Offences Bill comes into force.

28th – The British Steel Corporation is established.

31st – Appeal court judges overturn the jail convictions of Mick Jagger and Keith Richard. Their art dealer friend, Robert Fraser, does not enjoy the same good fortune. British pop's 'terrible twins' were assisted by a recent editorial by *The Times* newspaper, entitled 'Who Breaks A Butterfly On A Wheel?', which suggested that the pair were being unjustly made an example of, to deter other would-be drug users.

AUGUST

1st – Poet and writer, Siegfried Lorraine Sassoon, dies at the age of eighty. As well as expressing his hatred of war, he wrote 'The Memoirs of a Foxhunting Man'.

2nd – The Dartford Tunnel opens under the River Thames, at a cost of eight million pounds.

3rd – The Aberfan tribunal report blames the National Coal Board for the catastrophe. Lord Robens offers to resign, but his resignation is declined.

9th – Playwright John Kingsley 'Joe' Orton is murdered by his flatmate at the age of thirty-three. Orton, who specialised in black satirical comedies, wrote 'Loot', 'Entertaining Mr Sloane', and 'What The Butler Saw'.

14th – Most pirate radio stations reluctantly halt their broadcasts on the eve of the Marine Broadcasting Act.

15th – Pirate radio stations are now outlawed, as the Marine Broadcasting Act becomes law.

17th – Jimmy Hill announces that he will be resigning his position as manager of Coventry City football team, to pursue a career on television.

20th – The United States Embassy in London is on the receiving end of gunfire from three men, armed with automatic rifles.

21st – British troops start their phased withdrawal from Aden and Saudi Arabia. Also on this day, Home Office ministers announce a new Criminal Justice Bill, which includes a whole raft of new measures. They include a ban on ex-convicts serving on criminal juries, provision for the suspension of sentences, the ending of corporal punishment in prisons, and most significant of all, majority verdicts will be accepted in courts, when unanimous decisions are unachievable.

27th – Brian Epstein, the manager of the Beatles, is found dead, after an apparent overdose of sleeping pills. The homosexual entrepreneur's role in the Beatles had been significantly curtailed by the group's decision to stop touring twelve months ago. He also suffered from depression. Whether Epstein's death was accidental or suicide is open to question. Nevertheless, the Beatles are staggered by the news which reaches them in Bangor, north Wales, where they are attending five days of lectures and meditation from the Maharishi Mahesh Yogi.

28th – Herbert Bowden is appointed as chairman of the Independent Television Authority.

30th – The Chinese authorities forbid all members of Peking's British Mission from leaving China, without official permission. This development comes one day after extraordinary skirmishes between police in London and Chinese diplomats.

31st – Woburn Abbey's three-day 'Festival of the Flower Children' draws to a close, bringing the curtain down on a remarkable flower-power, summer of love.

SEPTEMBER

4th – The jury at the inquest into the death of Joe Orton are informed that he was hammered to death by Kenneth Halliwell. Meanwhile, the British Broadcasting Corporation recruits seventeen former 'pirates' (including Tony Blackburn and John Peel) for its radio stations.

8th – It is revealed that the relatives of the Aberfan avalanche victims are to be awarded five thousand pounds each as 'compensation'.

11th – The Conservative Party states that Edward du Cann will be replaced as Party Chairman by Anthony Barber.

18th – County champions for the second successive year, Yorkshire county cricket club decline an invitation to participate in a winter tour of Rhodesia. Also on this day, nuclear physicist, Sir John Douglas Cockcroft, dies at the age of seventy. Cockcroft shared the 1951 Nobel Prize with E.T.S Walton, and was directly involved in Britain's first nuclear power programmes.

20th – An estimated one hundred thousand people flock to Clydebank docks, to watch Queen Elizabeth II launch her name-sake, a £29 million Cunard liner.

21st – The Labour government's considerable parliamentary majority is reduced by four after the Conservative Party triumphs in by-elections at Cambridge and Walthamstow, in London's east end.

25th – Britain, France and West Germany bury their historical differences and sign an agreement to co-operate on a proposed 'Airbus' airliner.

27th – One week after the QE2 takes to the water, the Queen Mary arrives at Southampton, at the completion of her last transatlantic voyage.

30th – BBC Radio's new stations One, Two, Three, and Four begin broadcasting in place of the now defunct Light and Third Programmes, and the Home Service. The first track played on Radio One by disc jockey, Tony Blackburn, is 'Flowers In The Rain' by Midlands group, The Move.

OCTOBER

1st – Jim Clark fails to add to his two World Drivers' Championship titles, but he still manages to race to victory in the United States Grand Prix.

5th – The British Lawn Tennis Association plans to scrap the distinction between amateur and professional tennis competitors.

8th – Following his stint at the Gordonstoun private school, eighteen-year-old Prince Charles starts his studies at Trinity College, Cambridge University. Meanwhile, former Labour Prime Minister, Clement Richard Attlee (the first Earl Attlee) dies at the age of eighty-four. Attlee led the Labour Party from 1935 to 1955, serving also as Winston Churchill's Deputy Prime Minister during the Second World War.

9th – Rootes motor vehicle manufacturers reveal the production of the new Sunbeam Rapier. Also on this day, the Road Safety Act comes into force.

10th – Six undergraduate students at Oxford University are suspended for drug abuse.

12th – A BEA Comet aircraft crashes less than two hundred miles west of the Mediterranean island of Cyprus, causing the deaths of more than sixty people. Meanwhile, Dr. Desmond Morris's new study of man, entitled 'The Naked Ape', describes man (and woman) as "the sexiest primate alive".

19th – The bank rate increases by half of one per cent, to six per cent.

25th – A new foot-and-mouth epidemic originates reportedly in Oswestry, Wales. Also on this day, the Medical Termination of Pregnancy Bill (otherwise known as the Abortion Bill) completes its passage through parliament.

27th – The controversial Abortion Bill comes into force.

30th – Old age pensions and other benefits are increased. Meanwhile, not to be outdone by Mick and Keith, Rolling Stones' guitarist, Brian Jones, is sentenced to nine months in prison, following a drug bust on May the 10th.

31st – The Queen Mary departs the port of Southampton for the last time, en route to Long Beach, California. The talented, but increasingly fragile Brian Jones is released on bail, while a psychiatric report is compiled.

NOVEMBER

2nd – Winifred Ewing becomes the first Scottish Nationalist member of parliament since 1945, when she triumphs in the Hamilton by-election contest.

4th – A Spanish airliner crashes near London, causing almost forty fatalities.

5th – A train crash at Hither Green in south-east London results in the deaths of more than fifty people, while a further ninety are injured.

7th – Hugh Scanlon is elected as the new leader of the engineering trade union, the AEU.

8th – The British Broadcasting Corporation's first local radio station, Radio Leicester, begins broadcasting on the airwaves.

9th – The bank rate increases a further half a per cent to 6.5 %. Also on this day, Bernard Haitink presides over his first concert as the principal conductor of the London Philharmonic Orchestra.

10th – The Countryside Bill, which permits local authorities to create Country Parks, receives the approval of the House of Commons.

13th – It is reported that Britain has been the recipient of £250 million in international credits in an attempt to strengthen pound sterling.

14th – The Queen pays a state visit to the Mediterranean island of Malta. Meanwhile, disgraced fugitive, Kim Philby, gives his first interview to west European journalists in his adopted city of Moscow.

19th – Harold Wilson is obliged to give a special television broadcast in which he attempts to re-assure the British people that the increase in the bank rate to eight per cent and the devaluation of the pound against the dollar by 14.3 per cent are no cause for concern. In explaining devaluation, Wilson states that it does not mean "the pound...in your pocket...has been devalued." Nevertheless, Britain's recent financial crisis calls into question the political future of James Callaghan, the Chancellor of the Exchequer.

21st – The government releases figures regarding the cull of farm animals, apparently made necessary by the foot-and-mouth explosion. 134,000 livestock have now been 'put to sleep', whilst the scourge of farming now rears its ugly head in Cheshire, Northamptonshire, and Shropshire.

23rd – The 'Last Exit To Brooklyn' publication is deemed obscene.

27th – An eight-week unofficial London dock strike is halted. Also on this day, President de Gaulle vetoes Britain's proposed membership of the Common Market.

28th – All horse-racing events are suspended as a consequence of the foot-and-mouth crisis in the British countryside.

29th – James Callaghan, who had previously described the possible option of devaluation as "a flight into escapism" has been relieved of his duties as the Chancellor of the Exchequer. His replacement, Roy Jenkins, the Home Secretary, swaps ministerial portfolios with the outgoing economic 'supremo'.

30th – With trouble-spot Aden becoming part of the People's Republic of South Yemen, the last British soldiers leave, ending British involvement in the port city since 1839.

DECEMBER

1st – Tony O'Connor makes history by becoming Britain's first black principal, at Warley School in Worcestershire.

4th – Britain decides to ban imports of meat from countries affected by the foot-and-mouth virus.

10th – Britons Ronald Norrish and Sir George Porter are recipients of Nobel Prizes for chemistry in an awards ceremony in Stockholm, Sweden.

11th – The world's first supersonic airliner, Concorde, an impressive memorial to Anglo-French manufacturing, makes its first appearance, when the big bird is rolled out of its hangar, at Toulouse, in southern France.

12th – While the Rolling Stones' new psychedelic album, 'Their Satanic Majesties' Request', perches uncomfortably in a lofty chart position, one of the satanic majesties, Brian Jones, escapes a custodial sentence, but is fined one thousand pounds and placed on probation for the possession of illegal drugs.

17th – Alec Rose, a greengrocer by trade, completes his 14,500 mile solo voyage from Britain to Australia.

18th – Notorious defector, Kim Philby, is hailed as a hero in the Soviet Union.

20th – Britain and Egypt bury their previous differences and resume diplomatic relations.

21st – The premiere takes place in London of 'Half A Sixpence', starring former pop idol Tommy Steele.

26th – The Beatles' latest film, entitled 'Magical Mystery Tour', is broadcast on BBC1. The consensus of opinion is that although the music is still magical, the film (with no apparent plot) is at best something of a mystery. Paul McCartney appears on the *David Frost Show* the next day to defend the film, which was shot in the weeks following the death of Brian Epstein.

THE NUMBER-ONE HIT SINGLES OF 1967

I'm A Believer by *The Monkees*
This Is My Song by *Petula Clark*
Release Me by *Engelbert Humperdinck*
Somethin' Stupid by *Nancy and Frank Sinatra*
Puppet On A String by *Sandie Shaw*
Silence Is Golden by *The Tremeloes*
A Whiter Shade Of Pale by *Procol Harum*
All You Need Is Love by *The Beatles*
San Francisco (Be Sure To Wear Flowers In Your Hair) by *Scott McKenzie*
The Last Waltz by *Engelbert Humperdinck*
Massachusetts by *The Bee Gees*
Baby, Now That I've Found You by *The Foundations*
Let The Heartaches Begin by *Long John Baldry*
Hello Goodbye by *The Beatles*

1968

JANUARY

1st – Cecil Day Lewis fills the vacant position of Poet Laureate, a post previously held by John Masefield, from 1930 to his death last May, at the age of 88. Also on this day, five typists employed at Colt Heating and Ventilation in Surbiton, south London launch a 'I'm Backing Britain' campaign. Politicians and the press are quick to jump on the women's bandwagon.

14th – Malcolm Muggeridge stands down as the rector of Edinburgh University, in protest at plans to make the contraceptive pill available to students.

15th – Twenty people have been killed, apparently by hurricane-force winds which have terrorised Scotland in particular. Meanwhile, a new proposed piece of legislation is published which will render "irretrievable breakdown of marriage" the sole justification for a divorce.

16th – Harold Wilson announces cuts in public spending, to the dismay of some of his party members.

17th – Leyland motors and the British Motor Corporation reveal their intention to merge, under the title of the British Leyland Motor Corporation. Also on this day, more than forty Labour members of parliament refuse to support their own government's spending cuts, estimated to be over £700 million.

20th – Hastings in Sussex provides the venue for what would prove to be the last concert appearance by the original Pink Floyd, featuring their wayward genius, Syd Barrett. Barrett's increasingly erratic behaviour, a consequence of the consumption of 'acid' and other hallucinogenics, obliges the band to appoint David Gilmour as Barrett's replacement.

23rd – The Port of London states that it intends to close London Docks and sell St. Katherine Docks to the Greater London Council.

25th – Charlie Wilson, the fugitive great train robber, is arrested in Canada.

26th – Westminster Bank and the National Provincial Bank announce their decision to amalgamate as NatWest, which will become Britain's largest bank.

31st – The Indian Ocean island of Mauritius becomes independent of Britain, following days of race riots. Meanwhile, the Prime Minister absents himself from a meeting of the Labour parliamentary party, which suspends 24 rebel MPs. Also on this day, an announcement is made that 28-year-old former Cambridge University graduate, Trevor Nunn, will succeed Peter Hall as the director of the Royal Shakespeare Company.

FEBRUARY

4th – More than ninety Kenyan Asian refugees arrive in the United Kingdom.

5th – Nineteen Hull trawlermen are feared dead, after their boat sinks off Iceland's coast.

13th – It is reported that between 1,000 to 1,500 Kenyan Asians are migrating each week to Britain.

15th – The Royal Navy's first Polaris missile is successfully tested in the Atlantic Ocean.

17th – Sir Donald Wolfit dies at the age of 66. Wolfit formed his own Shakespeare Repertory touring company in 1937.

19th – The government publishes immigration statistics, which reveal that over sixty thousand people migrated to Britain from the Commonwealth last year, an increase of eleven thousand on immigration from the Commonwealth in 1966. Meanwhile, an anti-theft campaign is launched by the Home Office. It is entitled "Watch Out! There's A Thief About".

20th – The House of Commons approves a bill to increase National Insurance rates and end free milk provision in secondary schools. Nevertheless, almost fifty Labour members of parliament join forces with the Conservative opposition in refusing to vote in favour of the proposed legislation. Also on this day, England cricket international, Fred Titmus, loses four toes in a boating accident in Barbados, during England's winter tour of the West Indies. Meanwhile, film director, Anthony Asquith dies at the age of 65. Asquith directed films such as 'Pygmalion' (1938), 'The Winslow Boy'(1948), and 'The Importance of Being Earnest'(1952).

22nd – New Home Secretary, James Callaghan, announces new legislation aimed at restricting the migration to Britain of Commonwealth citizens with British passports.

23rd – The House of Commons votes in favour of the Theatres Bill, which will nullify the Lord Chamberlain's censorship powers.

26th – A blaze in a mental hospital results in the deaths of twenty-two people.

MARCH

1st – Royal Assent is granted to the Commonwealth Immigrants Bill.

2nd – A goal from future England international, Terry Cooper, provides Don Revie's Leeds United with a 1–0 victory against Arsenal in the English League Cup final at Wembley. Both clubs would return for another cup final four years later, which also produces the same result.

15th – Michael Stewart is re-instated as Foreign Secretary. He should prove a safer pair of hands than the outgoing George Brown, whose tempestuous relationship with his own cabinet colleagues, not to mention his fondness for alcohol, culminated in his almost inevitable resignation today.

17th – An anti-Vietnam War demonstration takes place in Trafalgar Square, London, attended by an estimated eighty thousand people. Trouble erupts however when protesters attempt to march on the American Embassy in Grosvenor Square. As a consequence, ninety policemen are injured and three hundred arrests are made.

19th – Roy Jenkins's first budget as the new Chancellor of the Exchequer increases purchase tax and raises the duty on petroleum, spirits, cigarettes, and gambling.

21st – The government is encouraged by statistics which reveal that road deaths fell by almost 25% in the first three months after compulsory breath tests were introduced. Another source of good news is a reduction in the bank rate to 7.5 per cent.

27th – New Foreign Secretary, Michael Stewart, maintains that sovereignty of the Falkland Islands will not be surrendered without the consent of the local population.

28th – The Conservative Party make further in-roads into Labour's large parliamentary majority, by winning four by-elections, three of which are gains of former Labour Party seats.

29th – Rolls-Royce are successful in obtaining a £150 million order for RB2-11 engines from Lockheed, which is Britain's largest aviation contract.

30th – Jump jockey Brian Fletcher guides Red Alligator to victory in the Aintree Grand National.

APRIL

3rd – A white paper is published which recommends a 3.5 per cent ceiling on wage increases.

5th – Barbara Castle is appointed to oversee the new Department of Employment and Productivity.

7th – Thirty-two year-old Jim Clark's glittering career is tragically cut short, when the racing driver is instantly killed in a Formula Two race at Hockenheim, in West Germany. Clark had won 25 grand prix races and two world championships in seven seasons.

9th – The Race Relations Bill is published in parliament.

16th – Britain withdraws from participation in the European Launcher Development Organisation, a new space project.

18th – It is reported that American oil tycoon, Robert McCullough, has purchased London Bridge for one million pounds.

20th – 122 people are killed when a Boeing 707 aircraft, bound for London, crashes in South Africa.

21st – Enoch Powell, the Conservative Shadow Minister of Defence, creates a political earthquake with a speech in Birmingham that warns of the perils of further immigration. According to Powell, Britain is a nation "busily engaged in heaping up its own funeral pyre." The public response to this speech is likely to be polarised.

23rd – The first decimal coins appear in circulation, for five New Pence (1/-) and ten New Pence (2/-).

26th – Britain's largest drugs haul takes place in London, when police officers seize LSD with a street-market value of £1.5 million.

MAY

2nd – Britain's first liver transplant is completed at a hospital in Cambridge.

3rd – Another medical first is achieved when Donald Ross and surgical staff at the National Heart Hospital, Marylebone, preside over the heart transplant of a 45-year-old patient. How the new heart behaves in the next fortnight is crucial.

6th – Enoch Powell may now be 'persona non grata' in Edward Heath's shadow cabinet, but a Gallup opinion poll indicates that almost 75% of British people share Powell's anxieties about continued rates of immigration.

8th – Reggie and Ronnie Kray are arrested again by the police. Joining them in custody is their brother, Charlie, and eighteen other suspected villains.

9th – All 21 police detainees are charged with a number of offences, including fraud and even conspiracy to murder.

10th – It is revealed that the ten shilling note is to go out of circulation, to be replaced by a seven-sided 50 New Pence coin.

16th – Britain's first lung transplant takes place. The patient, Alex Smith, is only fifteen years old. Also on this day, a block of flats in Newham, east London, called Ronan Point, collapses, killing three people. This tragedy calls into question the safety of prefabricated slabs.

18th – An extra-time goal from future England centre-forward Jeff Astle secures a 1–0 FA Cup final triumph by West Bromwich Albion against the Toffees of Everton.

22nd – Bobby Charlton nets a record 45th goal for England in a 3–1 home win over Sweden. His Manchester United team-mate, Alex Stepney, makes his only international appearance 'between the sticks', while Tottenham Hotspur's Cyril Knowles wins his first cap.

26th – Graham Hill drives to victory in the Monaco Grand Prix.

28th – Young lung transplant patient, Alex Smith dies.

29th – Sir Ivor wins the Epsom Derby, providing owner Mr. R Guest with his second triumph and flat jockey Lester Piggott with his fourth victory in this classic. Another monumental sporting milestone is achieved later that evening, several miles further north, at Wembley stadium, where Matt Busby's Manchester United defeat Benfica of Portugal 4–1 after extra-time. Bobby Charlton scores twice, while George Best and Brian Kidd also find the back of the net, to secure the first triumph by an English club in the European Champions' Cup.

30th – At the end of a month of European student uprisings, students at the Hornsey College of Art in north London engage in a sit-in protest.

JUNE

7th – Manchester United manager, Matt Busby, is awarded a knighthood.

8th – Forty-year-old James Earl Ray, masquerading as Ramon George Sneyd, is arrested by police officers in London, on suspicion of having murdered the American civil rights leader, Martin Luther King, on April the fourth.

10th – National Health prescription charges are introduced in Britain.

11th – Eyebrows are raised as French student agitator, Danny Cohn-Bendit, pays a short visit to London.

13th – A royal commission proposes the creation of a permanent Industrial Relations Commission.

14th – Restrictions are placed on entry into Britain by anybody associated with the rebel Rhodesian regime.

17th – Britain's first heart transplant patient, Frederick West, dies. Meanwhile, the Queen invests her son, Prince Charles, as a Knight of the Garter.

20th – Harold Wilson reveals a proposal to reform the composition and structure of the other house of parliament, the House of Lords.

24th – The National Union of Railwaymen take industrial action, in the guise of a work-to-rule, resulting in the cancellation of an estimated one thousand trains. Also on this day, melancholy comedian, Tony Hancock, commits suicide in a Sydney hotel room, at the age of forty-four. Born Anthony John Hancock, he came to fame alongside Sid James in *Hancock's Half Hour*, broadcast on radio and television.

30th – Women machine operators at the Ford car factory in Dagenham, east London abandon a strike for equal pay, but still demand that their grievances be redressed.

JULY

1st – A Nuclear Non-Proliferation Treaty is signed in London, Moscow, and Washington.

2nd – Rising star of the Labour Party, thirty-year-old Dr. David Owen is appointed as Under-Secretary for the Navy, thereby becoming the youngest member of the government.

4th – Portsmouth celebrates the return of Alec Rose, after he had steered his small boat, *Lively Lady*, through 28,500 miles of open sea, around the world.

5th – Greengrocer-cum-solo yachtsman, Alec Rose, is knighted at the age of fifty-nine.

6th – Australian Rod Laver wins the Wimbledon men's singles for the third time in eight years, when he demolishes fellow-countryman, Tony Roche, in straight sets. In the ladies' final, Billie Jean-King records her third consecutive triumph, when she defeats Australia's Judy Tegart, also in straight sets.

8th – Britain is reportedly promised 2,000 million dollars in credit by twelve countries, to revive the flagging pound.

9th – A proposed amalgamation by Barclay's, Lloyd's, and Martin's Banks is vetoed by the Monopolies Commission. Meanwhile, the Queen officiates at the opening ceremony of the new Hayward Gallery on London's South Bank.

13th – South African golfer, Gary Player, wins the British Open for the second time, after carding a total of 289, on the hugely difficult Carnoustie links golf course in Scotland.

25th – Barclay's Bank and Martin's Bank complete a merger.

31st – Hubert Selby Junior's controversial novel, 'Last Exit To Brooklyn', has its previous judgement of obscenity over-turned on appeal.

AUGUST

3rd – The Countryside Act becomes law, thereby enabling local authorities to designate country parks.

9th – A British Eagle Airways Viscount aeroplane crashes onto the Munich to Nuremberg autobahn in southern Germany, causing the deaths of almost fifty people.

18th – Colin Bland, a South Africa cricket international, is not allowed to enter Britain, because of his Rhodesian passport.

23rd – All is not well on planet Beatles, as easy-going drummer Ringo Starr storms out of recording sessions for the 'White Album', vowing not to return. He is coaxed back behind his drum kit eleven days' later. However cracks are clearly appearing, as four individuals start contemplating a career beyond the Beatles.

26th – Oxford University's Professor of Pharmacology admits that heroin addiction is now "a major emergency", as the likes of John Lennon and Keith Richard would later discover.

27th – On an uncovered pitch at The Oval in south London, Derek Underwood helps bowl England to a 226 runs victory against Australia.

28th – Basil D'Oliveira is surprisingly omitted from a cricket tour party chosen for South Africa, having recorded an innings of 158 runs against the Australians a few days earlier. It appears that D'Oliveira's colour influenced the controversial decision of the cricket selectors.

SEPTEMBER

1st – The first section of the new Victoria Line on the London Underground is opened between Walthamstow in the east end, and Highbury, in north London. The tube's newest line has reportedly cost an estimated eighty million pounds.

6th – GEC announces details of its £892 million amalgamation with English Electric.

8th – Britain's Virginia Wade causes an upset, when she defeats the local favourite, Billie Jean King, to become the first women's Open tennis champion of the United States.

11th – The epidural technique has been revealed today as a means of relieving the pain of childbirth.

13th – Despite protests from the police and retailers, the big banks announce that banking on a Saturday will not be possible from July of next year. Also on this day, the High Court of Rhodesia rules that the 1965 Constitution was legal.

15th – South-east England suffers its worst bout of flooding since 1953, resulting in hundreds of homes being evacuated.

16th – A two-tier postal service becomes operational in Britain. Consequently, a first-class letter costs 5d, while a second-class stamp can be bought for 4d.

17th – South Africa's Prime Minister, John Vorster, cancels the MCC's four-month winter tour, a day after Basil D'Oliveira had been drafted into the squad to replace the injured Tom Cartwright. According to Vorster, the cricket squad was "no longer a cricket team, but a team of troublemakers".

19th – The Labour administration reveals its intention to merge the Commonwealth Office and the Foreign Office into one government department from October.

24th – England's cricket tour of South Africa is officially called off.

26th – The Theatres Act, abolishing censorship, comes into force. Meanwhile, Jaguar motor company displays its latest model, the XJ-6 luxury saloon car.

27th – Britain's entry into the Common Market is again vetoed by France. Also on this day, the new musical 'Hair' celebrates the end of censorship by providing its west end audience with nudity, as well as obscene language.

30th – The Labour Party conference thrusts pressure on its own government by voting for an end to the imposed wage restraints.

OCTOBER

1st – The town of Coleraine, on the Causeway coast, provides the unexpected location for Northern Ireland's latest academic institution, the New University of Ulster, which becomes operational today.

2nd – Sheila Ann Thorns gives birth in Birmingham Maternity Hospital to Britain's first sextuplets. Five of the babies survive. Mrs. Thomas claims that fertility drugs may have contributed to this freak occurrence.

3rd – Booker McConnell and the Publishers' Association offer a five thousand pounds 'Booker prize' for the best British work of fiction in 1968.

6th – Captain Terence O'Neill's Northern Ireland administration is on the receiving end of worldwide condemnation at the heavy-handed response by its police force in previous days to marchers from the Northern Ireland Civil Rights Association, who were protesting in Londonderry about discrimination in employment and housing allocation. Meanwhile, British motor racing celebrates a unique triumph at the United States Grand Prix, when all three members on the podium after the race are British competitors: namely John Surtees, who finished third; Graham Hill, the runner-up; and Jackie Stewart, the winner.

9th – There is no love lost between Ian Smith and Harold Wilson. Nevertheless, both Prime Ministers attempt to patch up their considerable differences, with a fresh round of talks on board Her Majesty's Ship Fearless, at Gibraltar.

10th – The controversial Conservative, Enoch Powell MP, issues a fresh warning that new immigrants may "change the character of England."

13th – The publisher, Sir Stanley Unwin, dies at the age of eighty-three.

15th – Harold Wilson makes the House of Commons aware of his latest fruitless meeting with Ian Smith. Although Britain no longer insisted on the pre-condition of majority rule, Smith's hard-line associates are in no mood for compromise.

16th – As promised four weeks ago, the Foreign Office and the Commonwealth Office amalgamate into one government ministry. Also on this day, Robert Maxwell, a Labour member of parliament, makes a £26 million offer for purchasing the News Of The World organisation. Meanwhile, two constitutional referenda are held in the Republic of Ireland. The results indicate that sixty per cent of the voters reject the introduction of a plurality voting system to replace proportional representation.

17th – A new female joins the Labour administration, as Judith Hart is appointed as Paymaster-General.

18th – John Lennon and his new girlfriend, the Japanese artist Yoko Ono, are arrested and charged with possession of cannabis and of obstructing the police.

20th – Bud Flanagan, one half of the Flanagan and Allen comedy partnership, dies at the age of seventy-two. Born Chaim Reeven Weintrop, Flanagan appeared in the Crazy Gang, and he popularised songs such as 'Run Rabbit Run' and 'Underneath The Arches'.

23rd – Rupert Murdoch's News Limited joins the race to purchase the *News Of The World.*

25th – The Race Relations Bill receives Royal Assent.

27th – Fears of another bloody street battle are misplaced, as an estimated one quarter of a million demonstrators converge on the United States Embassy in London's Grosvenor Square, to express their opposition to American participation in the Vietnam War. Only a few arrests were necessary.

31st – The Pregnancy Advisory Service is launched, with chairman Alan Golding assuring women that a new clinic opening shortly in London would provide sympathetic treatment and help for anyone seeking a legal termination.

NOVEMBER

1st – The Family Law Reform Bill is published. It proposes, amongst other things, to lower the adult age thresh-hold from 21 to eighteen years of age.

3rd – A mixed year for British motor racing ends with Graham Hill crowned as world champion for the second time, following his triumph at the Mexico Grand Prix. This is some consolation for the loss of Jim Clark, who was tragically killed earlier in the year.

6th – More than two thousand jobs are lost, after British Eagle airline ceases to function.

8th – The one remaining fugitive from the great train robbery, Bruce Reynolds, is captured by the police.

9th – Previously called the New Yardbirds, an emerging quartet of rock musicians perform at the Roundhouse, London, under the new title of Led Zeppelin. The group's singer, Robert Plant, marks this historic day by getting married.

14th – Edward Heath chooses a new Shadow Transport Minister. She is called Margaret Thatcher.

17th – Artist and author, Mervyn Laurence Peake, dies at the age of fifty-seven.

18th – A blaze in a Glasgow warehouse results in the deaths of at least twenty people.

22nd – The Unionist-dominated Northern Ireland administration attempts to placate the Civil Rights Association with a new package of reforms.

24th – Lord Chalfont makes history as the first government minister to visit the Falkland Islands.

26th – The Race Relations Act becomes law. Also on this day, the Royal Albert Hall, in central London, is the venue for the last concert performance by the power trio, super-group Cream. Too much internal disharmony decreed that this group's existence would be short-lived.

28th – John Lennon pleads guilty to possessing cannabis, to protect Yoko Ono from possible deportation. Consequently, he is fined £150. Meanwhile, children's author, Enid Mary Blyton, dies at the age of 71.

30th – The Trades Description Act becomes law. Also on this day, the centre of Armagh is seized by loyalist extremists, as sectarian hostilities escalate in the 'six counties'.

DECEMBER

6th – Alleged racist agitator, Enoch Powell, is banned by the Conservative Party leadership from delivering a proposed speech on Rhodesia. Party chiefs fear a 'rivers of blood' repeat show.

8th – The Royal Naval Dockyard in Singapore is formally handed over to the Singapore government.

16th – Students at the University of Bristol call a halt to their eleven-day, sit-in protest.

17th – Eleven-year-old Mary Flora Bell is sentenced to life imprisonment for the strangulation of two small boys. The presiding judge at her trial laments the absence of a "hospital suitable for this girl", who is regarded as mentally unstable, rather than an evil killer.

19th – Colin Davis is nominated as Georg Solti's replacement as director of the Royal Opera House.

25th – At the end of a year of racial tension, arising out of the issue of Commonwealth immigration, the Queen's televised Christmas broadcast appeals for racial tolerance.

29th – The QE2 ocean liner is still deemed unfit for travel, thereby prompting Cunard to postpone the ship's maiden voyage.

THE NUMBER-ONE HIT SINGLES OF 1968

The Ballad Of Bonnie And Clyde by *Georgie Fame*
Everlasting Love by *The Love Affair*
Mighty Quinn by *Manfred Mann*
Cinderella Rockefella by *Esther and Abi Ofarim*
The Legend Of Xanadu by *Dave Dee, Dozy, Beaky, Mick, and Titch*
Lady Madonna by *The Beatles*
Congratulations by *Cliff Richard*
What A Wonderful World/Cabaret by *Louis Armstrong*
Young Girl by *Gary Puckett and The Union Gap*
Jumpin' Jack Flash by *The Rolling Stones*
Baby Come Back by *The Equals*
I Pretend by *Des O'Connor*
Mony Mony by *Tommy James and The Shondells*
Fire by *The Crazy World of Arthur Brown*
Do It Again by *The Beach Boys*
I've Gotta Get A Message To You by *The Bee Gees*
Hey Jude by *The Beatles*
Those Were The Days by *Mary Hopkin*
With A Little Help From My Friends by *Joe Cocker*
The Good, The Bad, And The Ugly
by *Hugo Montenegro and his orchestra*
Lily The Pink by *The Scaffold*

1969

JANUARY

1st – Sir Learie Constantine makes history, by becoming Britain's first coloured life peer on this day. Also on this day, it is claimed that Rupert Murdoch's News Limited, assisted by the Carr family, have successfully prevented Robert Maxwell's Pergamon Press from purchasing the *News Of The World* newspaper. Meanwhile, it is reported that the removal of trading licences for Asians in Kenya will lead to a large influx of Kenyan Asians in to Britain in the near future.

2nd – Leading loyalist, the Reverend Ian Paisley, and his supporters, are besieged at the Guildhall in Londonderry by nationalist opponents who demand "We want Paisley". The mob set fire to his car and hurl various missiles at the building. Tensions are running extremely high, as a civil rights march makes its way through Ulster.

4th – An airliner crashes into houses, not far from Gatwick Airport, resulting in almost fifty deaths. Also on this day, a loyalist mob ambushes the civil rights march at Burntollet bridge, near Londonderry. The Royal Ulster Constabulary is accused of failing to protect the marchers against their attackers.

6th – Police reservists, entitled the 'B Specials', are deployed to assist the regular police force, the Royal Ulster Constabulary, as sectarian tension persists.

10th – The Home Office Advisory Committee on Drug Dependence, under the supervision of Lady Wootton of Abinger, urges the need for a new law, which differentiates between 'hard' drugs (such as heroin) and 'soft' drugs (such as cannabis). Their report, issued today, advises less harsh criminal penalties for the likes of cannabis smokers.

11th – Richmal Crompton Lamburn dies at the age of 78. Subsequently known as Richmal Crompton, she created William, the scruffy, adventurous schoolboy, who was always in trouble. Altogether, she wrote more than thirty William novels.

12th – Police in London are required to cope with an estimated four thousand protesters, who attempt to 'invade' South Africa House and Rhodesia House.

14th – Manchester United's Scottish manager, Sir Matt Busby, announces his retirement, although he will remain on the club's payroll, in a more exalted capacity.

15th – Further problems with the ocean liner's turbines causes more cancellation for planned sailings on the QE2.

17th – 'In Place Of Strife', Barbara Castle's White Paper on the running sore of industrial relations, is published.

23rd – James Callaghan, the Home Secretary, insists that the current penalties for cannabis possession will not be downgraded, in light of the recent report.

24th – The Ford motor company reveals the new Capri, the latest sports saloon vehicle.

27th – The House of Commons reinforces the Home Secretary's view that proposed alterations to laws on cannabis possession should be ignored. Also on this day, loyalist hardliner, the Reverend Ian Paisley, is sentenced to three months' imprisonment for unlawful assembly. Meanwhile, an estimated one thousand students from the London School of Economics attempt to create an 'LSE in exile', by occupying the University of London union buildings. They are eventually evicted by the college rugby team.

30th – The Beatles, currently enduring less than harmonious recording sessions for the Get Back project, perform a hastily organised, open-air concert on the rooftop of the Apple building in central London. The surrounding area is thrown into a bemused standstill. John Lennon ends the proceedings by expressing "I hope we passed the audition." Also on this day, the Home Secretary orders a ban on the immigration of fiancés of Commonwealth citizens. Meanwhile, the longest--running radio show on the BBC, 'The Dales', is to finish its broadcasts at the end of April. Meanwhile, the High Court slaps a one week ban on thirteen student agitators from entering the London School of Economics, without official permission.

FEBRUARY

2nd – Boris Karloff dies, aged eighty-one. Born in Dulwich, south London, his real name was William Henry Pratt. 'Karloff' was a character actor, noted mainly for his roles in horror films, after his magnificent performance as the monster in 'Frankenstein' (1931).

3rd – Student protest at the London School of Economics prompts the director of this controversial academic institution to close it for the "immediate future". Also on this day, Captain Terence O'Neill announces that new elections for the Stormont parliament will be held in three weeks' time.

11th – Approximately one thousand, six hundred women employees at the Ford motor company celebrate being awarded the same wages as their male counterparts.

12th – Harold Wilson arrives in Bonn for talks with Dr. Kiesinger, the Chancellor of the Federal Republic of Germany. Wilson receives a hostile reception from African students, who chant "Wilson, murderer" for Britain's opposition to the breakaway Biafra state.

13th – A report is published by B.D. Bavister and R.G. Edwards of the Physiological laboratory at Cambridge University, which reveals that human eggs taken from women volunteers, have been fertilised in test-tubes outside the body.

14th – Marty Feldman is named as the television personality of 1968.

18th – Bee Gee member, Maurice Gibb, marries a fellow singer, Glaswegian pop star, Lulu.

20th – Lloyd's of London announce their intention to admit females from the beginning of next year.

23rd – Former England test batsman, the Reverend David Sheppard, prepares to start a new innings as the Bishop of Woolwich. Meanwhile, a new educational programme is broadcast on BBC2, presented by the art historian, Sir Kenneth Clark, called Civilisation.

24th – Harold Wilson plays host to new American President, the Republican, Richard Nixon, who pays a quick visit to London. Also on this day, elections are held for the Northern Ireland parliament at Stormont. Terence O'Neill has been awarded a fresh mandate to govern, but a substantial vote for the Reverend Ian Paisley is a major source of concern for the Unionist Party.

27th – The Trades Union Congress appoints Vic Feather as its acting general secretary.

MARCH

2nd – Concorde, the trophy of Anglo-French co-operation, takes to the skies on its maiden journey.

4th – Guilty verdicts are delivered upon Reggie and Ronnie Kray, and four associates, at the Old Bailey, London, for the murders of George Cornell and Jack 'The Hat' McVitie.

5th – The 35-year-old terrible twins, Ronald and Reginald Kray, are sentenced to life imprisonment, on the understanding that they serve a minimum of thirty years. Their brother, Charles, is also sent to prison for a lesser term, for a lesser offence.

7th – The Queen officiates at the opening of the new Victoria tube line, which extends from Victoria, in central London, east to Walthamstow.

11th – Science-fiction writer, John Wyndham, dies at the age of 65. Born John Wyndham Parkes Lucas Beynon Harris, his works included 'Day of the Triffids' (1951), 'The Chrysalids' (1955), and 'The Midwych Cuckoos' (1957).

12th – It is a day of mixed fortunes for the Beatles. George Harrison and his wife Pattie are busted for cannabis possession, while Paul McCartney marries Linda Louise Eastman at Marylebone Register Office in central London. Also on this day, Geoff Hurst records his first England hat-trick since the World Cup final, as Wembley is the venue for a 5-0 thrashing of France.

19th – No resistance was offered from the so-called Republican Defence Force, as Royal Marines and British paratroopers landed safely ashore on Anguilla, in the Caribbean. An "orderly administration" has been promised by the invaders.

22nd – The London Underground is on the receiving end of soccer hooligan misbehaviour, which causes considerable damage.

29th – Highland Wedding arrives home first in the Aintree Grand National steeplechase.

31st – A truce is signed between the rebel leaders of the island of Anguilla and Britain. Also on this day, with pilots taking industrial action because of concerns over pay and productivity, all BOAC flights are cancelled.

APRIL

7th – A burglary at the home of Sir Roland Penrose, a Tate Gallery trustee, results in the theft of 25 paintings, estimated at three hundred thousand pounds.

9th – The maiden flight of the British-built Concorde takes place. Meanwhile, Sikh bus drivers in Wolverhampton win a two-year fight to be permitted to wear their turbans while driving a bus.

18th – Twenty-two-year-old Bernadette Devlin causes something of a surprise, when she wins the Mid-Ulster by-election, with a majority in excess of four thousand.

20th – The O'Neill Unionist government announces that British Army units have been requested to come and guard important installations in Northern Ireland.

22nd – Robin Knox-Johnston wins a single-handed, round-the-world yacht race. Also on this day, after a delay of four months, caused by technical difficulties, the QE2 finally departs Southampton on her maiden commercial voyage.

24th – A new 1500 Austin saloon car, entitled the Maxi, is revealed by British Leyland.

25th – 'The Dales', BBC's longest-running radio programme, is broadcast for the last time. Meanwhile, continuing sectarian tension and unrest in Northern Ireland has prompted the announcement that five hundred more soldiers will be posted there.

26th – Manchester City win the FA Cup for a fourth time – courtesy of a 1–0 win against Leicester City. North of the border, Glasgow Celtic cruise to an emphatic 4–0 win against Glasgow Rangers in the Scottish Cup final, thereby securing 'the treble'. Amongst the goal-scorers is future Celtic manager, Billy McNeill. A mere 132,870 are in attendance at Hampden Park to see what would be the last appearance in a Rangers shirt by young Alex Ferguson.

28th – The Monopolies Commission states that any shop should be permitted to sell alcohol, subject to the granting of a licence for 'off-sales'. Also on this day, Unionist Party 'supremo', Terence O'Neill resigns as party leader.

29th – Captain Terence O'Neill predictably stands down as Northern Ireland's Prime Minister, after a tenure of six years. Divisions within Unionism as well as increasing trouble in the 'six counties' has prompted his resignation.

MAY

1st – Northern Ireland has a new Prime Minister: Major James Chichester-Clark, who yesterday defeated Brian Faulkner by seventeen votes to sixteen, to succeed Terence O'Neill as the leader of the Ulster Unionist Party. One of the decisive votes came from the departing O'Neill, who voted against Faulkner, his long-standing critic.

5th – The government announces that National Health Service charges for dental treatment and spectacles will increase.

6th – A wide-ranging amnesty in Northern Ireland is declared, which among other things, will allow for the prison release of Ian Paisley, a fierce critic of the Unionist Party.

8th – The omens are not good for the Labour government, as the Conservative Party achieve numerous gains in the local government borough elections.

12th – The voting age in Britain is lowered to eighteen. Meanwhile, Scotland bounces back from a 4–1 drubbing at Wembley against England a couple of days earlier, to demolish Cyprus 8–0 in a World Cup football qualifying match. Two Celtic players and a pair of Rangers players put their differences aside to score seven of the goals. Most prominent among the goal-scorers is Colin Stein of Glasgow Rangers, who finds the net no fewer than four times, having scored five times in Scotland's five most recent contests. Nevertheless, Scotland fails to qualify for the finals in Mexico.

13th – There are reports of a rift in the Labour cabinet, resulting from James Callaghan's opposition to Barbara Castle's White Paper, In Place Of Strife. The Employment Secretary's document has provoked the hostility of the trade union movement, with Callaghan and other Labour left-wing MPs expressing their displeasure. Having incurred the wrath of Harold Wilson, Callaghan is 'persona non grata' in the cabinet.

18th – The reigning World Drivers' Champion, Graham Hill, secures first place in the Monaco Grand Prix for an unprecedented fifth time. Also on this day, the last of thirteen Sunday broadcasts of the highly acclaimed history and culture series, 'Civilisation', presented by Sir Kenneth Clark, takes place on BBC Two.

22nd – Former middle-distance athlete, Christopher Chataway, finishes in first position in the by-election race at Chichester, on behalf of the Conservative Party.

26th – Recently married couple, John Lennon and Yoko Ono, take advantage of their celebrity status to promote their advertising campaign for peace. Consequently, they both take to their bed at the Queen Elizabeth Hotel in Montreal, Canada, for their second 'bed-in', following a previous stint at the Hilton Hotel in Amsterdam in March.

JUNE

4th – Blakeney finishes first in the 'classic' Epsom Derby, providing owner Mr. A Budgett with the first of two Derby winners.

7th – A fire overcomes the Maltings concert venue at Snape, in county Suffolk.

8th – The thorny issue of sovereignty of Gibraltar rears its ugly head again, as General Franco tries to bully the British colony with another siege.

9th – Controversial right-winger, Enoch Powell, suggests the repatriation of immigrants from Britain.

13th – The Queen's Birthday Honours List awards a Knighthood to poet John Betjeman. Other recipients of awards are Anna Neagle and Daphne du Maurier, who are allocated DBEs, while coloured cricketer Basil D'Oliveira is granted an OBE. Meanwhile, the Divorce Reform Bill continues to proceed through parliament, enabling couples to divorce with mutual consent, after two years of separation.

16th – Field Marshal Earl Harold Rupert Leofric George Alexander dies, aged 77. Earl Alexander of Tunis helped command Britain's counter-attack at El Alamein, before pushing the Germans out of north Africa. Alexander then assumed responsibility for the Allied campaign in Italy, before becoming Governor-General of Canada in 1946.

18th – The Labour government drops its plans to put legal restraints on unofficial strikes, in return for a T.U.C pledge to deal with disputes. Consequently, the Industrial Relations Bill is postponed until the next parliamentary session.

20th – It is reported that high-grade crude oil has been found on the borders of the British and Norwegian sectors of the North Sea.

25th – Veteran American tennis player, Richard 'Pancho' Gonzalez, successfully completes the longest-ever singles match at Wimbledon, when he defeats Charlie Pasarell 22–24, 1–6, 16–14, 6–3, 11–9 in a mere five hours and twelve minutes, at the age of forty-one!

26th – The Ladywood constituency returns Wallace Lawler to parliament, after his by-election victory renders him the first Birmingham Liberal Member of Parliament since the last century.

30th – 23 million viewers watch the joint BBC and ITV documentary, entitled 'Royal Family', which provides a behind-the-scenes view of the Queen and her family circle. The programme is broadcast on the eve of Prince Charles's investiture at Caernarfon castle.

JULY

1st – Despite violent opposition from Welsh nationalists, the Queen's eldest son is officially designated as the 21st Prince of Wales, at the age of twenty. Also on this day, John and Yoko Lennon, along with her daughter Kyoto and his son Julian, are injured in a car crash, whilst travelling around Scotland.

2nd – Demolition workers discover by chance the whereabouts of 25 paintings that had been stolen three months earlier from Sir Roland Penrose. Later that same day, Brian Jones goes for a midnight swim in his pool at Cotchford Farm in Sussex, but he never surfaces again. Aged only 27, Jones parted company with The Rolling Stones a few weeks earlier. Rumours abound that the versatile blond musician was murdered.

4th – Ann Jones becomes the new darling of Wimbledon, when she comes from one set down to defeat three times champion, Billie Jean King, 6–2 in the final set, thereby becoming only the second British ladies' champion since the last war. Meanwhile, General Franco 'generously' offers Spanish nationality to the people of Gibraltar.

5th – Rod Laver wins the Wimbledon men's singles for a fourth time, defeating his fellow-Australian, John Newcombe, the 1967 champion. Also in London this day, the notorious Rolling Stones perform a free concert in Hyde Park to an estimated one quarter of a million people, where new guitarist, Mick Taylor, makes his debut appearance in place of the departed Brian Jones. Butterflies are released from cages and Mick Jagger reads from Shelley's 'Adonais' in tribute to Jones.

7th – Brian Jones's premature death prompts the coroner to rule 'death by misadventure', or to be precise, an unhealthy cocktail of alcohol and drugs. However, subsequent revelations suggest something more sinister.

8th – The Church of England rejects a scheme for unity with the Methodist church. The Methodists accept their decision.

12th – A final round of seventy-two enables Tony Jacklin to become the first British golfer to win the British Open since Max Faulkner in 1951. Jacklin conquers the Lancashire links course of Lytham St. Anne's, with a total score of 280 shots.

24th – Gerald Brooke is released from imprisonment in Moscow, in an exchange for two Russian spies, who are similarly released by Britain.

30th – The High Court awards £33,600 in compensation to two boys who have suffered the consequences of the controversial thalidomide drug.

31st – Halfpennies cease to be legal tender in Britain.

AUGUST

3rd – A further eruption of street violence in Belfast necessitates the use of armoured cars to crush barricades.

8th – Britain's oldest aircraft manufacturer, Handley Page, is forced to call in the receiver, amidst financial ruin. Also on this day, the Beatles pose together for one of their last photograph sessions. The setting is the zebra crossing outside the E.M.I recording studios on Abbey Road, which is to be the title of their forthcoming album. The 'fab four' famously traverse the crossing in single file for the cover of their 'Abbey Road' album.

12th – Trouble flares in Londonderry, following the annual Apprentice Boys of Derry parade. More than one hundred people require hospital treatment after riots in the 'maiden city'.

14th – Sixteen people are killed after a bus crashes on a hill near Stanhope, in the north-east of England. Meanwhile, four hundred soldiers of the Prince of Wales's Own Yorkshire Regiment take up positions around the Bogside, Londonderry, in late afternoon.

15th – The initial reaction is one of relief and gratitude from the Roman Catholic nationalist residents, at the presence of British troops drafted in to cope with the 'Battle of the Bogside'.

16th – Irish republican areas of Belfast, notably Ardoyne and the Falls Road, have British soldiers to protect their streets from loyalist mobs. Unable to defend their own community, the I.R.A are taunted on graffiti as 'I Ran Away'.

19th – Northern Ireland's controversial police reserves, the 'B Specials', now come under the command of the British army chief, Lieutenant-General Sir Ian Freeland.

22nd – The 'B Specials' are requested to disarm. They have been criticised for not being an impartial police force, and the Roman Catholics have no confidence in them. Meanwhile, the Beatles are photographed together for the last time, in the grounds of John and Yoko's new home, Tittenhurst Park.

25th – Australia media tycoon, Rupert Murdoch, has reportedly offered to purchase 'The Sun' newspaper.

31st – An estimated 150,000 fans are in attendance at the second Isle of Wight Festival of Music. Star attraction is Bob Dylan and The Band, who entertain a crowd that includes three Beatles, their spouses, Jane Fonda, and Roger Vadim.

SEPTEMBER

2nd – The London Contemporary Dance Company kicks off its inaugural season.

3rd – The Trades Union Congress votes for the abolition of the Labour government's 1966 Prices And Incomes Act.

5th – ITV broadcasts in colour for the first time.

7th – Jackie Stewart continues the tradition of great Scottish racing drivers, by winning the Italian Grand Prix at the Monza circuit, to secure his first Formula One World Drivers' championship title.

10th – It is reported that no fewer than seven thousand soldiers are stationed in Ulster. Some of these troops start to dismantle the temporary barricades in Belfast, and establish a so-called 'peace line' in their place.

12th – The Cameron Report on the 'Disturbances in Northern Ireland' suggests that 'the troubles' have been provoked by extremists.

16th – The Biba department store for the fashion conscious, not to mention the well-to-do, opens on Kensington High Street, in west London.

18th – Lillian Board runs the eight hundred metres in a time of 2 minutes 1.4 seconds, to win gold for Britain in the European Games in Greece.

21st – The hippie commune of 144 Piccadilly is 'invaded' by an estimated two hundred police officers, who suspect the illegal possession of drugs therein. Consequently, 150 squatters are taken to a nearby police station, where thirty of them are charged.

26th – If a deal can be struck with the unions in the next two weeks, then Rupert Murdoch claims he will buy The Sun for an estimated cost of £250,000.

28th – The senior army officer in Northern Ireland, Sir Ian Freeland, denies that the new peace wall is Belfast's answer to the Berlin Wall.

OCTOBER

1st – Britain and France's big bird, Concorde 001, breaks the sound barrier for the first time.

5th – Monty Python's Flying Circus appears for the first time, as the British Broadcasting Corporation nervously grants the comedy show a late-night slot. One of the comedy team, Michael Palin, later suggests that the show's first viewers were probably burglars, insomniacs, and intellectuals.

9th – A mere three days after being appointed as Technology Minister, Labour Member of Parliament, Reg Prentice, resigns his portfolio.

10th – The Hunt Committee publishes its recommendations on policing in Northern Ireland. It advises the disarming of the Royal Ulster Constabulary and the disbandment of the 'B Specials'. The Unionist government agrees to implement the latter.

12th – Loyalist outrage at the disbandment of the B Specials has led to more street disturbances. This time, British soldiers have permission to fire back at rioters, and tear-gas is deployed against a loyalist mob in Belfast. Meanwhile, the number of troops in Ulster is now an estimated nine thousand.

14th – A new seven-sided 50 New Pence coin appears in circulation for the first time.

15th – Rupert Murdoch's proposed acquisition of The Sun newspaper is accepted by the print unions.

17th – Having previously been out of favour with his Prime Minister, James Callaghan comes in from the cold, to assume his place in Harold Wilson's 'inner cabinet'. Also on this day, the Divorce Reform Bill completes its passage through parliament, thus enabling the total breakdown of a marriage to be the sole grounds for a divorce.

21st – Leading female Conservative MP, Margaret Thatcher, is appointed by Edward Heath to the role of shadow education spokesperson.

24th – A prison riot at Parkhurst, on the Isle of Wight, results in injuries for almost fifty people. The inmates are venting their anger at the early release of the Russian spy, Peter Kroger.

27th – The Pacific and Orient passenger company announces that it will no longer provide a ferry service to India, from February of next year. Meanwhile, after two people are bitten by a dog, infected with the rabies virus, all wildlife in the surrounding area of Camberley, in Surrey, are to be destroyed, as a drastic pre-caution.

NOVEMBER

3rd – Reconstruction starts on London's National Theatre, following a century of delays and arguments.

5th – The government announces that the minimum wages of farm labourers will increase by 15/– to £13. 3*s.* –*d.* An appearance by the visiting South African Springbok rugby union team at Twickenham is disrupted by anti-apartheid protesters.

9th – Prince Philip expresses his concern that Buckingham Palace may have to be vacated, because the Queen's allowance barely meets the costs of running the palace.

10th – Sir David Rose, Guyana's Governor-General since 1966, is killed by falling scaffolding in London.

11th – The owners of the petroleum tanker, the *Torrey Canyon*, agree to pay damages to both Britain and France. As a result, each country will receive £1.5 million compensation from Barracuda Tankers.

13th – Thirty-three-year-old Mrs. Irene Mary Hanson gives birth to quintuplets. The five baby girls are apparently a product of the fertility drug, gonadotrophin.

15th – Another Springbok tour match is interrupted by anti-apartheid demonstrators, this time at Swansea, in south Wales.

19th – The House of Commons grants its approval of a new piece of legislation, which will replace Northern Ireland's B Specials with an Ulster Defence Regiment.

25th – Twelve regional radio stations have been given the green light by the government.

27th – Back on the road after an absence of three years, The Rolling Stones perform at Madison Square Gardens in New York, to promote their new album, 'Let It Bleed'.

DECEMBER

2nd – The South African rugby union team's efforts to play a match in Aberdeen are sabotaged by pitch invasions, which result in almost one hundred arrests. Also on this day, an EEC summit meeting at The Hague agrees on negotiations for a possible British entry into the Common Market.

6th – The bottom falls out of the hippie era of peace and love, as The Rolling Stones' performance at the Altamont festival in southern California descends into an orgy of violence. Over-zealous 'policing' from the Hell's Angels results in the death of a young black man, who is brutally murdered not far from the stage by Hell's Angels, wielding pool cues. Mick Jagger's pleas for the crowd to "cool it" are unheeded. The optimism generated by the Woodstock festival four months earlier is demolished, as The Rolling Stones beat a hasty retreat. It could be argued that this was the day that 'the sixties' died, or at least stopped 'swinging'.

10th – Ireland's Samuel Beckett is presented with a Nobel Prize for literature, while Britain's Sir Derek Barton receives a Nobel Prize in Stockholm, for chemistry.

12th – Bernadette Devlin, the darling of Irish nationalism or the arch-enemy of Ulster unionism, is sentenced to six months' imprisonment for incitement to riot, during August's 'battle of the Bogside'. She is however released on bail, pending an appeal.

17th – The Labour government publishes its Superannuation and Social Insurance Bill, which proposes to set up earnings-related pensions.

18th – The proposed creation of the part-time Ulster Defence Regiment completes its parliamentary passage. Meanwhile, in defiance of public opinion polls, the House of Lords follows the House of Commons, in accepting the abolition of the death penalty.

19th – It is announced that a new sterilisation clinic for men will open early next year in Birmingham, to follow the clinic in Cardiff, both of which are organised by the Family Planning Association. Apparently there is already a six-month waiting-list for the west Midlands clinic.

23rd – A reported figure of 294 people have perished in the last week, from an influenza epidemic.

26th – BBC radio's 'World at One' poll states that the current Prime Minister, Harold Wilson, is 'Man of the Decade'. His political opponent, Enoch Powell MP, comes second.

30th – Wolverhampton Council is found guilty of racial discrimination by the Race Relations Board. The sixties decade fittingly concludes with John Lennon as the British representative in a three-part ITV programme, entitled 'Man of the Decade', along with the late American President, John F. Kennedy, and China's supremo, Mao Tse Tung. The talented Beatle is a metaphor of the 1960s: colourful, controversial, larger-than-life, but ultimately unable to live up to the expectations of the peace and love idealism.

THE NUMBER-ONE HIT SINGLES OF 1969

Ob-La-Di-Ob-La-Da by *Marmalade*
Albatross by *Fleetwood Mac*
Blackberry Way by *The Move*
(If Paradise Is) Half As Nice by *Amen Corner*
Where Do You Go To My Lovely? by *Peter Sarstedt*
I Heard It Through The Grapevine by *Marvin Gaye*
The Israelites by *Desmond Dekker and The Aces*
Get Back by *The Beatles*
Dizzy by *Tommy Roe*
The Ballad Of John And Yoko by *The Beatles*
Something In The Air by *Thunderclap Newman*
Honky Tonk Women by *The Rolling Stones*
In The Year 2525 by *Zager and Evans*
Bad Moon Rising by *Creedence Clearwater Revival*
Je T'Aime...Moi Non Plus by *Jane Birkin and Serge Gainsbourg*
I'll Never Fall In Love Again by *Bobbie Gentry*
Sugar Sugar by *The Archies*
Two Little Boys by *Rolf Harris*

BRITISH AND IRISH SPORT IN THE 1960s

– APPENDIX ONE –

BRITISH OLYMPIC MEDALLISTS IN TRACK AND FIELD

1960 Rome Olympics – Peter Radford (Bronze) in Men's 100m
Peter Radford, David Jones, David Segal, Neville Whitehead (Bronze) in Men's 4x100m relay
Stanley Vickers (Bronze) in Men's 20km walk
Donald Thompson (GOLD) in Men's 50km walk
Dorothy Hyman (Silver) in Women's 100m
Dorothy Hyman (Bronze) in Women's 200m
Carol Quinton (Silver) in Women's 80m hurdles
Dorothy Shirley (Silver) in Women's high jump
1964 Tokyo Olympics – Basil Heatley (Silver) in Men's marathon
John Cooper (Silver) in Men's 400m hurdles
Maurice Herriott (Silver) in Men's 3000m steeplechase
Timothy Graham, Adrian Metcalfe, John Cooper, Robbie Brightwell (Silver) in Men's 4x400m relay
Kenneth Matthews (GOLD) in Men's 20km walk
Paul Nihill (Silver) in Men's 50km walk
Lynn Davies (GOLD) in Men's long jump
Ann Packer (Silver) in Women's 400m
Ann Packer (GOLD) in Women's 800m
Janet Simpson, Mary Rand, Daphne Arden, Dorothy Hyman (Bronze) in Women's 4x100m relay
Mary Rand (GOLD) in Women's long jump
Mary Rand (Silver) in Women's pentathlon
1968 Mexico City Olympics – David Hemery (GOLD) in Men's 400m hurdles; Lillian Board (Silver) in Women's 400m; Sheila Sherwood (Silver) in Women's long jump

– APPENDIX TWO –

ENGLISH COUNTY CRICKET IN THE 1960s

The County Championship Winners
1960 Yorkshire
1961 Hampshire
1962 Yorkshire
1963 Yorkshire
1964 Worcestershire
1965 Worcestershire
1966 Yorkshire
1967 Yorkshire
1968 Yorkshire
1969 Glamorgan

The Gillette Cup one-day finals
1963 Sussex beat Worcestershire
1964 Sussex beat Warwickshire
1965 Yorkshire beat Surrey
1966 Warwickshire beat Worcestershire
1967 Kent beat Somerset
1968 Warwickshire beat Sussex
1969 Yorkshire beat Derbyshire

The inaugural one-day Sunday League of 1969
Lancashire (winners); Hampshire (runners-up)

– APPENDIX THREE –

ENGLAND'S TEST MATCH CRICKET PERFORMANCES

1960: (away to West Indies) – won 1, drawn 4
(home to South Africa) – won 3, drawn 2
1961: (home to Australia) – won 1, drawn 2, lost 2
(away to Pakistan) – won 1
(away to India) – drawn 3, lost 2
1962: (away to Pakistan) – drawn 2
(home to Pakistan) – won 4, drawn 1
(away to Australia) – won 1, drawn 3, lost 1
1963: (away to New Zealand) – won 3
(home to West Indies) – won 1, drawn 1, lost 3
1964: (away to India) – drawn 5
(home to Australia) – drawn 4, lost 1
(away to South Africa) – won 1, drawn 4
1965: (home to New Zealand) – won 3
(home to South Africa) – drawn 2, lost 1
(away to Australia) – won 1, drawn 3, lost 1
1966: (away to New Zealand) – drawn 3
(home to West Indies) – won 1, drawn 1, lost 3
1967: (home to India) – won 3
(home to Pakistan) – won 2, drawn 1
1968: (away to West Indies) – won 1, drawn 4
(home to Australia) – won 1, drawn 3, lost 1
1969: (away to Pakistan) – drawn 3
(home to West Indies) – won 2, drawn 1
(home to New Zealand) – won 2, drawn 1

– APPENDIX FOUR –

THE BRITISH OPEN GOLF CHAMPIONS IN THE 1960s

1960: (at St. Andrews) – KDG Nagle of Australia; total score of 278
1961: (at Royal Birkdale) – A Palmer of the United States of America; total score of 284
1962: (at Troon) – A Palmer of the United States of America; total score of 276
1963: (at Royal Lytham St. Anne's) – RJ Charles of New Zealand; total score of 277
1964: (at St. Andrews) – A Lema of the United States of America; total score of 279
1965: (at Royal Birkdale) – PW Thomson of Australia; total score of 285
1966: (at Muirfield) – J Nicklaus of the United States of America; total score of 282
1967: (at Hoylake) – R de Vicenzo of Argentina; total score of 278
1968: (at Carnoustie) – GJ Player of South Africa; total score of 289
1969: (at Royal Lytham St. Anne's) – A Jacklin of Great Britain; total score of 280

– APPENDIX FIVE –

RUGBY UNION INTERNATIONALS AND THE CHALLENGE CUP FINALS

1960: (Five Nations) – 1st. England and France 7 points; 3rd. Wales 4; 4th. Scotland 2;5th. Ireland 0

1961: (Five Nations) – 1st. France 7 points;2nd. Scotland and Wales 4; 4th. England 3;5th. Ireland 2

1962: (Five Nations) – 1st. France 6 points;2nd. Scotland 5; 3rd. England and Wales 4; 5th. Ireland 1

(British Lions) – South Africa 3 Great Britain 3; in Johannesburg

South Africa 3 Great Britain 0; in Durban

South Africa 8 Great Britain 3; in Cape Town

South Africa 34 Great Britain 14; in Bloemfontein

1963: (Five Nations) – 1st. England 7 points; 2nd. France and Scotland 4; 4th. Ireland 3; 5th. Wales 2

1964: (Five Nations) – 1st. Scotland and Wales 6 points; 3rd. France 5; 4th. Ireland 2;5th. England 1

1965: (Five Nations) – 1st. Wales 6 points; 2nd. France and Ireland 5; 4th. England 3; 5th. Scotland 1

1966: (Five Nations) – 1st. Wales 6 points; 2nd. France and Scotland 5; 4th. Ireland 3; 5th. England 1

(British Lions) – Australia 8 Great Britain 11; in Sydney

Australia 0 Great Britain 31; in Brisbane

New Zealand 20 Great Britain 3; in Dunedin

New Zealand 16 Great Britain 12; in Wellington

New Zealand 19 Great Britain 6; in Christchurch

New Zealand 24 Great Britain 11; in Auckland

1967: (Five Nations) – 1st. France 6 points; 2nd. England, Ireland, and Scotland 4; 5th. Wales 2

1968: (Five Nations) – 1st. France 8 points;2nd. Ireland 5; 3rd. England 4; 4th. Wales 3; 5th. Scotland 0
(British Lions) – South Africa 25 Great Britain 20; in Pretoria
South Africa 6 Great Britain 6; in Port Elizabeth
South Africa 11 Great Britain 6; in Cape Town
South Africa 19 Great Britain 6; in Johannesburg
1969: (Five Nations) – 1st. France and Wales 6 points; 3rd. Ireland 4; 4th. England and Scotland 2

Rugby League Challenge Cup Finals (played at Wembley):
1960: Wakefield Trinity 38 Hull 5
1961: St. Helens 12 Wigan 6
1962: Wakefield Trinity 12 Huddersfield 6
1963: Wakefield Trinity 25 Wigan 10
1964: Widnes 13 Hull Kingston Rovers 5
1965: Wigan 20 Hunslet 16
1966: St. Helens 21 Wigan 2
1967: Featherstone Rovers 17 Barrow 12
1968: Leeds 11 Wakefield Trinity 10
1969: Castleford 11 Salford 6

– APPENDIX SIX –

BRITISH GRAND PRIX, AND BRITISH FORMULA 1 WORLD CHAMPIONS

1960 (at Silverstone) – 1st. Brabham (Cooper); 2nd. Surtees (Lotus); 3rd. Ireland (Lotus)

1961 (at Aintree) – 1st. von Trips (Ferrari); 2nd. P Hill (Ferrari); 3rd. Ginther (Ferrari)

1962 (at Aintree) – 1st. Clark (Lotus); 2nd. Surtees (Lola); 3rd. McLaren (Cooper)

1963 (at Silverstone) – 1st. Clark (Lotus); 2nd. Surtees (Ferrari); 3rd. G Hill (BRM)

1964 (at Brands Hatch) – 1st. Clark (Lotus); 2nd. G Hill (BRM); 3rd. Surtees (Ferrari)

1965 (at Silverstone) – 1st. Clark (Lotus); 2nd. G Hill (BRM); 3rd. Surtees (Ferrari)

1966 (at Brands Hatch) – 1st. Brabham (Brabham); 2nd. Hulme (Brabham); 3rd. G Hill (BRM)

1967 (at Silverstone) – 1st. Clark (Lotus); 2nd. Hulme (Brabham); 3rd. Amon (Ferrari)

1968 (at Brands Hatch) – 1st. Siffert (Lotus); 2nd. Amon (Ferrari); 3rd. Ickx (Ferrari)

1969 (at Silverstone) – 1st. Stewart (Matra); 2nd. Ickx (Brabham); 3rd. McLaren (McLaren)

World Formula One champions from Britain in the 1960s

1962 – Graham Hill
1963 – Jim Clark
1964 – John Surtees
1965 – Jim Clark
1968 – Graham Hill
1969 – Jackie Stewart

– APPENDIX SEVEN –

ENGLISH FOOTBALL IN THE 1960s

First Division Championship:

1960: 1st Burnley 55 points; 2nd Wolverhampton Wanderers 54 points

1961: 1st.Tottenham Hotspur 66 points;2nd.Sheffield Wednesday 58 points

1962: 1st.Ipswich Town 56 points;2nd.Burnley 53 points

1963: 1st.Everton 61 points;2nd.Tottenham Hotspur 55 points

1964: 1st.Liverpool 57 points;2nd.Manchester United 53 points

1965: 1st.Manchester United 61 points;2nd.Leeds United 61 points

1966: 1st.Liverpool 61 points;2nd.Leeds United 55 points

1967: 1st.Manchester United 60 points;2nd.Nottingham Forest 56 points

1968: 1st.Manchester City 58 points;2nd.Manchester United 56 points

1969: 1st.Leeds United 67 points;2nd.Liverpool 61 points

The FA Cup Finals (all played at Wembley):

1960 – Wolverhampton Wanderers 3 Blackburn Rovers 0

1961: Tottenham Hotspur 2 Leicester City 0

1962: Tottenham Hotspur 3 Burnley 1

1963: Manchester United 3 Leicester City 1

1964: West Ham United 3 Preston North End 2

1965: Liverpool 2 Leeds United 1 (AET)

1966: Everton 3 Sheffield Wednesday 2

1967: Tottenham Hotspur 2 Chelsea 1

1968: West Bromwich Albion 1 Everton 0 (AET)

1969: Manchester City 1 Leicester City 0

Football League Cup Finals:

1961: Aston Villa beat Rotherham United 3-2 on aggregate

1962: Norwich City beat Rochdale 4-0 on aggregate

1963: Birmingham City beat Aston Villa 3-1 on aggregate

1964: Leicester City beat Stoke City 4-3 on aggregate

1965: Chelsea beat Leicester City 3-2 on aggregate
1966: West Bromwich Albion beat West Ham United 5-3 on aggregate
1967: Queen's Park Rangers 3 West Bromwich Albion 2
1968: Leeds United 1 Arsenal 0
1969: Swindon Town 3 Arsenal 1

English teams in the European Cup:
1960: Wolverhampton Wanderers reach the quarter-finals
1961: Burnley reach the quarter-finals
1962: Tottenham Hotspur reach the semi-finals
1963: Ipswich Town lose in the first round
1964: Everton lose in the preliminary round
1965: Liverpool reach the semi-finals
1966: Manchester United reach the semi-finals
1967: Liverpool lose in the second round
1968: Manchester United beat Benfica 4-1 in the final (AET)
1969: Manchester United reach the semi-finals
1969:– Manchester City lose in the first round

England's major international matches:
1962 world cup; versus Hungary (lost 2-1)
1962 world cup; versus Argentina (won 3-1)
1962 world cup; versus Bulgaria (drew 0-0)
1962 world cup; versus Brazil (lost 3-1)
1963 versus The Rest Of The World (won 2-1)
1966 world cup; versus Uruguay (drew 0-0)
1966 world cup; versus Mexico (won 2-0)
1966 world cup; versus France (won 2-0)
1966 world cup; versus Argentina (won 1-0)
1966 world cup; versus Portugal (won 2-0)
1966 world cup final; versus West Germany (won 4-2 AET)

Personal milestones: Most league goals in a season – Jimmy Greaves (Chelsea); 41 goals in 1960-1961

European Footballer Of The Year in 1966 – Bobby Charlton (Manchester United)

– APPENDIX EIGHT –

SCOTTISH FOOTBALL IN THE 1960s

First Division Championship:
1960: 1st.Heart of Midlothian 54 points; 2nd. Kilmarnock 50 points
1961: 1st.Glasgow Rangers 51 points; 2nd.Kilmarnock 50 points
1962: 1st.Dundee 54 points; 2nd.Glasgow Rangers 51 points
1963: 1st.Glasgow Rangers 57 points; 2nd.Kilmarnock 48 points
1964: 1st.Glasgow Rangers 55 points; 2nd.Kilmarnock 49 points
1965: 1st.Kilmarnock 50 points; 2nd.Heart Of Midlothian 50 points
1966: 1st.Glasgow Celtic 57 points; 2nd.Glasgow Rangers 55 points
1967: 1st.Glasgow Celtic 58 points; 2nd.Glasgow Rangers 55 points
1968: 1st.Glasgow Celtic 63 points; 2nd.Glasgow Rangers 61 points
1969: 1st.Glasgow Celtic 54 points; 2nd.Glasgow Rangers 49 points

The FA Cup Finals (all played at Hampden Park):
1960: Glasgow Rangers 2 Kilmarnock 0
1961: Dunfermline Athletic 0 Glasgow Celtic 0
Dunfermline Athletic 2 Glasgow Celtic 0
1962: Glasgow Rangers 2 St. Mirren 0
1963: Glasgow Celtic 1 Glasgow Rangers 1
Glasgow Rangers 3 Glasgow Celtic 0
1964: Glasgow Rangers 3 Dundee 1
1965: Glasgow Celtic 3 Dunfermline Athletic 2
1966: Glasgow Celtic 0 Glasgow Rangers 0
Glasgow Rangers 1 Glasgow Celtic 0
1967: Glasgow Celtic 2 Aberdeen 0
1968: Dunfermline Athletic 3 Heart of Midlothian 1
1969: Glasgow Celtic 4 Glasgow Rangers 0

Football League Cup Finals:

1960: Heart of Midlothian 2 Third Lanark 1
1961: Glasgow Rangers 2 Kilmarnock 0
1962: Glasgow Rangers 1 Heart of Midlothian 1
Glasgow Rangers 3 Heart of Midlothian 1
1963: Heart of Midlothian 1 Kilmarnock 0
1964: Glasgow Rangers 5 Greenock Morton 0
1965: Glasgow Rangers 2 Glasgow Celtic 1
1966: Glasgow Celtic 2 Glasgow Rangers 1
1967: Glasgow Celtic 1 Glasgow Rangers 0
1968: Glasgow Celtic 5 Dundee 3
1969: Glasgow Celtic 6 Hibernian 2

Scottish teams in the European Cup:
1960: Glasgow Rangers reach the semi-finals
1961: Heart of Midlothian lose in the preliminary round
1962: Glasgow Rangers reach the quarter-finals
1963: Dundee reach the semi-finals
1964: Glasgow Rangers lose in the preliminary round
1965: Glasgow Rangers reach the quarter-finals
1966: Kilmarnock lose in the first round
1967: Glasgow Celtic beat Inter Milan 2-1 in the final
1968: Glasgow Celtic lose in the first round
1969: Glasgow Celtic reach the quarter-finals

Scotland's matches against the 'Auld Enemy':
1960: Scotland 1 England 1 (Leggat)
1961: England 9 Scotland 3 (Mackay, Wilson, Quinn)
1962: Scotland 2 England 0 (Wilson, Caldow)
1963: England 1 Scotland 2 (Baxter 2)
1964: Scotland 1 England 0 (Gilzean)
1965: England 2 Scotland 2 (Law, St. John)
1966: Scotland 3 England 4 (Law, Johnston 2)
1967: England 2 Scotland 3 (Law, Lennox, McCalliog)
1968: Scotland 1 England 1 (Hughes)
1969: England 4 Scotland 1 (Stein)

– APPENDIX NINE –

IRISH SPORT IN THE 1960s

Northern Ireland's Soccer League Champions:
1960: Glenavon
1961 and 1962: Linfield
1963: Distillery
1964: Glentoran
1965: Derry City
1966: Linfield
1967 and 1968: Glentoran
1969: Linfield

Northern Ireland's Irish Cup Finals:
1960: Linfield 5 Ards 1
1961: Glenavon 5 Linfield 1
1962: Linfield 4 Portadown 0
1963: Linfield 2 Distillery 1
1964: Derry City 2 Glentoran 0
1965: Coleraine 2 Glenavon 1
1966: Glentoran 2 Linfield 0
1967: Crusaders 3 Glentoran 1
1968: Crusaders 2 Linfield 0
1969: Ards 4 Distillery 2

Republic of Ireland's Soccer League Champions:
1960: Limerick
1961: Drumcondra
1962: Shelbourne
1963: Dundalk
1964: Shamrock Rovers
1965: Drumcondra
1966: Waterford
1967: Dundalk
1968 and 1969: Waterford

Republic of Ireland's Irish Cup Finals:
1960: Shelbourne 2 Cork Hibernians 1
1961: St. Patrick's Athletic 2 Drumcondra 1
1962: Shamrock Rovers 4 Shelbourne 1
1963: Shelbourne 2 Cork Hibernians 0
1964: Cork Celtic 1 Shamrock Rovers 1
Shamrock Rovers 1 Cork Celtic 0
1965: Limerick 1 Shamrock Rovers 1
Shamrock Rovers 1 Limerick 0
1966: Shamrock Rovers 2 Limerick 0
1967: Shamrock Rovers 3 St. Patrick's Athletic 2
1968: Shamrock Rovers 3 Waterford 0
1969: Shamrock Rovers 4 Cork Celtic 1
All-Ireland Football Champions:
1960 and 1961: Down
1962: Kerry
1963: Dublin
1964 to 1966: Galway
1967: Meath
1968: Down
1969: Kerry
All-Ireland Hurling Champions:
1960: Wexford
1961 and 1962: Tipperary
1963: Kilkenny
1964 and 1965: Tipperary
1966: Cork
1967: Kilkenny
1968: Wexford
1969: Kilkenny
All-Ireland Camogie Champions:
1960 to 1966: Dublin
1967: Antrim
1968 and 1969: Wexford
Personal milestones:
European Footballer Of The Year In 1968: George Best (Manchester United)

– APPENDIX TEN –

MUSICAL HIGHLIGHTS OF THE SWINGING SIXTIES

No study of the 1960s would be complete without reference to the music that provided the soundtrack to the extraordinary events featured in this volume. I have thus taken the liberty, as a self-proclaimed musicologist, to compile the following list of records, which arguably were the musical highlights of the swinging sixties. No mention is made of such sixties icons as The Beach Boys, The Byrds, Bob Dylan, or Elvis Presley, because this book has been exclusively concerned with Britain and Ireland. Also, on the subject of Ireland, the music scene there was dominated by the very localised phenomenon of the so-called showbands, who have earned their place in the culture of the whole island, but only the likes of The Bachelors, The Dubliners, and Van Morrison managed to appear on the international stage.

If I might start with an often under-rated area of popular music, I have listed ten tracks, which are among the best instrumentals of the 1960s. They are in alphabetical order:

'Albatross' by Fleetwood Mac (1968)
'Apache' by The Shadows (1960)
'Black Mountain Side' by Led Zeppelin (1969)
'Diamonds' by Jet Harris and Tony Meehan (1963)
'Flying' by The Beatles (1967)
'Ogden's Nut Gone Flake' by The Small Faces (1968)
'Pow R.Toc H' by Pink Floyd (1967)
'Stranger On The Shore' by Acker Bilk (1962)
'Telstar' by The Tornados (1962)
'Wonderful Land' by The Shadows (1962)

The following singles, I dare to suggest, are the best British-made number-one singles for their respective year:
1960: 'Shakin' All Over' by Johnny Kidd and The Pirates
1961: 'You Don't Know' by Helen Shapiro

1962: 'Telstar' by The Tornados
1963: 'Dance On' by The Shadows
1964: 'House Of The Rising Sun' by The Animals
1965: 'The Last Time' by The Rolling Stones
1966: 'You Don't Have To Say You Love Me' by Dusty Springfield
1967: 'A Whiter Shade Of Pale' by Procol Harum
1968: 'Everlasting Love' by The Love Affair
1969: 'Something In The Air' by Thunderclap Newman

The album, as a critically acclaimed art form, rather than a cycle of 'filler' material, did not take off until the mid to late 1960s, and the following represent my favourite British efforts from this era:

'Are You Experienced?' by The Jimi Hendrix Experience (May 1967)
'Sgt. Pepper's Lonely Hearts Club Band' by The Beatles (June 1967)
'A Saucerful Of Secrets' by Pink Floyd (June 1968)
'Ogden's Nut Gone Flake' by The Small Faces (June 1968)
'The Beatles' by The Beatles (November 1968)
'Beggar's Banquet' by The Rolling Stones (December 1968)
'Led Zeppelin' by Led Zeppelin (March 1969)
'Abbey Road' by The Beatles (September 1969)
'Led Zeppelin II' by Led Zeppelin (October 1969)
'Let It Bleed' by The Rolling Stones (December 1969)

Last but definitely not least, the following tracks, in my humble opinion, are the outstanding musical highlights of the British 'swinging sixties':

'End Of The Season' by The Kinks (1967)
'I Can See For Miles' by The Who (1967)
'Itchycoo Park' by The Small Faces (1967)
'Nights In White Satin' by The Moody Blues (1967)
'Strawberry Fields Forever' by The Beatles (1967)
'We Love You' by The Rolling Stones (1967)
'All Along The Watchtower' by The Jimi Hendrix Experience (1968)
'White Room' by Cream (1968)
'Cirrus Minor' by Pink Floyd (1968)
'Dazed And Confused' by Led Zeppelin (1969)